Between Times

Henry Mitchell

Printed in the United Kingdom

First Printing, 2014 Alfie Dog Limited

The author can be found at: authors@alfiedog.com

Cover image: Henry Mitchell

ISBN 978-1-909894-23-5

Published by
Alfie Dog Limited
Schilde Lodge, Tholthorpe,
North Yorkshire, YO61 1SN
Tel: 0207 193 33 90

DEDICATION

To my soulsister and fierce friend,
Deb Coulter.

ACKNOWLEDGMENTS

Grateful thanks to my editor at Alfie Dog Fiction, Rosemary J. Kind who made my best efforts better. Deep appreciation to ruthless readers David Longley and Michelle McClendon who were ever prompt to point out the errors of my ways. Boundless gratitude to my wife and lover, Jane Ella Matthews, who heard it all before I ever wrote it down, then heard it again, and listens to me yet. Special thanks to Iris and Ren, who let me dawdle over my pancakes and coffee while I scribbled after the story.

PROLOGUE

The American knelt beside her mother-in-law during prayers at Saint Mary's Cathedral in Urakami District. On her other side, the old woman's two daughters murmured their responses to the litany. They all addressed and introduced her formally, as if she were her husband's employee or business associate rather than his wife. Though they had received her into their circle with reserved friendliness and careful consideration, she was a gaijin still, as strange and foreign to them as they were to her. Still, she liked these women, especially her mother-in law, a quiet quick little woman whose external shyness cloaked a tough, resourceful, pragmatic nature much like her own.

Her husband, Tad, as she called him when they were alone, was not himself entirely at home in his native culture. Perhaps that was what had attracted them to one another in the beginning. They were both misfits among their own. He felt badly, was frankly apologetic about bringing her here where she was writing in a language that few she met could read, and there was no possibility of publication. They had intended an extended visit with his family, but the onset of war turned it into an indefinite exile for her, and to a lesser extent for her husband, who had more friends and interests abroad than in his own country.

Tad assured her that as soon as the war came to end,

they would return to her own people, that if she wished it then, he would free her from any obligation to remain his wife.

"And the war will surely end before long," he kept saying. "There is no way our side can win this thing without Europe. The longer it goes, the more likely we will lose. Cooler heads will prevail in government councils, and the same predicates that were used to justify war will serve to support negotiating a peace. All we need is a little patience, a little time, and the world will be sane again."

Tad would meet them here after Mass and walk them home. But for now, she listened gratefully to the priest's droning Latin cadences, as foreign to her ear as the language she swam in through all her days in this far country, but it was the same Mass as she would hear in a similar place in her own land, so it assumed a sort of familiarity, and comforted her. Unbidden, Benjamin Drum was in her mind, his presence as strong as if he sat beside her. Strange to think of him now, after all this.

She loved her husband, but it was Drum who had awakened her to love, with all its possibilities and complications. She marveled that these two men who held her heart had seemed so different yet proven in the end to be very alike in their self-containment, open acceptance, and refusal to own another soul. They might have become friends without her between them. When she set her mind on Tad, Drum had swallowed his hurt and handed all her promises back to her without one word of protest or accusation. She vowed that when she was home again, she would find him, ask his forgiveness.

The world ended without warning. No sound. No shift in the earth nor trembling in the August air. In the silence between two words, the windows imploded over their heads, streaming myriad shards of stained glass becoming molten drops of sun in the plasmic air before any there were aware of it, as the walls, roof, and all the souls they had sheltered were transmuted instantly into light.

JONAS

Jonas looked up from feeding his chickens and there the child stood under the trees, watching him with an expression of curiosity and mild awe, as if Jonas were an exotic specimen in a zoo.

"Hello, there," Jonas offered.

"Hello." The boy stayed where he was, waiting for Jonas to define their situation, while Jonas wondered how the urchin had come to his yard in particular. Most of the land around was national forest. Jonas knew his few neighbors. This boy didn't belong to any of them.

"What's your name, son?"

"Drum."

"That's it?"

"Benjamin, but everybody just calls me Drum."

"Drum it is, then. Your folks camping around here?"

"I'm by myself, I reckon."

"Then I reckon you're hungry. Come on in." Drum was probably a runaway, Jonas thought. He didn't have a phone, but he would feed the boy, give him shelter, try to keep him in one place until he could get into town and make some inquiries, let somebody in authority know he'd found a loose child. Jonas didn't consider Drum a lost child; there was no air of bewilderment about him at all. Either the boy had just gone on a wander without permission, or with premeditation, he had divorced himself from his assigned place in the world.

Beneath his concern for an unattended juvenile, Jonas

felt a minor elation at unexpected human company. He had been burdened with more loneliness than he usually felt so early in the day. He dropped his feed bucket beside the gate to the chicken pen as he closed it behind him and without looking back, started for the house. He heard his visitor's footfalls at his back as Drum ran to catch up, looked down at the boy as he came alongside, and bestowed on him a slightly crooked smile, "Well, Drum, everybody around here just calls me Bear. I haven't had my breakfast yet. Could you stand some pancakes and sausage?"

Drum's face came alight, "I didn't have breakfast yesterday, either, and pancakes and sausage be too fine to pass up if I had. I'm right thankful to you."

Jonas thought he might be having an interesting day for a change.

#

Jonas Bear had not always lived alone. Two years past he had been teaching painting and art history in a small women's college in Virginia, comfortably ensconced in a houseful of women, three of them, who doted on him. The doting was mutual.

It was an insular existence, surrounded by friends in a small academic tribe where every member knew their place and felt glad to be in it. Jonas taught his classes, worshiped his covey of flattering females, and painted. Every year or so, he would exhibit at one of the three galleries handling his work. His specialties were mountain landscapes and portraits of his family. He was comfortable and happy with his quiet, gentle routines and rituals, removed from all the major troubles of the world, or so Jonas thought. They were living a privileged life, he knew, and he was grateful for it, and said as much to God every Sunday when he packed his family off with all the other faculty dependencies to the campus chapel where they participated in a middling high liturgy and sang Welsh hymns.

Eventually, his daughters grew up. Emily went off to Brown to study Tudor history. Her plan was to become, like her father, a teacher at a small college, and continue to live in the regulated yet stimulating world she had grown up in. When time came for her summer vacation, Jonas was busy grading papers and preparing for the summer term class he was teaching, so Lorraine and their younger daughter Lucy set off to Providence in their brand new Nash Rambler to fetch Emily home.

Jonas was in his office, interviewing a prospective student and her parents, when the department secretary tapped on his door. In a fluster she blurted out, "Professor Bear, there's a policeman here to see you."

A trucker hauling a load of concrete pipe had driven too long, too far and fallen asleep on his way down a mountain. His overloaded rig ran right over the top of the new Rambler carrying all the love and joy in Professor Bear's life right out of the world.

Somehow Jonas sleepwalked through his summer term. Then he turned in his keys, sold their house with all its furnishings, bought a not too reliable army surplus jeep, and with his clothes and a few painting supplies piled in back, drove south through the Blue Ridge until he caught up with himself at the old house he lived in now. It had been priced for a quick sale, for which it had waited several years, empty and untended, was miles from anywhere on a map, and Jonas bought it, not because he thought he had arrived, but simply because he was too heart weary to keep traveling.

#

Jonas did not really enjoy living by himself. He had spent most of his adult life surrounded by loving family and convivial colleagues. He was used to having people to talk to, debate, touch, share ideas and enthusiasms, joys and hurts. But after the accident, the companionship of friends with their families only made him feel more acutely his own losses. Solitude was less painful. So here he was.

At first, he drank. Alcohol dulled the awful empty aching in his soul, until the day he ran a stop sign and narrowly missed doing for another man's family what a strung-out truck driver had done for his. He emptied his bottle into the sink, bought some chickens, began working on his ramshackle old house. He started to paint again, mostly solitary figures, sombre and intense, brushed and troweled in thick impastos, the faces of his pain. His dealers did not like his new work. "When will we see some more mountains?" they would ask.

"As soon as they feel like home again," he would answer.

Nevertheless, he sold a few paintings from time to time. He was spending more than he was earning, but not much more. He had few needs now, fewer wants. He had money from the settlement with the trucking company. He and Lorraine had always been savers and the sale of their house brought several times what he had paid for his present place. Most of what he had spent here so far had been to repair the house and build a little barn. At this rate, it would be years yet before he had to worry about a livelihood. He had replaced one very orderly and structured life with another. This one was not exactly rewarding and fulfilling, but it came naturally to him, did not require much effort, while he waited without daring to hope for his healing. He had waited pretty much apart and to himself until this morning. He didn't even have a dog. This was the first time he had cooked a meal in his house for anyone but himself.

#

They crossed the yard to the house, and Jonas was mildly surprised when Drum sat down on the steps to remove his shoes, thought about following the boy's good example, but it was his house, after all, so he crossed the porch and went in, stifling a fatherly urge to admonish Drum not to let the screen slam, and when he heard it close quietly behind him, was glad he had.

What had been two rooms before Jonas removed the wall between and added big windows across the back of the house was now his painting studio. Several easels stood in the space with paintings on them in various stages of incompletion. A score of canvases, most finished, leaned with their faces to the walls. Occasionally Jonas would turn them around and peruse them, but when he was working, he only wanted to see the piece in progress. Once he felt in flow with a project, he usually stayed with it until it was done.

Jonas walked across the room to the kitchen door, looked back to see Drum intently studying not the paintings, but the paints and brushes, standing before a worktable with his hands clasped behind him, as if reminding himself not to touch another's sacred objects. Jonas thought he should say something encouraging to his visitor, but no words came, so he went into the kitchen and took a couple of onions from a bin, skinned them and began to chop them.

Drum spoke at his elbow, "I can do that would it help." He said it like a statement.

So he's local, then, Jonas thought, alerted by the Southern highlander's penchant for eschewing subordinating conjunctions at every opportunity. He handed Drum the knife, "Count your fingers;" was about to add *and wash your hands first,* but Drum was already at the sink. While the boy began to dice the onions somewhat more deliberately, but just as finely as Jonas would have done it, he measured out some buckwheat flour and broke a couple of eggs and began to stir up batter for the pancakes. Jonas kneaded Drum's onions into a pound of sausage, divided it into four fat paddies, and when the griddle was freed of the sausage, it warmly welcomed the pancakes. Not long after, two human males made sausage and pancakes disappear, along with a cup of sorghum, all washed down with the barley brew Jonas sometimes used in lieu of coffee. He realized then with some astonishment that he had actually enjoyed his breakfast, and was looking forward to whatever pleasure the rest of his morning might bring.

They ate mostly in silence. Though evidently hungry, Drum didn't gulp down his breakfast as boys, hungry or not, often do. He ate slowly, looking at his food before he forked it up, seeming to savor each bite before he swallowed it. Jonas watched him, followed his guest's example. These were the same pancakes as he made for himself at least every other day, but these were really good. Jonas wondered how much trouble it could be to grow a little patch of sorghum and make himself some molasses of his own. He'd bought the homemade sausage from a neighbor. He thought he might go back there before he went to the store for sausage again.

After they ate all the food they saw, Drum, without being asked, helped gather the dishes and carry them to the sink. Then he stood by with a towel and dried and stacked them as Jonas washed. When Jonas began putting the dishes away on the high shelves above the counter, Drum took a damp cloth and wiped the table.

Jonas queried himself, *Well, what do I do with him now?* He posed a different question to Drum, "What brought you by my place, Drum? This is pretty much out of anybody's way off here in the woods."

"I was headed home, and you were on my way."

"Where's home?"

"Suspect I'll find out once I get there."

Jonas shot the child a keen glance, deduced from his expression that he was not trying to be flippant, but was speaking openly and seriously to him. Drum, he thought, was a puzzle. "School starts in a couple of weeks, Drum. Do you plan to be home by then?"

Drum looked genuinely thoughtful. "They were planning to send me off to Virginia to school, but that's too far. Ganny I should be looking for a teacher soon, who will teach me where I live."

Ask and Listen, Jonas told himself, as he had told a thousand students in their turn. Now he knew why Drum was making his own path through the woods. When they were done with the dishes, Jonas motioned to Drum to hang his towel over the back of a chair, and the boy followed him back into the studio.

"Drum, I usually work for a couple of hours after breakfast. You can watch if you want to." Jonas figured that would give him some time to decide what to do about his guest.

Drum had already been watchful. "You left your feed bucket outside. Do you want me to put it away for you?"

"Thanks, Drum; I forgot. Set it inside the barn door out

there. There's a broken bale of alfalfa there beside the feed bags. Put half of it in Mildred's trough, will you?"

"Mildred?"

"She's my milk goat, except she's not milking right now. Carrying her kid, as you'll notice when you see her."

Drum was out the door in a flash, remembering to close the screen quietly behind him. Jonas turned to his easel, spooned out some alizarin crimson and naples yellow onto the piece of window glazing that served as his palette, picked up a clean flat, stared a moment at the tortured visage emerging from the dark canvas before him, dropped the brush back into its can with the others. "Dear Lord, I need some air," he prayed to the windows. Jonas picked up a couple of sketchbooks and stuffed a fistful of markers into his pocket. He would ask Drum to walk with him.

Jonas found Drum engaged in earnest conversation with Mildred, who gazed adoringly at her visitor as if he were a learned sage come to impart to her all the wisdom of the Mountain. Jonas felt himself in need of some of that wisdom. He had lived in this place for a year. People came from across the continent to experience the mystery of these mountains around him, and he'd seen precious little of any of it past his own yard. He looked around him in the golden late summer morning, realized he'd been asleep since he fled Virginia. He'd looked but not seen, listened but not heard, touched but not felt. He'd lost count of the days that had dawned and faded since he came among these laureled hills to hide from the world's outrage and from his own agony. This was the first morning among them all that lay new and fresh upon his soul. A spark of awareness that had died to darkness with his beloved three feebly now flared to life. He didn't acknowledge it yet, even to himself, but he felt the light coming in, felt his spirit beginning to open imperceptibly, like a willow bud after last frost.

Mildred and Drum turned to stare at him as if he had suddenly sprouted wings. "Drum, can you take time off from your travels today to go look at some trees with me?"

Drum's face unfurled like a flower into a broad grin, "I'm just a boy, don't you know? Time is everything I've got."

#

A steep, rutted dirt track meandered up from the graveled county road to the two-storey clap-boarded house, now needy of paint, and continued past, between the house and its new barn, which, somewhat contrary to tradition, was quite smaller than the house. Traversing the yard, the track wound off up the mountainside to the boundary of the forty-odd acres attached to the dwelling, and presumably off into the wild steeps of Moriah National Forest beyond. Jonas had never ventured up this road beyond sight of his house. He marveled now that he had breathed a cycle of seasons on his plot of earth and never once traversed its limits.

Under the kind sky of a late-summer's morning, a boy older than he knew and a man growing younger than he had been in a while set off along this road with an air of companions on a quest.

"Where are we going, Mister Bear?"

"You can call me just Bear." He almost said Jonas, but only Lorraine ever addressed him with his given name. To his friends, he had always been Bear.

"Where are we going, just Bear?" They both laughed.

"You can just call me Bear."

"Where are we going, Bear?"

"There's something along here I need to see today."

"What do you need to see?"

"Suspect I'll find out once we get there." They laughed again. Jonas felt his mood lifting beyond what he had gotten used to. He didn't feel quite like singing yet, but if he had recalled a tune at that moment, he might have, just for the change.

A high thin haze of cloud paled the blue overhead, but failed to dim the sun, warm on their backs as they walked. Jonas thought he should have brought some water for Drum. This afternoon or tomorrow he would need to go into town and try to ascertain something of the child's status, but for now he was content to accept the proximity of a friendly soul as a gift and a comfort. They were both solitary travelers, bereft of familial bonds, strangers who had met on the way and forged solidarity against their loneliness. It was a momentary respite in both their journeys, Jonas reckoned, but it was a respite, and he would not be so ungrateful to the life that was left to him that he would refuse it.

#

The road lifted them gently around an overgrown field to their right. There had been no farming here for years, hence no traffic, except perhaps an occasional trespassing hunter. Once along the way they passed a broken whiskey flask. Other than that, there was not even trash to signify a past human presence, only the traces they walked, in places overgrown with grass and weeds to their knees. Beggarlice clung to their jeans as they pressed through. Somewhere down among the trees to their left they could hear the singing descent of a creek.

Past the field, the creek drew nearer the road until they

crossed it as it chorused through a boulder field, then the road turned sharply right and began climbing seriously to follow the creek up the mountain's face. Erosion had kept the track clear here, but had rutted the traces and left a multitude of stones protruding from the soil. Walking was not difficult, but required concentration. Jonas wished he had a walking stick. If Drum missed the staff he had left beside a door two mornings past, he didn't complain.

As they climbed into a more ancient and robust forest, hemlock and rhododendron yielded to hickories and laurel. A few old poplars, tall and straight as masts of clippers, pillared the canopy. Crows and jays called and cackled from branches overhead. A great dark owl, harried by sparrows, glided soundlessly past them down the open air above the road.

After less than a mile, the road bore left, away from the rowdy little stream and steeped north toward a clearing within sight of the crest of the ridge they were on. The trees thinned away, and broad decaying stumps of an old growth forest testified to the predations of long dead humans. This area had been logged, then burnt over. Fire had sterilized the soil, and little grew yet apart from tall wavy grass and a scattering of blueberries. Lichen-covered stumps protruded from the grass like tombstones in a graveyard. With a clear view, the man and the boy looked back to see away below, the little house with her minuscule barn huddled beside her like a calf. Mildred was just a dot in her lot behind the barn. Ahead the road forked, the left branch only a dim memory of travel there. Within the fork was a huge pile of quartzite boulders. In the sunlight they seemed to shine from within. Jonas held his sketchbooks over his eyes to shield against the glare. Drum squinted into the light, wrinkling his face into a parody of a grin.

Abruptly, Jonas sat down on the lip of a stump. "Well, Drum, this is what we came up here to see."

#

Jonas opened one of his sketchbooks and addressed his muse. Three blocky quartzite boulders leaned into one another before him. Taken together, they were bigger than his house. Smaller chunks and splinters of the gleaming stone littered the ground around. Some turning their cloven faces to the light, some more worn and weathered. Patches of moss and gray lichens clad several. Other glared white and bright as snow.

Amid the largest boulders, like a crown of thorns, three old sourwoods clawed upward to craze the sky with their frantic asymmetry. Here, fire had found less organic to feed upon, the inferno had been therefore less intense, sparing some random seed or root. Now the resurrected trees bore their mute witness to the transience of death and the abidance of renewing life.

Sourwoods never grow straight to their height; they lean into the light or away from the wind. Their growing form is like an orgasm stilled in a photograph, wild, irregular, ever turning, twisting toward some unrealized direction, seemingly drunk with all the possibilities of growth. They are not pretty trees by nature, but beautiful in their lust to become.

With one of his markers, Jonas made a few deft lines to indicate the basic shapes of the stones. While the lines were still wet, he rubbed the heel of his hand across the paper in the general directions of the trees' spread. Then he settled into his moment, observing the slant of the light, claiming an outline here, placing a shadow there. As his hands moved and hovered over his pad, he heard crows somewhere off in another world, felt the sun's heat on his arms, noted the tug of breeze in his hair, but mainly he saw. Jonas opened his soul to the stone and drank in its song of permanence. Over eons even mountains were broken and brought low, but some deep things endured and were not taken from the world before their time.

Out of the corner of his eye, Jonas saw Drum watching him work, looking back and forth between the emerging drawing and the motif, weighing the act against its inspiration. Jonas held out his other sketchbook with some of his markers, "Are you an artist, Drum?"

"I reckon I'm not a real artist. I can't draw but the things I see."

Jonas pretended to continue working on his drawing, but he watched, intrigued, as Drum set to work. He had a sure hand for one so young. Jonas thought he must have had a teacher somewhere. Drum pulled across his page a continuous angular line, traced fairly accurately the top edges of the three large boulders. With little hesitation then, as if before he took up his tools he had already seen and internalized the pathways of their growth, he began to draw the trees in free, unbroken swirls and thrusts that wove a lively and complex labyrinth pouring upward into the paper sky from the heart of an invisible mountain.

They spent the rest of the morning working on their drawings, then clambering over and among the boulders, pocketing a few sticks and shards as souvenirs. They debated for a time about which fork of the road to explore. Jonas suggested the way to the right.

Drum counseled, "The widest road takes you quickest to your own undoing."

"Who told you that?"

"I don't remember; I think I might have dreamt it." If it

were more than a dream to Drum, he chose not to admit it.

When hunger and thirst won out over wanderlust, they started back down the way they'd come. "What would you say to some ham and grits, Drum?"

"I'd say to them, 'I'm going to eat you.'"

Jonas kept a straight face, "I think I may have a little okra, too. We can fry it with the ham."

"I'm right partial to fried okra." Drum declared with obvious enthusiasm, "Africans brought us okra, don't you know. After they'd been made slaves."

"So you are a historian as well as an artist."

"No, sir, but I'm a good listener."

Drum and Bear were both good listeners as they made their way back to the house. Jays scolded them, Crows admonished, Mockingbirds sang them all the songs they knew. The creek told them her best jokes, chuckling and chortling down among the trees, the wind whispered unspeakable secrets, the air sang warm in the sun and cool in the shade, the grass rustled their legs in a persistent snare. Mildred bleated her greeting as they came into the yard. Her belly bulged out to either side like an inflatable goat in a big city parade.

"There will be four more feet on the ground around here shortly," Jonas observed.

Drum changed the subject, "Bear, I'd really like to go back up to the rocks sometime."

"You know the way, but you'll need to get home soon now, don't you think?"

"I reckon I might like to go back for a visit once I'm grown."

"Don't you think your family might miss you?"

"I think you might miss me more than they would."

Jonas doubted that what the boy had told him was true. He did not doubt that Drum believed it true. And yes, he would miss this child when he was gone. He wished they had more time. He would think about that after he fed Drum his lunch. It wouldn't do to send him home hungry.

Together they filled Mildred's water barrel, forked up the soiled straw in her stall, lay down fresh bedding, then hauled the refuse in a barrow to the compost pile in a fence-corner. Coming in from the porch, Drum looked around at the walls of the studio, "You have logs inside."

"This house was built of chestnut logs, Drum. Some farmer who lived here prospered, maybe by selling off all his timber, and covered the logs up outside with clapboarding, and bead-boarded all the rooms inside. He might have wanted his house to look like the houses of his acquaintances in town, I guess, or maybe he had a wife with social aspirations. Anyway, when I opened up the center rooms for the studio, I took out all the boarding so I could see the square-hewn log walls. It's a little dark, but it doesn't seem right to paint over them. The logs are the bones and soul of the house."

"Every tree is somebody's house." Jonas understood the child was not referring to human habitations.

He pointed Drum to the bathroom while he scooped his morning paints back into their jars. When both humans were clean and unburdened, they went off to the kitchen to tackle lunch. While Jonas was heating the pan for the ham and readying a pot for grits, Drum began cutting the okra. Contrary to what Jonas considered the standard method, the boy, after chopping off the tips, sliced the pods lengthwise.

"Drum, do you always cut your okra like that?"

"That's how Mary does it. She says there's less cutting and turning that way. Do you have any cornmeal to batter this in?"

"Who's Mary?"

"Mary's my aunt. If I could have stayed with her, I wouldn't be at your house right now." Jonas set a small bowl and a canister of cornmeal on the counter. Drum looked up at him, solemn and earnest, "Bear, are you going to turn me in now?"

"Not today," Jonas answered truthfully.

Lunch was tasty, and left them feeling properly weighted and centered in their world. Jonas had always enjoyed cooking. His talents tended toward basic and straightforward fare. Robert, Lorraine's brother, a chef who owned a fancy restaurant in Chicago, told Jonas once, "You are a good rustic cook." Jonas regarded that as a high compliment. Even in his painting, he sought simple forms with a minimum of adornment. He used big brushes, urged his students to do the same, "Any detail too precious to render with a one-inch flat belongs in a photograph." His criticisms were never mean or belittling, but were always blunt and unsparing. From time to time he had reduced a student to tears. Anyone who finished his studio courses left better painters than they had ever supposed they could be. A gifted painter, Jonas possessed perhaps a better gift for teaching.

They cleared the table, washed and put away the dishes, hung their pot and pan on the rack over the gas range, and still had an afternoon ahead. Neither man nor boy seemed inclined to dwell on tomorrow. Jonas wasn't sure how to include a young visitor into his accustomed routines. Usually, he would have taken a nap after lunch, not because he was tired, but just to escape thought for awhile. Now, he offered a different invitation, "Let's go see if we got some eggs today."

They found eggs enough for a breakfast or two. After they checked the nesting boxes and picked up a couple of eggs that had been dropped off at undesignated locations, they cleaned and filled the waterers, threw out some scratch for the hens, stood in the pen for several minutes watching a pair of red-tail hawks circling and soaring round and round one another away off above the Shining Rocks, riding and rising effortlessly on some invisible upcurrent of air, or perhaps lifted by a gyre of Spirit power sprung from the mountain itself. The hawks posed no threat to the chickens, were both oblivious to all but the form of the other and wind against wings. One called in that wild free voice peculiar to raptors that made the tiny hairs on the humans' forearms stiffen and lift in the afternoon sun like a multitude of minute invisible wings.

For long moments, Jonas and his visitor stood entranced by the hawks' high dance, feeling connections that could not be put to words or music, but that drew them into a song nonetheless, rendering their very stillness a movement in a cosmic choreography whereby their watching and listening bound them into unity with the mountains around and the air above and all the creatures within that breathed and moved toward light and life.

While Bear and Drum were soaring in their heads with the hawks, a car horn from down the drive brought their gaze to earth. A dusty black Ford bumped and rumbled into the yard. Drum held the egg basket before him as if he might hide behind it, "Who's that, Bear?"

"That's Marcus Dill; he's the sheriff."

Marcus opened the door of his Ford, emblazoned with

a white star camouflaged by mud and dust. "Morning, men. Bear, we've got a couple of teenagers, boy and girl, hiking up around here a couple of days back, and their folks haven't heard from them. Have you boys seen anybody walking through?"

Jonas laid a hand on Drum's shoulder as he answered, "Nobody at all, Marcus, but we'll be watchful," then let his hand drop as the sheriff continued, smiling at Drum, "I didn't know you had a fine looking boy like this around, Bear."

"I'm just visiting," offered Drum hopefully.

"He's Mary's nephew, just up for a breather before school starts." That was not exactly what Jonas had planned to say the next time he saw the sheriff, but the words outed before he thought, and he let them stand.

Another time, Marcus might have, if only for curiosity's sake, inquired as to just exactly who Mary was and how she figured into this situation, but he was not looking for a lost little boy today, and Drum didn't look lost standing with an adult whom the sheriff knew as a responsible if somewhat reclusive citizen of his jurisdiction. He apparently assumed, as Jonas had counted on, that Mary and Jonas were somehow relations. The sheriff didn't have leisure at present to sort out family connections, a subject upon which, Marcus knew from experience, mountain folk could palaver for hours on end. He had two sexually potent young adults unsupervised and unprepared loose in his woods. His plate was full enough to keep him occupied for a spell. "Let me know if they turn up, Bear. Their folks are scared and worried and ready to nail my hide to the door if I don't find them quick."

"I'll drive in straight away if they come by, Marcus.

Good luck."

Marcus sat down behind the wheel of his Ford, swung and folded his long legs until his big feet were safely enclosed, then slammed the starred and dusty door with a resounding thud, stirring the hens to cackling anxiety. He waved, backed his car around and headed back down the hill, gathering and scattering more dust as he went.

Drum gave a long, serious look at Jonas, who returned it. Then they both burst into a laughing fit that carried them all the way back to the house.

"You didn't tell him," Drum gasped between giggles.

"I didn't lie, either," said Jonas, managing to hold his mouth straight for an instant before they both laughed some more.

As they washed the eggs - there were nine of them, varying slightly in size with shells shaded from tan to chocolate - some residual mirth would occasionally rise to the surface and they would laugh together again, whether at their big joke on the world or the world's big joke on them, Jonas would have been hard put to say. He put the eggs in the fridge, pulled two caps from the rack by the door, clapped one on Drum's head, and put the other on himself as he went out the door, "Come along, Drum; we've work ahead."

Drum's cap was a little large for him, but he tucked the band behind his ears and flipped up the bill so he could see out from under it, "What are we doing?"

"A wee bit of farming to while away our afternoon. You planning to stay long enough to help?"

"Well I guess I owe you some for delivering me from the law," which unleashed another round of high hilarity; but as they headed toward the barn, Jonas patted Drum between his shoulders to assure his attention and said,

"We're going to have to have a serious talk about your future real soon, you know. There are people somewhere sick with worry about you, and I'm not equipped here to bring up a boy, not to mention all the trouble that could come to us both if I don't get you back home."

"But this feels like home to me."

"A boy needs to be with his family, Drum."

"You don't have a family."

"I used to, but something happened."

"Did you run away like I did?"

"Nobody ran away; a truck ran over them and killed them."

"Everybody?"

"Everybody in the world I loved, Drum."

"I'm sorry Bear. That must have hurt you awful."

"It will always hurt awful, Drum, but it doesn't hurt so bad now that I have a good friend like you."

"Will we still be friends after you take me back?"

"Drum, once you become a friend, you can't unfriend yourself. We are friends wherever we are."

"But you said you wouldn't turn me in today, Bear."

"We won't do anything drastic today, Drum. Let's enjoy it. In the morning, we can decide what you need to do."

"Bear?"

"Yes, Drum?"

"When I go home, my dad won't let me draw."

"I'm sorry, Drum. Maybe I can talk to him."

With that they came to the barn. Jonas opened the door and told Drum to bring out the barrow. He pulled a spade and a hoe from inside the door, put them over his shoulder, and motioned to the barrow, "Bring that along, and follow me."

Behind the barn, on the other side of Mildred's lot, was a long row of raised garden beds, bordered by stacked stones. Grass grew in them now, but there were stalks remaining from recent squash and bean vines. The creek murmured somewhere among the trees below the garden.

Drum set the barrow down. Jonas pushed his cap back on his head and laid out their drill, "We're going to spade up a couple of these beds, Drum, so we can plant some kale and turnips and have something green to eat this winter."

"But I won't be here to eat any, will I?"

"If I make a good impression on your folks, they might allow me some visiting rights. You'll have to convince them when you get back home that I've been a good influence on you. Right now, though, I'd like to influence you to help me out here. As I spade up this bed, we're going to turn up some rocks, unless somebody carried them all off since I picked my squash. It would be a great help if you could pick them up as I dig them out and put them in the barrow. When you have what you think you can push along without trouble, take them down to the end of the row and dump them. I can use them to put around the next bed."

"I'm good at picking up rocks. I did that for Mary a lot."

"Your aunt's a gardener, then?"

"She grows right good tomatoes, and she's the one told me where okra came from."

"You like her a lot, don't you?"

"When you take me back, maybe you could talk her into letting me stay with her."

"Sometimes, Drum, we just have to stay for awhile wherever life puts us down. Sometimes, we don't get to decide the turns our life might take."

"What do we do then, Bear?"

"We pray, Drum, until we can hope again." Jonas was surprised when he said it, to realize that his whole year in this place had been a wordless despairing prayer, and that he actually did believe again now in the possibility of hope.

They fell silent then and turned to work, each of them taking refuge from their past and from their future in the gentle and kindly toil that bound their wounded souls to this holy moment of communion and trust.

Jonas worked his way through one bed, end to end, and started on another. The soil had already been turned once this season, so wasn't hard. As he dug, he loosed occasional stones, some of them fairly hefty, flipped them aside with the tip of his spade. Drum gathered them in his barrow, hauled them to the end of the row, then stacked them carefully as if he were building a witch's tower. *He has an artist's eye,* Jonas mused, *and an artist's knack for play.* To every new class of students in his custody, he preached that the most important skill for a visual artist was not an ability to draw, which could be learned with practice, but a capacity for seeing deeply into the soul of things, to sense the spirit within the movement, and to translate that into activity that elevated labor to play and play to ritual.

They fell into the rhythm of their doing. Drum's little circle of stone rose straight and taller until it measured nearly half his height. Now and then Jonas glanced up to gauge the tower's progress, but mainly was lost in his own remembering as over and over he pushed his spade into the good dark loam, lifted it full, and turned it before letting the earth receive its own again.

Not a day had passed during his year on this land that

he had not relived a hundred times his secretary's tap on his office door and the conversation with the state trooper that followed. Today his sadness and anger lifted enough to allow him to dwell on the years before that rending of his life. Jonas saw in his mind his woman, his girls, the light on their hair, heard the lilt in their voices. He felt Lorraine's hand upon him, his daughters' breath on his cheek as he held them up. His loss, the awful impersonal unfairness of life, still lay heavy upon him, but all the love they had shared remained with him as well. Their lives and his love had been stolen from them as they had been stolen from Jonas, yet other lives continued and held promise. Jonas and this stranger boy could still breathe and seek and love in the world, and mark the earth with their striving.

Jonas thought that tomorrow he would drive into town and ask Marcus to find out where Drum belonged. Probably by now the sheriff would have had some notice of a runaway child. They would contact the parents or aunt or whoever was waiting for him, and take Drum back to his place to get on with his life. Jonas figured he had found his own place right here, or perhaps his place had found him. While he was in town tomorrow, he would order a phone put in. There were people out there who loved him yet, and he was ready at last to be loved again. He was considering the prospect of resuming a shared life, when Drum screamed.

Jonas jerked his head upright to face his dread. A few feet away, a terrified Drum, crying and swatting the air around him, danced frantically amid an angry cloud of bumblebees. Unawares, Jonas had knifed into their underground nest with his spade, sealed it in a stroke with a stone he turned, and when Drum lifted the stone, the bees launched their vicious assault on the unsuspecting child. Jonas dropped his spade as he ran, scooped Drum up in his arms and fled the scene. He did not feel the stings that rewarded his misstep when his foot plunged into the nest cavity as he passed.

Jonas thought later they should have made for the barn, but he spared no time for thought now. Instinctively, he ran with the child through the trees, trying to shield Drum's face as the thicketed branches whipped and lashed them in their flight. By the time they reached the creek, the bees were left behind and cruised the open air around the garden seeking other culprits to punish. By some obscure bee logic, they did not bother Mildred who stood by her fence, chewing placidly on a clutch of vine she had pulled through the wire, gazing after her vanished humans.

The humans by now sat breathless and shivering in the cold creek. Drum, in silent agony, managed not to cry. "Let me see," Jonas commanded, and began to inspect the damage. Drum bore several stings on his face and in his hair, and perhaps a dozen more on his arms and torso that Jonas discovered when he opened the child's shirt. "Stand up, Drum," he said, as he stood himself and turned to the creek bank, rife with jewel weed. He grabbed it by the handful, crushed it in his fists and rubbed the juice liberally on Drum's face and arms. It would ease the pain, but would not do much for the already considerable swelling.

They climbed out of the creek, and once on the bank, Drum retched and threw up his lunch. The beginnings of a rash manifest on his neck and chest, no doubt, Jonas surmised an allergic reaction to all the stings the boy had taken. Jonas felt the pain now in his left ankle, reached

27

down it to find it tight and swollen. Jonas himself had a severe allergy to bee stings, kept a bottle of Benadryl on hand as a precaution.

So without further dally, they headed back to the house, giving wide berth to the garden and the patrolling bees. Jonas fetched the Benadryl straight away, dosed himself and Drum as well. Then he put the child to bed on a sofa in the corner of the studio, and sat with him until Drum fell into a fitful sleep. He kept watch for another hour and when Drum's breathing remained clear, Jonas finally remembered to take off his shoe, a painfully difficult maneuver now due to the swelling in his foot and ankle. Thanks to the Benadryl, he didn't feel really ill, but the medicine did nothing to keep his leg from burning like it had been scalded. Jonas lay down on the floor beside the sofa, rolled Drum's shirt under his neck, which felt slightly stiff, and was himself asleep before he could ward against it.

#

"Bear, I'm thirsty." Drum's voice was clear and he seemed alert, if sleepy, mitigating considerably Jonas' guilt at falling asleep on his watch. He sat up and studied his patient. Though no worse, the rash still presented. Drum's puffy cheeks and brow narrowed his eyes to slits, but there was a lopsided grin on his swollen face. Angry red welts marked his points of contact with the maddened bees. His breathing was steady, no wheezing. Drum would have gotten up and gone for his own drink, had not Jonas been sprawled unconscious on the floor in his way.

"Stay put, Drum; I'll fetch you a drink." Jonas lurched groggily to his feet. His leg still hurt, his back and neck felt as if he'd slept on gravel, but his stomach was steady.

28

The Benadryl had done its work. He took off his other shoe and hobbled off barefoot to the kitchen to get Drum's water. Drum did not stay put, but headed for the bathroom. As Jonas stood at the sink filling a mug with water, he peered out into the foggy dark toward the barn. He had forgotten to put Mildred in for the night. In the morning, before light, he would take the can of gasoline he had stashed in the back of the Jeep and apply a generous anointing to the bees' nest. He didn't have any real insecticides at hand. Jonas gardened without them, and seemed to harvest about as well as his neighbors.

The clock on the windowsill showed nearly midnight. *Us boys have had a full day and survived to tell about it,* he thought to his distorted reflection in the wavy window glass. It looked like one of his demented portraits. Jonas grinned. The uneven pane refracted it into a grimace. "That's not me," he spoke aloud to the mirage. He had to laugh at the spectacle of a grown man conversing with his shadow self.

Jonas poured some water. When he and Drum converged in the studio, they washed down another round of Benadryl. Drum had commenced scratching himself somewhat tentatively, for the itching wounds were also sore. In the bathroom Jonas found a bottle of calamine lotion, applied some to Drum's stings. Then he put a liberal dab on each of his own. The zinc oxide in the lotion would relieve the itching.

"You hungry, Drum?"

"Just a little."

"Good sign. We might live."

Jonas went back to the kitchen, took out half a loaf of bread, cut a couple of slices, and set the frying pan on the stove. While the pan was heating, he broke a couple of eggs into a bowl, added a dash of sorghum, whipped the mix together and baptized the bread slices, then laid them in the hot pan.

Drum padded into the kitchen to supervise, clutching his rumpled shirt at his side. "I look like a giraffe or something," he observed, looking down at his pink calamine spots.

Jonas turned around to see, agreed, and lifted the splinter of black gneiss suspended from a braided leather cord Drum wore around his neck, "Tell me about your talisman here."

"Talisman?"

"A talisman is a sacred token, an object that carries spiritual power."

"Mary gave it me. Owl told me it's a binding stone. Said he was glad I had it, that it would always pull me back to people who love me."

"Is Owl a relative?"

"His name is Ethan. An old man who lives all by himself up aside Pinnacle. Mary says he's a hermit. I think he's maybe an Indian. He knows all about special bones and stones and feathers and things - he knows all about talismans." Drum lingered on this last word, as if he liked the feel of it on his tongue.

Ask and listen, Jonas reminded himself again, "Where's Pinnacle, then?"

"By Jonas Gap, where Mary lives."

"Jonas, that's my name."

"Aren't you Bear?"

"Bear's my family's name. I'm Jonas Bear."

"It must be good to be named after such a fine place."

Jonas flipped the toast in the pan, not with a fork, but jostling the pan just so as to make the slices lift and turn before falling back.

Drum watched, intent, "I bet you could teach me to do that."

Jonas nodded as he turned the toast one last time, pleased that the simple maneuver had made an impression. He spoke sincerely then, not as a patronizing adult, "You have interesting friends, Drum. You have an interesting life."

"My life happens all in the summer, don't you know."

"What happens the rest of the year?"

"I have nightmares and nosebleeds."

By the time they ate their french toast and drank cups of the cider Jonas heated to go with it, Drum was almost asleep in his chair. Jonas took him to his one furnished bedroom and turned down the covers on the bed, which he had neatly made up immediately upon rising that morning, one of the small daily disciplines he maintained to ward himself against total dissolution. "You can sleep here tonight, Drum."

Drum did not protest being tucked in like a wee child, but queried Jonas, "Where will you sleep?"

"I'll figure that out when I get sleepy."

Jonas turned out the light and was closing the door when Drum raised his head to peer after him, "Bear, could you leave that open?"

"I'll be knocking around out here for a while yet; won't the light bother you?"

"The dark gives me dreams sometimes. I can sleep in the light."

"I'll leave it open just a bit here. Good night, Drum."

"Goodnight, Bear."

Jonas put on a pot of real coffee to brew, washed their plates and cups, threw Drum's dirty shirt and trousers into the washer. The house seemed cool. He'd build a fire in the studio and hang the clothes by the stove to be dry in the morning. While the washer ran, he sat at the kitchen table, sipping his strong coffee black, and studied the drawings they had made that morning. Drum had not tried to copy Jonas, but engaged the scene through his own vision. Where Jonas had communed with the weighty stability of the rocks, merely suggesting the sourwoods in their midst, Drum had dismissed the boulders with a single skirting line, and with a throng of fluid, yet almost violent gestures, had chronicled the trees, distilling their forms to the essential lineaments of their life. The lines did not rest flat on the page; Jonas perceived space and air around and among them. As he looked, they seemed almost to move, to reach toward him to touch. The raw energy of the image astounded and stirred him. If he had not been there when it happened, Jonas would not have believed a soul so young could grasp and appropriate so much of what was seen.

Jonas folded the sketchpads, left them on the table. He poured the remains of his cold coffee into the sink, refilled his cup from the pot, carried it into the studio. He turned on the work lights over his easel, looked for a time at the unresolved portrait there, sipping his drink occasionally without really tasting it. "You're not me at all," he whispered to the image he had wrought.

Jonas set the cup beside his palette, took the canvas off the easel and turned it to the wall behind him. He put up a blank canvas, freshly stretched and primed, the largest he had on hand. He inhabited his palette with several heaps of ultramarine, cerulean, viridian and cadmium yellow, as an afterthought, added a dip of alizarin. He laid the colors out in a circle and last dumped a generous pile of titanium white in the center. Jonas filled a small widemouth jar with turpentine, dipped his finger in and rubbed it on the most eloquent of his bee stings. It felt much quieter when the smarting subsided. Then he wet a large flat brush in the turps and began to drag some color into the mass of white.

A few broad strokes laid a predicate for a sky. The edge of a fresh brush anchored an arcing outline for a buttery sun. Violet shadows rooted the great shining stones. Drum's trees sprouted and blossomed from them like flowers. While he painted now, Jonas deserted thought, abandoned ego. He obeyed as he saw, breathed and moved from his soul's bright core, deeper than his hurts, beyond all his losses, falling upward into morning.

#

At the first glance of dawn on his window, Jonas dashed out to eliminate the threatening bees. He did not see Mildred, but when he looked into her stall on the way back to the house, she was standing with her newly arrived kid, who had already found her way to breakfast. There was nothing much left for Jonas to do but admire his goats. He admired and petted, cleaned and fed and watered, then came back to his house and stood in the open door gazing at the painting on his easel. More than Mildred's kid had been birthed this night. His dealers had been begging for landscapes, but they hadn't seen any like this one. Jonas thought his career might be about to take an interesting turn. If it turned out to be profitable for a change, he could live with it.

The fire had gone out during the night, but Drum's shirt and jeans hanging behind the stove were dry. Jonas took them down, folded them and left them on the sofa in the studio. When the boy emerged in the kitchen, awake, aware and fully dressed, Jonas was scrambling a saucer of diced peppers and onions into some eggs.

The swelling in Drum's face had subsided to the point he once again resembled a child more than a frog. Jonas was relieved "Drum, do you feel up to feeding and watering the hens for me while I get our breakfast in order here?"

"As we speak," Drum had learned the phrase from his uncle Ronan, Mary's husband. He was already headed toward the door.

"And while you're out there, look in on Mildred, will you?"

When Drum came back to the house. Jonas sat on the porch steps with their breakfast plates in his lap, an expectant grin on his face, "Bear, guess what! Mildred's had a little she-goat."

"Yes, Drum, a little doe. What should we name her?"

With no hesitation at all, Drum proposed, "Emily."

Jonas mutely handed him the plate with his breakfast, then turned away so the boy would not see his stunned expression, or the tears glistening in his eyes, but his silence gave him away.

"Is something wrong, Bear?"

"No Drum, you picked the most beautiful name I could ever think of. But why Emily?"

"I had a dream last night about a girl named Emily and her little sister Lucy."

"Was it a good dream?"

"I think so. They said their daddy had been lost, but they were happy now because he was coming home."

Jonas pulled two forks from the pocket of his checkered flannel shirt. His eyes were still ashine with moisture, but his crooked smile won out as he held out a fork to Drum, "Let's eat. We have another big day ahead of us."

They sat on the steps and finished their eggs, biscuits and grits in silence. If Drum wondered how long he had before Jonas turned him in, he didn't ask. Jonas tended his battered spirit. Drum's dream opened up his wound again, but also brought new healing. The hurt done to him now in such innocence released the dregs of Jonas' anger and resentment toward his God and toward himself. A seething rage that had hidden from him behind the barricade of his anguish, poured out of him in an instant and evaporated in the clear morning light. He would know sadness all his life, for all that was lost and all that would never be, but he could not blame God for taking his family, or for sparing him. The love he had known had not been erased, remained just as much a part of his being as his grieving, and he would carry them both as long as he breathed, for he lived now not only for himself, but for each soul who had been joined to his. The present held the future open to him. The past lived on in Jonas Bear, flowering toward tomorrow.

It wouldn't occur to Jonas to try to fix this turning of his soul in words, to write it down like a story, but he sensed it nonetheless, felt his burden beginning to lighten, starting its long slow transmutation into the sustaining treasure of his heart. Jonas downed his last bite of biscuit, wiped a bit of egg from his lip, and looked at Drum. "You still hungry?"

"Reckon I've plenty for now. It was awful good."

"I have to go into town for a little while. You want to go with me?"

"I'd like to stay here, if I can, say good bye to the hens and Mildred and Emily. Maybe I could go up to the

Shining Rocks one more time."

"Well, be careful if you do. Don't stir up any more bumblebees. Will you be here when I get back?"

"I don't plan to run off."

Jonas knew the truth when he heard it.

They carried their plates into the house, washed and dried and put them away, cleaned the pan and hung it on its rack. Jonas made them hot chocolate, which they drank in the studio as Jonas photographed his painting with his beat up old Leica.

"Where did you get that funny looking camera, Bear?"

"I found it beside a road in Germany. Someone in a hurry had forgotten it."

"It's easy to lose things when you're in a hurry, I guess."

"It's easy sometimes to lose things, Drum, even when you go slow and try to keep them close."

Jonas meant to send the photograph to his dealer in New Orleans, tell her if she liked this, there would be more. When he had several exposures of the painting, he turned suddenly and fired at Drum, catching him perched on the arm of the old sofa, his mouth puckered to blow on his hot chocolate. The flash went off, startling the boy, and he laughed, nearly spilling his drink. Jonas took two more quick shots. Then he mounted the camera on a tripod and carried it into the yard, set the self-timer, and they sat on the steps together like family. They went to the barn after that, and Jonas photographed Drum with the hens, with his arms around Mildred, and one showing Emily sucking on his fingers.

"How long before you have pictures?" Drum wanted to know.

"They'll be back in a couple of weeks."

"I don't reckon I'll get to see them."

"I'll know where you are. We'll still be friends. I'll send some prints to you."

Drum stood with his hands in his pockets, squinting into the low morning sun, as Jonas started the Jeep and turned it around.

Jonas put the Jeep in gear, called, "Don't burn the house down," and lurched away on his mission. Before starting the hill, he glanced in his mirror and glimpsed Drum sitting down on the porch steps again, with his hand in the air, poised to wave. It looked like a gesture of blessing.

#

The Jeep dropped out of sight below the hill. The sound of its descent settled with the dust. Drum stood up and went to the bathroom, found the calamine and anointed his stings once again. Mary's rock with its rough edges irritated his inflamed hide, so Drum lifted the cord over his head, laid the stone beside the sink before he rebuttoned his shirt. He would go up to visit the Shining Rocks first. He might take the sketchpad and draw something for Bear. If he had time before the Jeep returned, he would say goodbye to Mildred and Emily. He hoped if he had to go back to his kin today, Bear would take him, tell them what he needed. More than that, he hoped Bear would take him back some other day.

Drum stepped out onto the porch, heard the rumbling growl of a vehicle laboring up the drive. He thought Jonas must have forgotten something until a green International pickup crested the hill and rolled to a stop in front of the house. The truck though dusty, looked new. A big wooden box with a padlock filled half the bed. A man with a neatly trimmed beard, perhaps a little younger than Bear, who reminded Drum a bit of his father, stepped out of the cab. He looked surprised, almost shocked, to see a boy there. He hesitated, then "Hi, Is Mr. Bear at home?"

"Bear had to go to town; he'll be back soon if you want to wait."

Strangely intent, the bearded man scanned slowly around the yard, then climbed back into his pickup. "No thanks; I've come too soon. I'll catch him another day." He looked at Drum as if he wanted to say something more, then waved, and drove away down the hill.

Drum stood on the porch listening until he heard the pickup grumbling low, like distant thunder, down the county road. It was thunder, in fact. Drum looked up to see a bank of grim cumulus piling up over the ridges to south. He'd have to hurry, or risk getting damped upon. Clutching his sketchpad and a couple of markers, Drum crossed the yard at a trot, skirted the overgrown field and charged among the trees along the creek. He could hear the water urging him on. As he crossed the stream, it seemed to be laughing at him, *Time to* go, *don't you know, don't be slow.* The jays and crows were trying to tell him something as well, but he didn't stop to listen. Thunder boomed and rumbled louder now and he realized no sun dappled the road before him. Almost at a run, he came clear of the last of the trees and crossed the graveyard field. The bright boulders with their torturous crown of sourwoods towered up before him and the grassy ridgetop beyond sloped up and away against the lowering gloom. A momentary rift in the clouds admitted a spear of sunlight seeming to set the quartzite ablaze with heaven's fire. Then shadow reigned and all was gray and the world was awash.

Drum spied between two of the more massive

boulders, a dark triangular cleft that looked large enough to fit a boy. He made for it, squeezed himself in. He and his sketchpad were already soaked. He had thoughts of bees and snakes. A flash of lightning lit his stony refuge. An enormous crack of thunder deafened him, made the earth under him seem to pulse. The air thrummed with power.

The wind roared and screamed at him, He could see debris and limbs of trees sailing by outside. Water and leaves blew in upon him. Drum tried to squirm deeper into his burrow, saw reflected on the rocks ahead of him daylight coming in from the other side. He came up against a sharp wedge of quartzite and attempted to worm around it to get leeward of the wind. The rough stone pulled at his clothes and scraped his tender hurts. He found it hard to breathe. The boulders closed around him. Drum felt if he did not get from this place immediately, the mountain would swallow him. Terrified, suddenly and without reason, he screamed aloud, scrambled and grappled and struggled and strove as much against his own clumsy fear as against the confining stone, and suddenly he was through. He lay winded and bruised on his back in the shade of the boulders. Tall russet grass swayed gently above him. High and away, a pair of red tailed hawks circled one another in the unbroken blue.

ANNIE

Jonas stepped into Marcus Dill's office, shaking his soaked jacket at the door. The tattered top on his jeep had offered only minimal protection from the sudden downpour. Marcus was nowhere in sight, but Wilma Longshadow, the deputy, looked up from her desk as Jonas dripped on her floor.

"Been for a swim, Bear?"

"Close to it. Marcus in?"

"He's at the hospital. Their boy Josh tangled with a copperhead and got himself bit."

"How is he?"

"Marcus called in a little while ago. The doctor says Josh will be fine, but he's a sick young'un right now, and it scared Marcus and Ethyl to death. You know Marcus, nothing gets to him, but he was a scattered man when he left here. You want me to call him and tell him you're here?"

"His plate's full right now, Wilma. I'll talk to him tomorrow." "

Marcus said to call if anybody needed him."

"No, don't bother him; it'll keep." Jonas decided one more day of Drum's company wouldn't be a bad thing for either of them. "Be good, Wilma. I'll check with Marcus later."

"I can't be good, Bear."

"Well, have a good time, then."

Jonas was thankful for his jeep as it crawled and

slipped up his muddy drive. Once secure in his yard, he yelled, "Hey, Drum, back the same day." Mildred bleated greeting from her stall.

He didn't find the boy at the barn nor in the house, hoped he'd been in the dry when the storm came over. In the bathroom, he saw Drum's talisman lying by the sink. Jonas picked it up and held it to the light. Bits of quartz sparkled in the dark stone. It was warm to the touch, as if it had been lying in the sun.

After an hour, Drum had not reappeared. Jonas walked up to the Shining Rocks. He stood among the mouldering stumps and called again. Only a hawk's cry answered somewhere high above. He looked up, saw two of them, circling one another as they flew, each the other's center. Jonas walked slowly around the boulders. In a shadowed crevice, something bright caught his eye. He had to kneel on the wet earth to reach in and retrieve a page from the sketchpad, torn, smeared, sodden, but still alive with vision. Drum must have crawled in here to get out of the rain. But he was gone now.

#

When Drum could draw a measured breath again, and hear the strumming of cicadas over the pounding of his heart, he sat up and tried to get his bearings. The sourwoods were gone from atop the boulders that had sheltered him against the storm. The ground around the quartzite outcrop was grassy as before, but when he looked up the slope above him, only one track wound away to his right into a forest of mature fir and maple blocking any view of the crest of the ridge. He stood up and stared wonderingly all around. Except for the little meadow right around the stones, all he could see were trees. When he climbed up onto the boulders and looked down toward the house, the forest blocked his view. The track he had climbed quickly lost itself in the shadowed wood below.

He took deep breaths. The air seemed lighter, without any sign of the gray haze that often settled in over the mountains in summer. Drum shivered, not from cold but with a thrill, as if the clock of his being had somehow been reset. He wondered if he might be dreaming. Fleeting images and faces gathered in his mind and were gone again. He had a strong sense that something like this had happened to him before, but when he tried to recall it, even the feeling slipped away. There was nothing he knew to do but go back to the house and hope Bear was there.

Drum scrambled down from his perch. When he couldn't find his sketchpad and markers, he started back the way he had come. The road was where it should be, but seemed not quite the road he knew. "This looks new," he told the trees. When he crossed the creek again, it looked the same as far as he could tell, except there was more water in it now, maybe from the rain, he thought, although the woods and all the land around seemed dry, bearing no trace of recent wind or storm, no broken limbs, no scattered branches. The creek still chattered at him, *You belong, come along, mind the song.* Drum knew that creeks don't talk, but he heard the laughter of the water and the words were in his head.

He came to the field, still right where he'd left it, but full now of corn, dark and green, taller than a man, ready for harvest. An elderly mule stood in the road, hitched to an unpainted wooden sledge with several bushels of unshucked corn heaped upon it. The John held a broken corn stalk in his mouth, chewing the middle as both ends twirled about his long face. He peered at Drum with studied unconcern, as if the boy were an accustomed fixture in his days. An industrious snap and rustle issued from the cornfield. Somebody nearly hidden by the tasseled stalks hummed to themselves a cheerful tune. The voice was pleasant enough, sounded to Drum as if it belonged to a grown woman, maybe old, but not real old. He glimpsed a basket already full of fat ears, a flash of apron and a checkered sun bonnet. He could see nothing of the face owning them, and the woman, unaware of him, never looked up from her gathering.

Drum waved furtively at the mule and slipped on past. He was not ready to talk to people he didn't know until he could ask Bear how the world had gotten turned bottom up. "Don't be surprised at anything you see now," he said aloud to the road, but when the trees were behind him and he had a clear view of the house and the yard around, Drum was surprised.

Hens ran loose in the yard, their pen gone. Mildred and Emily had disappeared, along with their barn. A large vegetable garden, rowed and hoed, occupied that whole end of the yard. A log barn, bigger than the house, stood just beyond it. The house was where it should be. Its log walls looked to have weathered only a few seasons. Their hewn sides still shone pale in the noonday sun. In place of Bear's metal roof, the house, like the barn, was topped with cedar shakes. Drum didn't see the jeep, but when he walked to the front of the house he saw a buggy in a lean-to on the side of the barn.

Drum stepped up on the porch. The boards of the floor were wider than the ones Drum sat on earlier that morning. They looked as freshly cut as the logs. There was no screen to slam at the open door. In the studio, half its former size, no easels or paintings, no worktable or paints or brushes, just a small desk and two long tables with benches down one side of each. Three tall stacks of books perched at the end of one of the tables.

"Bear?" He said it without much hope for an answer.

Drum went into the kitchen, found a table in the center of the room, and a couple of chairs, but no fridge, and Bear's propane fueled range was gone. So was the washer. The kitchen had been deprived of its cabinets and sink. A cupboard stood by the windows, and a long table beneath them. A cedar bucket and a basin sat side by side on the table. Shelves with plates and bowls and cups and pots and pans and assorted other implements and needfuls covered the opposite wall.

Drum retreated back to the studio and opened the bathroom door. It had become a pantry of sorts, with jars and jugs and bags of supposedly edible contents. On the back of the pantry door someone had tacked up an antique calendar adorned with a lithograph of a cheerful boy maybe a little younger than Drum, barefoot, wearing overalls and a somewhat frayed and bedraggled straw hat. Three spotted puppies crowded onto his lap, one of them licking his face. Some of the pages had already been torn away. September was set to go next. Four bold red numerals in the upper right-hand corner Drum took to represent the year. He read it aloud, wondering what it was, beside the date, *1913*, that troubled him. Then he knew what bothered him about the calendar; old as it was, it looked new, as if it had been hanging on a pantry door months rather than decades.

While he was trying to figure this out, a voice from the door behind startled him back into his moment, "I wish thee no harm, boy, but I'm about to swing my stick right through the air occupied by thy noggin, unless thee can inform me now and accurately what business a total stranger to me might claim to be prowling through my house."

The voice sounded like the one singing among the corn. The face that spoke strove mightily to maintain a severe expression, which was a hopeless task, given the suppressed merriment in the blue eyes and the wide mouth threatening to blossom into a laugh any instant. A cumulus of pewter locks surrounded the mobile features. Expressions flickered across the face too rapidly to register, as if the weather of a year had been contained in a single day. Every second was a departure and an arrival.

That face, not young, not really old, maybe a little older than Jonas would be in thirty-five or forty years, seemed quite pleased to have thoroughly rattled her visitor. "Don't faint, young friend, for I am a Friend indeed and would not smite nor flail thee for the world and all its gold. My name is Annie. I am a teacher and this is the place I live and do it in. Thee is perhaps a student, come to learn and study, or be thee skulking about in my house just because thee has no place that is properly thy own? Tell me now honestly, and we will remain friends."

Drum's penchant for speaking honestly had gotten him into trouble from time to time, but now it seemed the most promising course open, "I'm lost from all who know me, Miss Annie, and I need to be in school soon. My name is Drum and I don't know how I got here or where to go."

"In the manner of Friends, I am ever Annie to thee, Drum. If thee can work and be honest with all, there is a place right here for thee to learn and become."

Drum faced all the love smiling down upon him there and began to cry. He did not sob or wail or whimper. His chin did not tremble. His mouth did not twist. His face did not fall ashamed. Drum stood where he was and looked steadily at Annie, saw in her eyes her caring for an equal soul, and without embarrassment let tears of release and relief come as they would. Annie for her part, did not say, *Don't cry,* as solicitous adults are prone to do confronted by juvenile weeping. She did not say, *It will be all right,* when she had no idea what history of hurt and trial she was speaking to. She did not lift a hand to wipe away tears before she could touch the suffering. She simply stood where she was, returning Drum's gaze, her smile holding, until the tears glistening on her cheeks matched those of the boy before her.

When they were both fully present and aware to one another, she reached out and took his hand. "Come along," she whispered, and led Drum away to the kitchen. Annie seated him at the table, poured out a glass of milk in front of him. "Is thee hungry, Drum?"

Drum was thirsty. He took a swallow of the milk, recognized the taste of goat's milk, and wished he could have drunk Mildred's with Bear. "I had a right good breakfast."

"Well, it's dinnertime now. Thee won't skip a meal under my roof. There's half a cured ham left hanging in the pantry; would thee fetch it for me? There's a stool by the door there if thee need it to reach the hook."

Not quite sure what he was looking for, Drum located the ham by its smell. It hung by the shank, suspended from a hook in the middle of the little room, wrapped in a cloth bag gathered around the top. Drum brought it back to the kitchen, bag and all, and laid it on the table under the windows where Annie pointed him.

She laid back the cloth, with a broad knife sliced a

couple of thick slices from the ham and retied the bag. "Go hang this back for me, please thee."

When Drum returned to the kitchen, Annie had stoked the coals to life in her wood cookstove and already added several splints to heat the black iron pan atop. She shot her welcome home smile at Drum as he finished his milk and wiped away his pale mustache, "While I fix our nourishment here, please thee go loose Johnny and put him in, and bring me back a few ears of that corn from the sled."

"I don't know anything about mules," Drum confessed.

"Mercy then, Drum, where has thee been all thy life, down in Asheton?"

Drum knew about Asheton- a small resort city between mountains about thirty miles from Jonas Gap. It comforted him to hear he was still in the same world he had been born into.

#

Jonas walked into his bedroom, saw Drum had made the bed when he got up, done a better job of it than a grownup might expect from a boy. He hung Drum's talisman on the head of his iron bedframe. Drum wouldn't forget it. Either the boy planned to come back, or he'd left a parting gift. Then Jonas went out and tended his animals, feeding chickens, cleaning the goats' stall, stripping Mildred of whatever milk Emily had left. He might just let Drum's name for the kid stand. He came back to the house, set aside the landscape and started a portrait. When daylight began to fail, the only Drum he had seen since returning from town was the one on his canvas.

Jonas thought then about supper, but the idea lacked

47

appeal. He wasn't hungry; he was tired, and his eyes hurt. He lay down on the sofa in the studio and was asleep with one foot still on the floor. Not long past midnight, he woke suddenly from a dream. Lorraine had come to visit, smiled down at him that wise sad sweet smile of hers and laid her hand lightly on his chest. He closed his eyes and savored the warmth and pulse of her touch until he realized that her hand was not resting against his chest but inside it, her fingers cupping his heart the way one would hold an apple.

For one eternal instant of terror, without reason at all, Jonas feared she would squeeze his heart and still its beating. Every day since the accident he had cursed himself for being alive when his family was dead, wished he had been with them in the Rambler when the truck shredded it. But now, he was not done with his life. Even alone and bereft, he was not ready yet to die. He opened his eyes. Lorraine withdrew her hand and delivered to him the sweetest brightest smile she had ever bestowed. He hoped she was about to kiss him and she was gone and Jonas awoke to the cool dark and the distant proclamations of owls and the whisper of a gentle rain on his roof. "Drum?" he inquired of the night. None answered but the owls.

#

Drum braced himself for judgment. What he got, as Annie set the pan off the stove and wiped her hands on her apron, was an offer of instruction and fellowship, "We'll go together then, thee and me, and the little I know will shortly be in thy own head to wield."

Annie was true to her word. Before Drum darkened her door again, he would know the difference between reins and lines, between stay and latch, between collar and billet. He would know trace from chain and what to buckle first and what to loose last. In time, he would learn about saddles, too, and he would ride a horse or a mule if necessity called for it, although Drum was never comfortable with large animals. Having learned as a child to be slow about trusting humans larger than himself, he would grow to manhood being wary of beasts bigger than him. He made exceptions for individuals he knew well, who returned his gentleness and patience in kind.

With Annie's guidance and assistance, Drum liberated Johnny and turned him into the barn lot with water and feed, then hung the tack away before heading back to the house with several ears of corn for dinner. Annie did not do lunch. She informed Drum, that although the town folk in Asheton might eat lunch if they were pretentious, all plain souls ate breakfast, dinner and supper.

Back in the kitchen again, Drum demonstrated that he did at least know how to shuck corn and pull the silks and cut the kernels from the cob. This much Mary would teach him one day when he was almost Annie's age, if the calendar in Annie's pantry told the truth. He was still puzzling about the calendar when he heard Annie say, "Thee has a good hand in the kitchen, Drum; maybe we could take in boarders."

Drum recognized it as sincere praise; he didn't think Annie ever offered anyone less than her honest appraisal. "Annie, it might be a long time before I can go home again. Could I be your boarder and go to your school if I work hard and help out around?"

Annie stopped her work, took a couple of steps toward him, stood hands on hips regarding him intently as if she were examining his soul. Then she laughed at the light of her revelation, "Drum, thee may stay for thy refreshing company as long as thee has need, and thy labor will be thy gift to God."

#

Annie Starling possessed a strong will to believe. She believed in a guiding Spirit, the sanctity of life and Love's power to prevail. Any evidence she encountered that might indicate the contrary, she could usually arrange to align with her personal predisposition. Against all advice, she used her inheritance from her Aunt Cora, who married rich and died widowed and childless, to come to this wilderness, as her friends called it, and have a house put up to shelter her and her school, which so far had drawn pitifully few students and none regularly. The mothers in the cove needed their daughters, they said, to help care for the house and their younger siblings. The fathers required the sons to assist with field or mill or still, and the sons for their part saw more to be learned in the woods than in books.

An old Quaker proverb held that *When you go with God, you go alone,* and in Annie's case, the say seemed to fit. Her Monthly Meeting down east at Sandy Spring had given her their prayers, but little else. They felt led to save their funds for their new meeting house, and for benevolences that were closer home, more accessible and therefore more readily supervised.

Where Annie's new neighbors lacked in education they excelled in imagination. Her unique manner of speech and dress marked her as different and alien and therefore most likely dangerous. Before long, Annie was rumored by some to be a witch, and found herself often addressed and referred to as Warwoman, an appellation she was inclined to suffer with good will as long as it was assigned in the same spirit. Over time, she gained a reputation as a healer, and a kind and generous soul, and so was tolerated by all and accepted by most as a good and helpful neighbor, though not entirely to be trusted with the minds of their offspring.

Houston Coggins and his son built her house for her and most of the furniture in it, with her helping more than they thought a female should properly be able to do, and came back the next summer to build her barn. Houston said no more than three words a day even to his family, directing them with signs and grunts to do his bidding. If he ever had any curiosities, he kept them to himself, but his son James, not so shy, asked one day as Annie handed him an armload of shingles she had split, "Warwoman, whatever on God's earth made you think to put a school here?"

Annie gave him her own simple truth, "Spirit led me up this road, James, and this is where it ended." If James thought this an inadequate response, he never let on.

#

Before the sun set that evening, Drum had been fed dinner and supper, helping with the preparation more than Houston and James would have thought proper for a boy to be able to do, surprising and mightily delighting Annie. It confirmed an inkling that had struck her the instant she had spied an unknown boy standing in her pantry.

Her father, a teacher, loved his work, but had few illusions about it. When she told him she wanted to become a teacher like him, he said that was a fine thing, "But Annie love, thee best brace and prepare. Thee may teach for years and count thyself blessed if thee meet just one student with a gift and a passion for learning, and the will and skill to use it for betterment. But that one, will make thee count thy life well spent." She felt Spirit telling her in that meeting moment with this young stranger that her greatest joy as a teacher was standing before her. Now at the end of the day, as she and Drum ate their gritty bread and baked sweet potato, the conviction still held.

"Drum, be those all the clothes thee has?"

"Annie, these are all I have of anything." He stood up and spread his arms wide, grinning broadly as if it were a great joke, "This is all there is of me in the world."

"Come along then." Annie beckoned him to follow her into the classroom, "We must expand thy wardrobe promptly. Thee must need some to wear and some to wash." Annie kept a sewing box in her desk, for she never had a student who wasn't wearing something that an older brother or sister, or maybe two or three, had not worn before them, and there were ever holes and tears requiring emergency repair. She was adept at patching and joining what life and struggle had pulled apart.

She took her cloth tape from the basket and sized Drum for shirt and trousers, noting but not remarking on the strange cut of his attire, which looked to her too flimsy and carelessly sewn to be of long use.

When she had finished, Drum asked, "Where's your bathroom?"

"You can bathe in your room, Drum; there's a basin and soap, but the privy's yonder," and she pointed out the back door. Drum could see in the shadowed verge of the yard the object of his search.

Later, when her boarder and new student was abed, Annie turned up her lamp and began on one of the long tables to lay out and mark for cutting, the fabric she would use to make Drum's new clothes. He would never know he was wearing the resurrected remnants of Annie's own skirts and jackets.

Sometime in the wee morning Annie set her sowing aside and went upstairs to bed. She blew out her lamp and opened her window to the foggy dark, heard above the frogs and crickets the whisper of the creek and the shuffle of men going through her yard, headed up the track by the Shining Rocks. She was certain it was the McMinn brothers. She knew that somewhere past there, they had a still. A few years before, the state legislature had declared the unlicensed manufacture of corn whiskey illegal, but the practice persisted in the mountain districts since the market for spirits was far more reliable and rewarding than the demand for corn, and the product was more transportable over roads that were at best no more than marginally passable.

A few hours later, the less stealthy passage of a somewhat larger party wakened Annie again. Among the voices there, she recognized the twangy protests of William McMinn, and the jovial growl of Zebulon Pounder, the sheriff. Apparently the brothers had neglected to pay their blind money, and Zeb had led the agents of the State to their operation. Annie slept little after that, pondering the strange boy Spirit had dropped upon her out of the air.

When the easterly sky began to pale and she could see against the dawn the silhouettes of trees outside her window, Annie threw a shawl about her bare shoulders to ward the morning chill, and stepped onto her porch to greet the day. She nearly stumbled over the figure stretched out before her on the floor, lying on his side, an empty glazed jug beside his head.

Shoeless, therefore unable to kick him effectively, she fetched her stick from beside the door and poked the sleeping man in the small of his back, hard enough that later in the day he had reason to recall how he had been roused. The stricken man yelped like a puppy, rolled onto his back and lay gasping for his breath, staring in her approximate direction as he tried to focus his eyes.

"Wallace McMinn," she intoned, "Why be thee asleep on my porch while the day is aborning?"

"Oh, Warwoman, you've hurt me here," Wallace wheezed, when he could breathe. "I was watching for the Revenue; it commenced to drismal on me, and I could see the road from your porch."

"Then thee better keep to thyself for a few days, Wallace," she advised him, "The Law came through with thy brother in tow two hours past."

#

When Drum woke to gray morning light, and ventured as far as the kitchen, Annie had eggs and gritty bread already on the table, "I pray thee had a good night's rest, Friend Drum, and that thy long sleep did not tax thee unduly before thy day ever started."

Drum could tell by the light in her blue eyes and the smile in her voice that she teased. It eased his embarrassment at having slept far longer than he intended. Annie motioned for him to sit, set a bowl of fried apples on the table, then sat herself, poured for them both coffee, heavily milked, folded her hands in her lap and bowed her head. Drum followed suit, anticipating either a long blessing like his parents would inflict, or some brief exclamation of praise or thanks as he experienced at Mary and Ronan's table. But only after two full minutes of absolute silence, Annie lifted toward him a grand smile and whispered, as if it were a secret between them and God, "All praise and ever thanks."

"I'm sorry, Annie, that you had to make breakfast by

yourself."

"Thee is forgiven, Drum, for thee has gladdened me beyond measure by coming to help me eat it."

Drum had been taught strict manners; he was careful to chew his bite of biscuit thoroughly and swallow it totally before he spoke, "You talk different from most folks, Annie. Are you from afar?"

Annie laughed, as if this were the first time anyone had ever called attention to her mode of speech, "Sandy Springs in all but distance is as far from Sorrow Cove as Paris is from Asheton, but I was born and grew up among Friends, Quakers. Does thee know of Quakers?"

"I know about William Penn, and Pennsylvania."

"Then thee knows much already, but there are Friends in Carolina, too, and I be one of those."

"Why do you say *thee* instead of *you*?"

"Because over the water, wealthy and powerful folk were fond of speaking of themselves as *we* and *you*, as if one soul were favored more in the sight of God than many with lesser means." *Thee* counts only one, as each one of us must stand equal and alone before God."

Drum considered this as he sought unity with his apples. He wished his Baptist preacher grandfather were here to consult. "That makes sense to me, Annie; maybe I could become a Friend like you."

"Methinks perhaps thee is already, Drum, but only thy heart can tell thee so."

After their breakfast, as they were drying and putting away the dishes, Drum pointed toward the classroom, "Annie, will we have school today?"

"Thee has gotten adrift from thy times, Drum. This is First Day, no school today, but thy eagerness gratifies considerably."

"First Day?"

"Has Spirit sent me an English boy, then? God has a fine sense of humor. Sunday, Drum. Would thee care to keep Meeting with me, now? Thee would find it more peaceable than classwork, and likely more enlightening for thy soul than studying skills for accumulating property and getting thy own way in society."

"What kind of meeting?"

"Meeting for Worship, but none like in a steeple house, Drum. We will sit still and quiet and listen for Spirit."

Music was Drum's favorite part of doing church, "Do we sing hymns?"

"We share any song or word Spirit might lend us, but mainly we listen, for God needs to hear our prayers and praise out loud much less than we need to see holy Light within. God already knows anything we might think of to say or ask, but all Spirit means to move and make in our lives we have never yet dreamed."

Like most in her tradition, Annie felt an abiding need to maintain solidarity with the body of her faith in matters of religious practice. There was no Friend's meeting within a hundred miles, but she maintained regular and timely worship on her own. The only organized Christian congregation in the community was the small and newly gathered band of Methodists, whose shepherd did not think Annie quite qualified as a redeemed-by-the-blood daughter of Christ. He regarded Annie as possibly a pagan influence in an already depraved population, and certainly competition for his enterprise. He did not even pretend to wish her well. In his view, if his congregants needed enlightenment on any subject under heaven, they should ask him.

Although she likely prayed for her neighbors more

than the zealous young preacher did, he never went out of his way to welcome her to his church. She had friends in the congregation, and if there were a christening, wedding or funeral in one of their families, she would attend the service. Once when a neighbor asked her why she went to church so seldom, she responded, "Sula Mae, I reckon I'm mainly interested in hatchings, matchings, and dispatchings."

As soon as the kitchen was cleaned and cleared, Drum followed Annie to the barn to take food and water to Johnny and turn him out of his stall. It did not take long to toss into a crib the remainder of the corn Annie harvested the day before. They shelled a few dry ears, threw out some kernels for the chickens, who had free range of the place. The hens had nesting boxes in the barn. They sometimes used them when they could not find more imaginative venues for hiding their eggs. Annie knew their favorite places, and with Drum's sharp eyes to help, managed to claim most of them before they started back to the house. "We'll wash these and put them by, and it will be time enough for Meeting, Drum."

"Where do we go to Meeting, Annie?"

"Meeting comes to us. It is such a lovely morning, why not on my porch?" And only a little later they were sitting down beside Annie's door in two big rockers that Houston and James had made for her.

By necessity, the inhabitants of the cove made most of their possessions for themselves. Annie's chairs were examples of the highlander's craft elevated to an art form. With none but the simplest of hand tools, Houston and James built furniture more durable than any made by machines in a factory. They felled the trees, split and planed and shaved each part by hand. Annie's rockers had been cut and joined without nails or glue, right on her porch on rainy days when the men could not work on the barn. The stretchers, rails, arms and splats were made from dry red oak, and the legs were shaped from green hickory, so that when they dried and shrank they would grip tightly all the parts pegged into them. James made splits from white oak, and Houston wove them onto the frame for seats. Houston came back several months later and fitted the rockers, which had been shaped from freshly cut maple. The chairs would last longer than the hands that made them.

Drum sat as Annie did, folded his hands in his lap like her, and waited for Meeting to commence. Annie glanced at him, smiled, then lifted her chin and closed her eyes, and appeared immediately lost in herself, as if she were the only soul for a thousand miles around. Not wanting to disturb her, Drum sat as still and quiet as a boy could manage, found it easier than he thought it would be as he looked around and the world began to draw his attention out of himself. He felt the heat of the sun reflecting from the baked yard before the house. He heard the sputter of grasshoppers, a discussion among crows away somewhere past the barn. Johnny snorted. A hen announced her new egg. Cicadas chanted a hypnotic cadenza, *Listen to this; listen to this; listen to this...* Somewhere high and away above the porch roof, an unseen hawk cried for the sheer joy of flight. Drum lost count of all the sounds of the day; they blurred and blended slowly and subtly into a single ceaseless voice. Drum closed his eyes, tried to concentrate and catch the words.

Through his eyelids, he could see the russet glow from the sunwashed yard. The glow brightened, paled, shaped into a square, and within the square coalesced a face, painted on a canvas upon an easel, and Bear stood before the easel working on a portrait, nearly finished. Drum recognized his own likeness as it wavered, then dissolved into a formless golden luminescence pulsing with the throbbing of the cicadas, *Follow the light; follow the light; follow the light...* Drum tried to follow in his mind that sparkling and rippling becoming sunlight reflecting from a wide river far below, flowing away westward between dark green mountains. The reflection blazed like a great fire burning in the water's depths, and Drum was falling down toward the river, sparkles and ripples rushing up at him. Then a voice, calling his name, "Drum."

Annie stayed Drum's rocker with a hand, looking amused as two startled eyes peered up at her, blinking against the light. "Drum, is thee sleeping through Meeting?"

"I wasn't asleep, Annie, I was just away for awhile."

Annie tried hard not to laugh, "And pray, Friend Drum, where was thee all that time?"

"I was falling, Annie. I was falling in the Light."

#

Roused from a dream about the Shining Rocks by the mad cackling and flailing of his chickens, Jonas pulled on his pants and rushed out barefoot into the night to find four large hounds in pursuit of his hens. Several birds already lay bloodied and scattered about the pen. All the dogs but one cleared the fence and disappeared into the dark with his first shout. The largest crouched back on his haunches, faced Jonas with bared teeth, growling low. Jonas cursed himself for not owning a gun. He had nothing in hand but his big flashlight, threw it at the hound as hard as he could. His aim was lucky. The heavy light hit the dog squarely between the eyes. The hound howled, shook his head and fled after his gang.

Jonas retrieved his light, surprised that it still worked. He found six hens dead, and another he had to dispatch for mercy's sake. Mildred and Emily, frantic with fright, were safe in their stalls. If the dogs could have reached them, Jonas had no doubt he'd be goatless. He finally got a hand on Mildred and stroked her to calm. As she settled, so did her kid. "Mildred, he said soothingly, we need to get us a dog of our own, and a gun."

The following afternoon, Jonas had just returned from town and was ejecting the first shell fired from his new shotgun when he heard a vehicle laboring up his drive. A tan Plymouth Belevedere crested the hill and stopped beside his Jeep. A neat handsome woman with short gray hair got out of the Plymouth and walked toward the house as Jonas laid his weapon on the porch and stood by the steps to greet her. He was out of practice, but he tried to summon up his company smile, "I hope you didn't have too much trouble with my hill. I haven't kept the road as I should."

His visitor returned his smile as if she were used to smiling at strangers. Jonas guessed a smile probably came naturally to her in most situations. She held out her hand, shook his strongly, "Believe me, I've traveled much worse in my time. I grew up in the Cove when the quickest way to go anywhere was to walk. I'm Emma Truelight."

"I'm Jonas Bear; how can I help you, Emma?"

"The house looks quite different from my remembrances, but is this the old Starling place?"

"I bought it from Jim Coggins, but he called it the Starling place. You may recall the house as built of logs; it's been altered somewhat over the years."

"Well, I don't want to disturb your privacy, Mr. Bear, but I just wanted to see the place again while I was here. I used to go to school in your house."

#

Classes commenced on Second Day, which Drum learned was Monday, September eighth, nineteen thirteen, according to what Annie called *the English calendar* on her pantry door. Drum, sat with three other pupils at one long table when Annie called for their attention. Drum and Emmalou Truelight were the oldest of the students; she seemed to him about his age. Another girl, Polly Coggins, maybe a couple of years younger, turned out to be James' little sister. The youngest was a boy called Owly by all but Annie because of his habit of staring intently with his big brown eyes at anyone who spoke to him. Annie steadfastly addressed him as Willard. A pale frail child who was so myopic that he almost touched the page with his nose when he read, he was unlikely ever to shed his nickname, reinforced as it was by his surname. His father was Daniel Hoots.

Drum and Emmalou were the best readers in the group, so were enlisted as assistant teachers in that subject. Owly, though not more than eight, evidenced a genius for numbers, and his nose was often smudged more than his eraser after a spell of intense calculation. Occasionally he would stay after classes for extra study. Numbers were more reliable friends to him than rowdy children his age, and since his vision was too poor to be of much use farming or hunting, his father allowed him the time he needed to pursue his passion. Drum was not too proud to accept Owly's tutoring when it was offered, for arithmetic was not Drum's consuming interest, although he wanted to do well enough at it not to disappoint Annie.

He was impressed when Owly told him that after class he and Annie had begun to delve into a mysterious subject called *algebra*. Owly tried to explain it to him, but the main impression Drum gleaned was that it involved trying to calculate with numbers that didn't exist. That seemed to him a lot like counting eggs before the hens laid them.

Annie discouraged Drum from drawing in class, which he habitually did whenever their studies tended toward numbers or grammar, but she recognized his gift, and employed the limited resources she had at hand to encourage him to practice it.

#

Summer lingered longer that year. Usually Annie was up before first light to open her kitchen window to the warm September dark and gather herself toward the new day. On a Seventh Day barely two weeks into the Ninth Month, someone stood watching in her yard when she lit the lamp on her kitchen table and turned to let in the air.

William McMinn held his breath and took careful aim through the open window. He was near enough to hear the clatter as Annie made her morning's coffee, and far enough out in the dark to be into the woods before she made it out her door. People would know it was his rifle that fired, but he didn't mean for anyone to prove it.

He wasn't planning to shoot the woman, just frighten her, and perhaps murder a piece of her good crockery. Neither he nor his brother really thought Annie had informed the law of their still operations, but after their arrest, pride and reputation demanded some sort of dramatic response. He didn't want his neighbors ever to be too sure of what McMinns might do if crossed.

William could see Annie clearly as she washed a cup, could smell the coffee she poured. He pulled the trigger of his rifle, aiming for the clock on a shelf opposite the window. The hammer fell with a resounding tock, amplified in the still foggy air. The rifle did not fire.

Annie heard it clearly, recognizing the sound for what it was. She did not flinch, but turned toward the window, knowing without seeing him, who was there. She smiled on William McMinn her sweetest smile.

William ran for the trees, not trying to be quiet. He was certain Annie had recognized him; he would avoid her in the future. He never admitted to a soul that in his nervousness he had forgotten to load his weapon, but like most highlanders, he was too fond of a good tale to keep the morning's adventure to himself. The version of events he told abroad only added to Annie's reputation as a woman with powers.

#

Owly was not the only student who came sometimes to study with Annie outside of class. Emmalou wanted to be a writer when she grew up, having gotten a taste for narrative from the Walter Scott novels she found at home, Waverly, Rob Roy, and Bride of Lammermoor, which had been handed down through generations of semi-literate Truelights from some forgotten ancestor whose life was likely as adventursome and improbable as any of the tales in the books. Emmalou wanted to live a wild and important life, and since there seemed to her little chance of doing that in the Cove, she wanted to make one up and write it down. Annie herself had a weakness for writing and imagination and was only too happy to encourage her. "If thee wants to write a book, Emmalou," she counseled the girl, "Thee must read a great number of them first, and as thee sees how others write, thee will learn all the ways to avoid when thee comes to write for thyself."

Emmalou took Annie's advice to heart and over time discovered she preferred reading books to writing them, and so became a teacher instead.

As the extended Indian summer gave way to a sudden and snowy winter, Drum became used to the sight of Annie and Emmalou sitting by the stove in the kitchen or the classroom, their heads together over a book, as they took turns reading and questioning. In true Quaker tradition, Annie would usually frame even her explanations as questions, leading her students to find the answer waiting in mind and heart to be claimed and lifted into life.

Emmalou was at Annie's door as often as she could get permission from her mother, and sometimes, in spite of Annie's disclaimers, even when none had been given. Once, on the way home with two borrowed books under her arm, she met her mother on the path coming to fetch her.

"Emma Louise," Maude Truelight spoke sharply, "You'll find a proper dose of hickory tea awaiting if you go slipping off to that Warwoman again when you've chores undone. All the time you pass with her, people will say she's spelled you."

"She has books, Mama," the girl said it like a plea. "She lets me read and then we talk about them."

"Your life is not in a book," Maude pronounced, then softening, laid her hand on Emmalou's head, and almost in a whisper, "I had big dreams once, Child, but bythebys the world shrinks down to what the eye can spy between these hills. Be content with the Cove, daughter, or you will reap only sorrow and regret for your last years." After a reflective pause, in a stronger voice, "Find yourself a husband and you can have plenty of both without all the wearying travel."

Emmalou told the Warwoman what her mother had said about living close to home and not reading too much, and was rewarded with a fleeting smile that hinted of something wistful. "Don't discount everything Maude tells thee just because thee doesn't want to be her," answered Annie, then added, "Travel wonderfully narrows the mind."

#

Annie was a source of endless curiosity and speculation for all her neighbors. Mainly, they wondered how she managed to get by, and what the Warwoman did all day by herself when she wasn't corrupting the minds of their children with foreign notions,

She got by through keeping her needs simple and her wants few, and with a meager continuing grant from a small foundation dedicated to preserving Southern Appalachian history and culture. The families on the creek never guessed they were as much a field of investigation for her as she was for them. Day by day in her little study off the classroom, she was putting down their lives in incisive, yet loving sentences. Their stories would long outlive them. Decades later, when life in their cove had changed beyond all their imaginings, Emmalou Truelight would come across the stories in a bookstore in Asheton, and recognize herself among the pages.

Although Annie remained a curiosity to her neighbors, in truth she was no more eccentric than any of them, who never forgot she was an alien flatlander. The Warwoman was their flatlander, though, respected by most and loved by some. When anyone was sick or hurt, Annie would hear of it and show up offering food and help. She never interfered with their convoluted feuds and alliances, never offered advice, although she had a penchant for posing troubling questions, never talked down, even to a child, and regarded all the world, including herself with compassionate humor. Only the most conscientious misanthrope could have managed to dislike a soul like Annie. Even those who were a little afraid of her would never imagine she meant them anything but good.

The people of the cove had for generations lacked all opportunity for formal education, but their beautiful and unforgiving wilderness taught them wisdom and an instinct for survival. They knew the world outside their Cove was changing rapidly and would soon intrude into their mountains and drastically alter the landscape of their lives. Some of them recognized that if their children prospered in that strange new world, they would need to know its ways, Until the county built a school in their cove, Annie offered the only way to that knowledge open to them. None in the Cove could have afforded to send their children to the boarding school in Asheton, even had they been able to spare young hands from the unending work of wresting a living from a steep, rocky and ungenerous soil.

#

The long mountain summer was followed by an abbreviated autumn. Mid-way through October, the weather cooled precipitously and for weeks rain, sometimes mixed with snow or sleet fell more days than not. The creeks filled, topped their banks, became raging rivers, flooded the bottomlands and fields, washed away yards and barns, and a few houses.

On a rare sunny morning, Emmalou slipped away to read with Annie. Within an hour after her arrival, the clouds closed again, dusking noon, and unleashed a deluge. The rain had slacked only a little when Emmalou said, "I've got to get home, Annie." Annie tried to persuade her to wait for a clearing, but the girl insisted, "I didn't tell anybody I was here. They'll worry."

Annie called Drum, who was in the kitchen drawing storm and flood on his tablet, "Drum, please thee go with Emmalou and see she gets safely across the creek."

Drum was pleased to oblige, as he had an unspoken crush on Emmalou. Owly's cousin Eldon, who showed up at the school seldom more than once in any given week, picked a fight when he saw Drum drawing a portrait of Emmalou. Eldon was older and bigger, but Drum was quicker, and the fight wound up more or less a draw before Annie intervened. At that point, both boys were too tired to continue the contest and glad to be contained. When Drum showed Eldon the drawings he had made of Eldon and all the other students, he was appeased. For his part, Drum after that studiously ignored Emmalou whenever Eldon was around.

The footpath between Annie's place and the Truelights' was much shorter than the road, but crossed a creek that was bold and riotous even in normal weather. When Drum and Emmalou reached it on this day, the roiling water was splashing against the bottom of the huge chestnut footlog spanning the stream.

The top side of the log had been flattened with an adze to provide stable footing. Normally, either of them would have skipped across without a thought. Today was not a normal day. They had to shout to hear one another over the roar of the swollen stream, and the soggy earth vibrated with the power of the torrent. Drum was uncharacteristically fearful, "Maybe we should wait for the flood to ease, Emmalou."

"I've got to get home, Drum; Ma will skin me alive. I'll be fine." Emmalou was half way to the opposite bank when a huge square-hewn beam from somebody's barn surged around the bend upsteam and struck the footlog just ahead of Emmalou. She kept her balance and made to dash the rest of the way when the forward end of the beam dipped and began to slide underneath the log, lifting its far end from the earth. Emmalou was about to leap for the shore when her log rolled and spilled her into the raging creek.

As the two logs swept on below, Drum ran at the bank and jumped as far as he could toward the girl. He would have never reached her at all had not the swirling current brought them together, and in her panic, Emmalou would have pulled him under had that same current not swept their way an uprooted maple sapling. Drum clung to it. Emmalou fastened herself to Drum, and the maple delivered them alongside a sizable boulder jutting out from the shore. In the relative calm of the eddy behind the obstructing rock, they managed to pull themselves up onto the boulder where they stood in the driving rain, shivering as much from fear as from cold.

Emmalou, all her speech washed away, offered Drum a hysterical smile. He felt that somehow he had a duty to speak to the moment for them both, and could think of nothing at all to say other than his confession, "I can't swim, don't you know."

The words were scarcely out of his mouth, when the maple of their deliverance turned in the shifting current and slid away past their perch. The brushy top snagged Drum's shirt and pulled him over backwards. Emmalou screamed and reached for him. Their fingers touched an instant and he was gone. Emmalou saw an arm flailing out of the flood, and a terrified face bob behind a wave once, maybe twice, and then a raft of debris rode by on the brown water. "Drum!" she shouted, and ran for home.

Tom Truelight was standing in his door, about to go out into the storm to fetch his daughter when she ran into their yard, barefoot, her dress torn, her straggled hair covering her face. Tom ran out to meet her, grabbed her up in his arms and started for the house, "What's befell you, Daughter? Where have you been to?"

"Oh, Pappa, if it weren't for Drum, I'd be drowned and dead, and now he's lost!"

HORACE

"Doctor Truelight, it's time." Emmalou peered at the earnest young woman who had waked her, silently rebuking herself for falling asleep in her chair. It had been a long flight, rough and stormy. The plane arrived in Asheton late; tourist traffic ensnarled the drive from the airport, and there had been no time to rest at her hotel. No one called her Doctor Truelight except students and strangers. Her friends called her Emma. Richard had called her True.

Richard was a photographer, traveling in China when he contracted some sort of avian-borne fever. "Nothing serious," his letter said. Four days later, the call from National Geographic, a kindly, somewhat fatherly sounding voice telling her Richard was dead.

"Let's do it then," she answered the pretty graduate student who had been assigned to shepherd her through the occasion. As Emmalou shrugged into her gown, her right hand paused involuntarily to touch the tiny silver Celtic cross hung around her neck. Richard's gift to her before he left for his last assignment. The Cross had defined her life. That Love was ultimately lived out in sacrifice and surrender she never doubted. She didn't forget for a day that she lived and breathed and moved in the world because a fatherless boy had delivered her from the waters of death. While she was here, she meant to go back and say thank you.

Emmalou followed her warder into the dark hall, and

during the overblown introduction by the Dean of the College, she studied the nearest of the indistinct young faces emerging from the dim void before her. When the masculine droning ceased, she moved to the podium and began, "Before we evolved as a species to the point where we could form thoughts and words, there is the Word that Spirit is ever speaking..."

When she had delivered her deep Truth to souls who would promptly forget it, and spent two more interminable hours making small talk that would be remembered only a little longer, Emmalou found a phone and dialed the number for Earlham. "Saul, I need someone to cover my classes next week. I must spend a little time at home." Then she opened the phone directory and looked up High Country Photography.

The next day, she was navigating her rented Plymouth up the intimidating incline of Jonas Bear's drive.

#

Emmalou's frantic face was Drum's last sight before the flood pulled him under. He saw her lips shape his name, but only heard the roar of the creek, then the whole world was a brown blur as he submerged and the silty soup stung his eyes and the current tried to push water into his nose and mouth, stealing his breath. How could this be the same creek where he and Jonas Bear had and would again one far off day find refuge from the bees?

Now, it seemed intent on erasing him from the flow of time altogether. Yet, when he was desperate for air, once, twice, three times, the flow buoyed him to the surface and allowed him to gasp one breath before he was plunged immediately once more into the murky maelstrom. Rocks battered and scraped him, roots and limbs of unlanded trees tried to snag and impale him, yet somehow, he was swirled away to suffer more.

After minutes or millennia, the stream overran its bed and broadened over a flat bottomland, the current slowed enough for Drum to gain purchase on the butt end of his maple nemesis and hold his head above water long enough to see his situation. Ahead, a wooden bridge cleared the water now not much more than a foot. Already, debris had begun to drift against it. A mud-splattered model T stood in the road just right of the bridge. Two men were in earnest conversation beside the Ford, apparently trying to assess their chances of getting the car across safely.

The older man, wearing overalls, Drum recognized as Polly Coggins' uncle Walt. Walt glanced up stream, spied Drum, and pointed. The younger man sprinted out to the center of the bridge as the maple's brushy top snagged it, then the trunk swung about to slide beneath. The man knelt on the rain-slicked planks. Drum raised his arm, the stranger grabbed his wrist, got a hand on his shirt and hoisted him through the air, depositing Drum sprawling and breathless beside his rescuer. They looked mutely at one another as the bridge trembled and heaved under them, then the maple came clear. The man, whose rain-drenched khaki shirt and trousers looked as if he too had been adrift, pulled Drum to his feet, observed mildly, "You picked a rough day for a swim," and they made unsteadily for solid ground.

Safe on the road, Walt Coggins greeted them with as much amusement as relief, "Well now Horace, looks like you landed a big one there."

#

Jonas breached his shotgun, held it under his arm and gestured toward the door, "Would you like to see inside the house? There might be something there you'd remember."

"I don't want to intrude on your day, Mr. Bear."

Jonas offered Emma Truelight his crooked smile, "Folks around just call me Bear, or you can call me Jonas if you like. I'm up to no good today; you won't interrupt a thing."

"Then thanks, Jonas, I'd love to in that case. This old place has some dear memories, although it looks very different now." Emma followed Jonas up onto the porch, "You must be a hunter, everybody around here is."

Jonas held the screen open for her. "No; I've never kept a firearm until today. Dogs after my chickens." He made a sweeping gesture as they entered, "The log walls had been covered over inside as well as out. I took down the beadboard on the lower floor here. That probably looks pretty much the same as you remember it. Look around and I'll start us some tea." Jonas laid his shotgun on the kitchen table and lit the gas under a kettle.

As he spooned out tea into a pot, Emma called from the studio, "I don't remember this room being so large."

While the water heated, Jonas came back and leaned against the jamb of the kitchen door, "It was two rooms originally. I took out the partition between, and put the large windows in across the back wall."

Emma stood before a window, gazing at the line of trees bordering the yard. Above and beyond the woods, sunlight glinted like a beacon on the Shining Rocks. "Annie loved this land so. She was a Quaker, you know."

"I don't know anything about Annie, or the school. I bought this house from James Coggins through an agent. Maybe you can tell me something of the history of the place, when you have some time." He was about to say more when the kettle whistled from the kitchen. He carried the pot to the stove and filled it from the kettle, fetched a couple of mugs and carried them back to the studio. He set the pot on his worktable to steep, and put down the mugs beside it.

Emma walked from the window and stood by his easel, studying the portrait of Drum, almost finished. "You are an artist, then? Don't tell me I'm wrong about you again."

"Guilty as charged, Emma. I taught art at Mercy College for years. Now I pretend to be a real painter."

"I'm a teacher, too. American Religious History at Earlham. I know the face in your portrait. Did you find an old photograph in the house?"

"No, I did that from memory. I don't like working from photographs."

"But that is Ben Drum; He and I went to Annie Starling's school together."

"I think our tea is ready," Jonas filled the mugs and held one out to her. "I don't know how that can be, Emma. He was here a couple of weeks ago." He gestured at the painting, "As you can see, just a boy, maybe eleven or twelve."

"Jonas, the likeness is uncanny. I would never forget that face. He saved my life."

"Well, Emma, the boy in that painting told me he was Benjamin Drum."

"The boy in your painting is grown up now, Jonas. I had dinner with Ben Drum in Asheton last night. He owns Highland Photography."

#

Rain poured down unabated as Drum sat huddled with Horace and Walt under the canopy of the model T. They watched the bridge buck and groan several times as large timbers and trunks of trees surged underneath. Horace was not inspired to trust it. "Let's go back to camp and wait this out." Walt raised no objection. Drum thought he'd had enough of swimming for one day.

The car had an electric starter, the first model to be so equipped, Horace informed them, so nobody had to get out into the downpour to crank the engine. He had trouble turning around on the narrow and slippery road, but after several starts and retreats, they were headed back away from the creek. In less than a half mile, Horace pulled over in a place where the road widened before a turn. A steep side track, now awash, wound off to the right up through a laurel thicket into a shadowy stand of hemlock and pines.

"This car won't make it up there now," Horace appraised. They got out into the wet and began slogging up the hill. All three soaked to the skin already, none considered this a great inconvenience. Hardly beyond sight of the road below they came to a cabin in a small clearing. A faint wisp of smoke still straggled from the chimney to be promptly dispersed by the wind. The place looked to have been long abandoned, but evidenced some recent repairs. Without hesitation, Horace stepped up on the rickety porch and led them through the door. This was his camp.

Once inside, Horace began building up the fire in a little iron stove. Walt made belated introductions. "Horace, this drowned boy here is little Polly's friend Drum. He lives with the Warwoman I told you about. Him and Polly go to her school. Drum boy, this fancy man is Horace Kellett. He just wrote a book about our cove, and it's been printed up in New York City. Gannies we'll all be famous now and be overrun with tourists and foreigners."

Horace, satisfied that his fire was sustaining, closed the lid on the stove and turned smiling to shake Drum's hand as he would any grown man he might happen to shelter with from a storm. "Glad to meet you, Drum. Tell Walt he needn't worry about tourists and foreigners. It's the timber companies that will spoil this place, and they are already here."

They hung their sodden clothes behind the stove to dry, and set their shoes underneath. Horace pulled out something dry for them to wear. His pants were a tight fit for Walt, way loose on Drum, who had to hold on to keep them from dropping to his knees, but at least they had decent cover as they sat around the stove toasting the soles of their bare feet and listening to the rain and the wind. The roof leaked in a couple of places. Horace set pots under the drips, adding a little percussive accent to the rustle and rattle of the storm. He made some coffee, but after awhile he and Walt began pouring the contents of a bottle into tin cups, which as they drank it, seemed to relax them considerably. After Horace had downed three cups full, Walt advised, "Horace, you'd better taper off on that; we've got a boy with us here."

Horace seemed surprised, as if he had forgotten Drum were there. "You're right, Walt; I've had enough," then he lifted the stove lid and emptied the bottle into the fire. The flames flared for a moment, reminding Drum of the time Mary threw a handful of corn flour into a fire and he thought it magic.

Walt started up from his chair, "Lord have mercy, Horace, Don't waste it!"

Horace winked at Drum, "If it isn't here, I don't have

to drink it, do I?"

After Walt got over the loss of his spirits, he picked up a week old newspaper from the floor. On the front page was a picture of a long row of shrouded human corpses with people going down the line, apparently trying to identify the dead. Walt stabbed the picture with his finger and handed the paper over to Drum, "Drum boy, put the Warwoman's schooling to some good use and read me what this picture's about."

The picture was about an explosion in a coal mile in Wales. Over four hundred miners had been killed. A week after the accident, bodies were still being found. Walt Coggins was not totally illiterate. He probably could have labored over the article and made out enough to get the gist. Once, when he had been called to serve on a jury at the county court, he had pled his ignorance to get out of it. State law required that jurors be literate. When the judge asked Walt if he could read, he responded, "Sort of, your honor."

"What do you mean by *sort of*, Mr. Coggins?"

"Well, sir, when I come to a road sign, I can read how far, but I can't read where to."

When Walt had heard all about the disaster at the Universal Colliery, and Drum told them all the details of his adventure in the creek, and the crackle of the fire in the stove became louder than the rain on the roof, Walt shed Horace's khakis and began slipping back into his own clothes.

Horace raised an eyebrow, "Those things are still wet, Walt."

"They're not wringing, Horace. Ganny while it slackens some, I'll trundle up to Truelight's and tell them Drum ain't drowned, afore somebody goes and spreads false sorrow."

Drum felt guilty. Until this moment, it had not occurred to him that Annie might be fearing for his life.

#

An hour passed while Emma and Jonas sat on his porch steps as she related one tale after another about her years growing up in the cove, and how her sojourn at Annie's school planted seeds that would flower into her life. Finally she stood, and handed Jonas her cup. He held their cups cradled in one hand while she shook the other, "Thanks for the tea, Jonas, it has been lovely getting acquainted and seeing this old place again. You've done well by it. You need to find somebody like old Houston, though, to make some big rockers for your porch."

"Well, Emma, if you plan to drop by again, I'll make certain you find a couple waiting. Why don't you come back for supper and finish the history lesson? I'm a fair cook for somebody who has only himself to cook for most days."

"I'd like that, but I'm leaving for Richmond in the morning, and I need to spend this time with my mother. I see her so seldom now. But next trip down, for sure." Emma got into her Plymouth and put the key in the ignition, then rolled down her window, "And let me know when you've finished with that portrait. I'd like to buy it if it isn't taken already."

Jonas promised he would, they exchanged addresses, agreed that Benjamin Drum was a wildly improbable coincidence, for there was no other logical explanation. Emma waved, and was off and away to Maude, who, for what turned out to be her last time, waited impatiently for her wandering daughter to come home from the Warwoman's place. Tom Truelight died several years before, but Maude still held out alone at the old homestead, resisting all Emma's pleas to come north with her, "All I've loved except you, Child, is right here. I've never been a traveler."

About a week after Emma's visit, Jonas walked down his hill to fetch the mail, and a package bearing an Indiana postmark waited in his box. He opened it to find a copy of *National Geographic* from ten years before, with a strip of paper inserted between the pages and folded down over the front cover. He read in Emma's studiously legible script, *Look what I found!* The paper marked an article titled *Deadly Rain on London*, which consisted of several pages of tight text wedged around thirty sharp focus black-and-white photographs of a bomb ravaged city and people who lived in it. The byline credited Benjamin Drum as the photographer. A small photo in the *Contributors* blurb inside the front cover presented a thin bearded fortyish face under a broad-brimmed canvas hat. The face executed a smile Jonas remembered, bore a familial resemblance to the portrait on his easel.

#

Walt arrived back at the camp next morning before daylight, in time to share in the biscuits, corn grits and bacon Horace cooked on his little stove. Walt was hoping to ride into Asheton with Horace. They had trouble getting the Ford started. Horace finally resorted to the crank. They found the bridge where they had left it. A couple of loose planks, but when they had walked it, they deemed it essentially sound. The model T rattled across without impediment, and slip-slided along the road as far as Annie's turn-off, which Horace judged impassible for his auto, so they parked at the foot of her hill, and trekked up the steep to the house, where they found Tom

Truelight and Emmalou in the yard talking to the Warwoman, having just gotten across the subsiding creek with Walt's good news. When Annie saw the three approaching, she knelt in the mud to peer level into Drum's face, and with tears streaming down her own, wrapped her arms tight about him. Drum could feel Annie's heart beating against his chest. Of all the times in his life when Drum had felt loved, at this moment he could remember no other.

Horace promised Annie that he would stop for supper on his way back from Asheton. It turned out he was delayed and overnighted in town, but the next evening, he did show, with apologies, and a gift of dried figs and cheese. After supper he and Annie talked long and late, while Drum listened and remembered all they said. They had much to talk about, for both had deep and abiding love for the Cove and the mountains around, and for the people who lived there. Each of them had been writing seriously about a way of life and a sense of place they saw passing away never to be recovered. Annie had several articles published in various historical society journals. Horace's book, *Highland Faces* had just come out, and on his next visit, he brought Annie a copy as a gift.

Horace Kellet became a frequent visitor to the Warwoman's house, to the point his friend Walter Coggins took to teasing him about being spelled. Spells or not, Horace and Annie became deep and good friends, bound by their common love and concern for their neighbors and their place, but they were never more than friends, for Horace had wife and children far away, and though he was unable to share their life now, he still loved them dearly, and had married the one great love of his life.

#

Winter settled into the cove swift and hard. Snow drifted three or four feet in places along the road, rendering it impassable for days at a time. In January, the first cases of influenza appeared, and by spring, few houses had escaped. Often only Emmalou and Drum appeared at the school, and some days Drum studied solo. Annie was the closest to a doctor the Cove could muster, so many days found her afoot on the slopes, carrying food and comfort to households where the whole family might be ill and abed. She was usually alone on these missions. Drum always offered to go along, but Annie tried to limit his exposure to the sickness. Should he offer to help carry her load, she was likely to respond, "When I go out walking, I'd rather be alone; then I can stride or gawk as I please with no soul but my own to stay or rush me."

As long as the epidemic raged, Annie would be abroad on the mountain in all weathers, as solitary as a raven. And she had not lied to Drum; she enjoyed the lack of company on her rounds. She loved the mountains best in winter, she said, for then she could see the bones of the Earth. Once, on her way home in a flurried dusk from the Truelight place, she became aware she had company. She knew the animal following her, had met her on the mountain several times, and heard her cry an hour past. *Painter*, her neighbors called the big cat, *panther*. She could not see nor hear her uninvited companion now, but sensed her presence. The Warwoman was not afraid; to her, just a cat, no more nor less a cat than the two who twined around her feet at Maude and Tom's house. All the same, she crossed over the stream then, risking going home with cold and wet feet, rather than pass close by the overhanging boulders crowding the path ahead.

When Annie herself came down with the flu, Drum took care of her as best a boy could. Thanks to Walt Coggins, word got to Horace in Asheton, and he came out to the Cove and stayed for four days, plying Annie with soups and teas until she was on her feet again. When he wasn't fetching or cooking or acting as nurse, he often sat beside her bed and read to her when she was sleepless.

Once, midway through a particularly melodramatic passage in George MacDonald's *Lilith,* Horace said teasingly, "Oh, Annie; if my life were arranged differently, I would have pursued you for sure."

Annie had to laugh, even though it made her chest hurt, "Horace, if my life had been arranged differently, I would have had no use for thee at all."

#

The spring of 1914 arrived late. The first thaws of the season were brief, and the relapses into icy chill were deep and lengthy. Eventually, the coves and valleys did green, and over the course of three weeks the emerald tide rose up from the creeks until it topped the highest peaks and ridges. From a distance, the steeps and knobs looked inviting and accessible. Traversing the landscape beneath the canopy of trees revealed a different reality. Such roads as there were followed the streams and sought the lowest gaps. Anyone who wanted to reach the higher elevations would do so afoot, carrying their provisions on their back. They would also pack their shelter, unless they were adept at rigging their own from whatever materials the mountain allowed them. Horace had a hunger for the "high lonesome," as he called it. And as soon as Annie declared classes at an end for the summer, he invited Drum to go with him to stay for two or three weeks at a place he had permission to use for the season several miles further on up the ridge beyond the Shining Rocks. "It would ease my mind to have somebody along to notice if I fall down and break my leg," he told Annie when he asked her to release Drum for the expedition.

Drum joined in the jest, "We'd better be careful then; I wouldn't be able to carry you out."

"Well, you could shoot me so I wouldn't have to starve by myself."

They acted as if this exchange were exceedingly funny, but they failed to win a smile from Annie. "Thee both deserve each other; maybe thee will just decide to stay up there," was all she said before disappearing into her kitchen, which provoked another round of laughter from the males trailing after her.

When they realized they had really hurt her feelings, they were properly contrite, and it was not in Annie's nature to withhold forgiveness. She agreed to let Drum go along when Horace promised that if any shooting had to be done, he would do it himself. "I promise, Annie. We might have to do a little shooting, though, unless you want us to live for the next couple of weeks on nothing but roots and berries."

As Annie handed Horace the plates to set the table, she patted his belly and surrendered the smile they had been trying to provoke, "Horace Kellett, that would do no hurt to thee."

#

Late on a cloudy August morning in 1945, Tadahito Kitamura walked up a street near Urakami Cathedral toward his studio. Under his arm, he held the 1913 vintage Eastman Empire Number Two view camera he bought a few minutes before. Antique photographic equipment was his hobby. Photography was his livelihood and his passion. As a child, he wanted to grow up to be an artist. When a photographer friend of his father gave him a camera, he decided that film was the way to capture the true essence of what he saw in his world. After months of documenting victorious defeats for the war ministry, he now knew that in skillful hands, a camera could be made to lie even more convincingly than a brush.

As he stopped to cross the street to his studio, the clouds parted, bathed the whole scene in sunlight. Most of the people on the street were busily into their day and seemed not to notice. As Kitamura neared his door, fishing in his pocket for his keys, the world dissolved instantly in blinding brilliance and searing heat. Before he heard a sound, Kitamura felt the skin on his arms crisping and curling. Then, neither darkness nor light, sound nor silence, for what might have been an instant or a forever.

Somewhere nearby, crows called to one another. Kitamura heard a faint dry rustling around him, and when he could see, beheld a forest of ripe cornstalks, blocking the immediate view on all sides. Away beyond the tasseled tops he could see the humped contours of green mountains, and over his head a deep blue sky. His Eastman Number 2 was still under his arm. His skin itched as if he had a sunburn.

He looked down at the dirt under his feet. No pavement, no buildings, just endless green corn rattling insistently in the slight breeze. When he realized he could still command his body, Kitamura began walking down the long row and as it made a slow turn he could see trees past the end. Emerging from the corn beside a dirt road, Kitamura looked along it to where it hid in a grove of oaks, then heard at his back a progressive rattle and clatter. He turned to see a long-bearded Caucasian in overalls sitting on a rickety wreck of a wagon pulled by a single mule and heaped with corn. The bearded man, either singing or arguing with himself as he jostled along, pulled up short when he drew abreast of Kitamura, and peered at him from underneath a broad-brimmed hat, well-worn and carelessly kept.

"You're a tad far out in the sticks to be taking pretty pictures, don't you know." Kitamura recognized the speech as something akin to English. He did not regard himself as fluent, but had done business with Americans before the war, and spoke the language at home with his American wife. This man, however, assaulted him with a burr of consonants shorn of most of their vowels, bearing faint resemblance to any English Kitamura had encountered before. *Pictures* was about all he gleaned from the driver's strange dialect.

"Afraid I am lost." Kitamura offered tentatively.

"Where then be you lost from?"

Kitamura understood the *where* part. He looked down at his Eastman. There was a faded and torn label affixed to the top, *Elliot Photography, Asheton, N. C.* He knew of Asheton, though he'd never been within a thousand miles of it. He'd bought the antique Eastman in part because his wife came from there. Lacking any further clue as to where he was, or how he got there, "Asheton," was all the answer he had.

"Well, you're in Deep Laurel now. Climb on up here, then; I can get you part way home, though you can't hardly get to Asheton from here. You might have to cross a mountain or two and start from there."

#

Before light on First Day, Drum brought water and fodder

to Johnny and turned him into his lot, fed the chickens and Lucy, the new cow Annie bought the week before from Tom Truelight. Drum named her after one of the sisters he had dreamed about in his other life. Whether it was a life before or a life to come, he could never quite decide. The dream seemed to him now the most real thing about that time apart.

At breakfast, as he poured sorghum on his biscuits, Drum thought Annie looked as if she had missed her sleep, "Are you sure you won't be needing me here, Annie?" Horace was due to show up today to begin their sojourn on the mountain.

"Worry thee none on my account; I'll do fine. Thee needs a man to mentor thee some, and Horace, poor soul, pines for youthful companionship. He misses his own children dreadfully."

"Why do they live so far away then?"

"Because Horace and his family are at home in different worlds, Drum. Love can bridge all distance and differences, but it can't erase any. We may not always choose the people we love or the life we live. Love and life choose us. The choices we live are seldom our own to make."

It had not rained in more than a week. The road was firm and Horace was able to get his Ford up Annie's hill. When he parked beside the house, and Drum saw all the gear and provisions piled in back, he thought they might have to beg to borrow Johnny. "Horace, how are we going to carry all that?"

Horace laughed, "We'll tote enough to keep us for a day or so, until Walt Coggins can bring his mule and haul up the rest. Walt will keep us company until you're ready to come back, then he'll deliver you to Annie on his way home."

"What about you?"

"I'll probably hang out up on the balds for most of the summer, but whenever Annie can spare you for a few days, you can come up and visit when Walt resupplies me at the camp."

"Maybe I should just stay the summer and give you a hand up there,"

"You'd be good company, Drum, but you wouldn't feel right leaving Annie all on her own."

Drum didn't argue because he knew it was so.

Horace sat with them for Meeting, then they shared at table the season's first green beans from Annie's garden, simmered with onions and potatoes, and fried chicken, which Annie had cooked especially for Horace, who, she said, with a twinkle in her eye, had "a fox's fondness for recently dead birds."

While they ate, they gossiped amiably about their neighbors, especially Horace's friend Walt Coggins, of whom Horace had enough tales to fill a book.

Drum spoke to a lingering curiosity, "Annie, why does Walt call you *Warwoman?*" Annie could not quite stifle a laugh, "Because Walter Coggins has a fine imagination. *Warwoman* means *witch.*"

Horace set down his fork, looked at Annie with mischief in his eye, "You know, there are a few in the Cove beside Walt who say you are a witch."

Annie's laugh cut short, "You know what I am, so don't encourage any. That goes for both of you. These people were brought up on fairy tales; they believe witches eat little children."

After they finished their lunch, and helped Annie clear the table and clean the dishes, Horace looked at Drum,

"Where's your clothes?"

Drum brought them out, already stacked and folded, set them down on the porch in front of Horace. He nodded approval, then brought from his car two haversacks. The big bulging one was for Horace. He opened the lighter pack, fitted Drum's clothes neatly inside and buckled the flap. Horace motioned for him to turn around, adjusted the straps over his shoulders, and stood back to appraise his sidekick's trailworthiness, "Can you stand up under that?"

"I can walk all day," Drum hoped that wasn't a lie.

"You have anything in case we get wet upon?"

"I won't drown."

"If you get wet up there, you might freeze," I have an extra poncho in my pack. You're going to need a stick."

Annie reached inside the door and handed her staff to Drum, "May this prop thee aright as well as it has me." She filled their canteens and bid them traveling mercies. Horace hauled his pack onto his shoulders. His had a rifle strapped to it. He pulled his stick out of the Ford and they were off across the yard toward the track up past the cornfield and over the creek toward the Shining Rocks. Annie stood watching them until they were lost to sight among the trees.

#

Moving like a ghost through the morning fog, Nancy, with Walter Coggins on her back, picked her way down to Sorrow Creek. The name came not from the grief it caused in flood stage to every generation daring to live close beside it, but because an old farmer named Isaac Sorrow once tended a large cornfield along its banks, until he got tired of having his crop drowned before harvest more years than not. When Nancy reached the rowdy water, she stopped, wanting Walt to go first. Walt and his mule had an understanding about these things. He climbed down, whispered Nancy reassurances and carefully led her across to the opposite bank. They had made a late start, for his cow got loose again, and had to be secured before she raided the Warwoman's garden one more time. Walt knew he would be forgiven for it, but he also knew how hard food was to raise amid the unforgiving stones of this land. Beautiful as the mountains were, they yielded sustenance for the soul more readily than they did food for the belly.

The Warwoman was his nearest neighbor, and he and Nancy were on their way to her place now, to pick up the supplies Horace Kellett had left there for them to carry up to Horace's camp on the divide by Haynes Knob. Whenever Walt's friend decided he was drinking too much, which if not frequently, was more or less regularly, he would go hide out on top of a mountain somewhere until the urge got weathered out of him. As Walt and Nancy came up from the creek by the Warwoman's garden, they met her mending the low stone wall she laid up from the stones turned in her garden, in a token effort to keep Walt's errant cow out of her vegetables.

Walt stood unspeaking for a few moments, admiring her stonecraft. When he could contain his opinions and curiosities no longer, "Warwoman, that is large work for one wee as yourself; Gannies you've a spell to lighten those stones. Why ain't your boy Drum doing that?"

Annie bent to pick up another stone, "He's gone with thy Horace on his wander, Walt. It seemed good for them and for me to have them both off and away for some days."

"You need yourself a man up here to do such chores

for you."

Without pausing or looking up from her task, Annie lifted the melon-sized stone into place as she answered, "Walt Coggins, naught but sweat and toil will raise these stones, and as for a man, there isn't a human male in the cove used to lifting anything heavier than a jug. Before the sun was above the trees, he'd be away to nap and nip, and I'd be left to finish it myself in the heat of the day."

Walt thought that a slight exaggeration, but too slight to sustain an argument, so he tipped his hat and went without further speech, whistling on his way. Whistling, he believed, would confuse any mischievous spirits or weefolk who might notion to follow after and bedevil Nancy.

#

Drum could scarcely remember their now familiar way as it would be one day when Jonas Bear lived in this place. To their right, the turned earth of the cornfield lay dark as a storm's shadow. With Annie's assistance and direction, Drum and Johnny had hauled out several loads of composted manure and straw from the barn, and plowed it in with the stubble of the cornstalks.

Drum still was not at ease with the big mule, but he and Johnny had achieved a working arrangement based on tolerance and patience. Johnny would do about anything Drum directed him to do unless Drum became inclined to rush him. Each was sensitive to the other's moods, and as considerate of one another as their routine allowed, and they were developing a measure of mutual respect and regard. The fact that Drum usually brought food and water to Johnny helped to cement their relationship. They were able to work together and get things done. Increasingly, Annie was able to guide their activities from afar.

Once across the creek and moving up the slope through the trees, Drum became acutely conscious of the weight of his pack. He supposed he might be used to it by the time they reached Horace's camp, which Horace said would be near sundown. Drum hoped the whole distance would not be uphill. As the day progressed, Drum realized that most of it was.

The steepest mile came early, between the Shining Rocks and the crest of the ridge beyond. They stopped at the Shining Rocks so Horace could have a good look at them. "I usually come up by the other side of the ridge on Pigeon Timber's land. I've only glimpsed these through the trees from above. They look more impressive from close and below."

Horace slipped off his pack in the shadow of the boulders and walked all around them, peered into the crevice through their midst. Drum looked over Horace's shoulder, thought he saw a glimmer of light coming through from the other side. It seemed to flash brighter as he looked, but Horace didn't seem to notice, stood up and clambered up on top of the outcropping like a boy would do. Drum climbed up right behind to stand beside. They could see ranks of blue ridges over the trees to south but the forest all around blocked any view of the near terrain beyond the clearing around the rocks.

Horace sat down on the boulder where he'd been standing, with his feet hanging over the edge, so did Drum. Horace reached out a hand to steady him as he sat, but didn't try to discourage the maneuver.

When his companion had settled, Horace patted the stone between them, "Drum, did you know that the people of the Old Nation believed this is the very spot where Maker brought the first people into the world?"

Drum had not known, but considered it now, "Maybe Maker brought them here from some other time." Drum fancied he could feel the power in the stones. The sun had made the surface hot. His hands tingled. Drum folded them in his lap. He was glad when Horace stood up and they went back down to grassy ground. Drum liked this man. He was not ready to be snatched out of his life again before he had a chance to get to know it.

#

Firmly grounded and settled, they shouldered their packs again. Horace helped Drum adjust his load, and they continued upward into the high forest. As they climbed, oak and hickory supplanted ash and hemlock. Fir and spruce succeeded those in turn. The woods crowded close and dark, filled with rustlings and whisperings and pipings brimming with mysterious portent verging on revelation. Man and boy climbed without speaking, loathe to break the pregnant and holy silence. They listened to the sounds of the forest and the scuffling and thud of their footfalls and the measured blow and sigh of their own breathing, and for something else, just beyond the edge of sense, something neither of them knew or guessed but would have recognized immediately had it given voice.

A raven croaked once from a dead spruce just ahead. Drum looked up to see the Watcher gazing fixedly at the two human pilgrims in his domain. Horace raised his stick in salute and mustered a fair imitation of the corvid's grating gutturals. The dark sentinel rasped once more, either in greeting or warning, then flew away up the slope.

Horace looked after him, grinned at Drum, "He's telling us that we are in his world now, and had better behave ourselves and follow his rules if we want to get to where we are going before night." Drum thought Raven's rules might be a lot more sensible and easier to follow than the rules of his parents who were due to be born in another year or so. He had seen enough of their world in his short and previous life that he was in no hurry to live his way back into it.

A mile into the forest, the wagon track dwindled into a foot path, rocky and circuitous. Horace slowed, matched his pace to Drum's. When Drum thought he'd done about all the climbing that was in him, the forest ended abruptly at the crest of the ridge. Before and below them spread a scene that would pass for Armageddon. Raw stumps and fallen trees littered the whole upper face of the mountain. A narrow gauge railway snaked along the slope a couple of hundred yards below. A locomotive towing three flat cars heaped with huge logs belched smoke and sparks on its downward run. Steel draglines anchored near the top of the ridge guided great bundles of logs down toward the tracks, where cranes loaded the cars as fast as they could be delivered.

The logging was brutal and dangerous work, with no thought for the continuance of the forest or the lives of the men who harvested it. Hardly a day passed that somewhere on the mountain a human did not lose his life, or an arm or leg. When the trees were gone, the machines would move on to rape yet another mountain, leaving barren ground and broken lives behind. Nature, if left unmolested, would require generations to restore order and vitality to this place.

Horace waved his arm over the tortured and destroyed landscape, "Look at this, Drum. If greedy men have their way, this is how your children's world will look. When you are old, you will tell them what the Cove and the mountains were like, and they will not believe you, for they will have nothing in their lives from which to imagine it."

Very soon they had beheld more of the ravages of civilization than either wanted to see. Horace pointed southwest along the ridge with his staff, and they took a track along the crest that wound gradually up to a rounded knob topped by a small grove of pines and spruce. To their left, the vast verdant forest rolled down and away until it began to rise up the side of the next ridge. In the free air above the valley and a stream so far below they could not hear it above the wind, a multitude of crows wheeled and plunged, scraps of night against the day, until the sun on their wings flared and flashed against the shadowed hills beyond. To their right tumbled the smoky waste that had once been a haven for multitudes, now a desolation of clamor and confusion.

Once they topped the knob and followed the trace down into far gap, the wind carried away the noise of geocide and the acrid smoke from burning brush piles as big as houses. Halfway through the afternoon, Raven croaked to the wind somewhere up the ridge, and the wind carried his message to the humans, reminding them that the world was not made for them, but they were made for the world. Tall red-tipped grasses carpeted the high gap, and they stopped there leeward of the next rise, to eat the hard-boiled eggs, biscuits and cheese Annie had packed for them.

Horace seemed as hungry as Drum, "Let's take time in this pleasant place and enjoy this mercy, Drum. We'll be suffering my cooking soon enough." Drum would discover, however, that Horace was an accomplished field cook. He had, in fact, written a book about it that was still being read by a lot of people when Drum stood at woods edge watching Jonas Bear feed his chickens.

After they ate, Horace stowed their greasy wrappers in his pack. "We can use that to start our fire tonight. We'll need one where we're going."

As they began to climb up the next knob, which seemed a little higher than the one before, the grass gave way to blueberries and turkeypaw and a multitude of flowers, wild and nameless, praising the sun with their unceasing gaze. Drum told Horace he thought it strange that people talked about flowers as frail and delicate, when flowers eat dirt and stare at the sun all day. Horace agreed that most humans view life backwards from the way it really is. "We are the weak ones, Drum. If we destroy all the trees and flowers and all the creatures that move among them, we will not be able to survive on our own. It is so obvious, but most people have a hard time understanding that. Money and towns make most men near-sighted, unable to see much beyond their pricks."

This seemed to Drum as funny as it was sad, and as sad as it was true. As they walked on, whenever he thought of Horace's observation, funny usually won out and he had to laugh. Horace seemed amused at Drum's amusement, "At least, I'll have some cheerful company up here."

They crested the knob ahead, picking their way through clumps of low blueberry bushes and assorted briars, punctuated by an occasional straggly spruce. The sun slipped behind a swath of cloud and left Drum shivering and wishing for his jacket. Horace, too, felt the change, rubbed his arms, warming himself with the friction, "We'll need good cover tonight, Drum."

Making their way downward again through a shadowy grove of spruce and fir into the far gap, once out of the wind, they immediately felt warmer after the exposed bald they had just traversed. As they came clear of the trees on the slope below, the path intersected a circle about twenty feet across, worn bare from traffic of beasts or humans, with eight short sections of a barked log upended around the perimeter. Horace slipped loose from his pack and set down on one of the stumps. Drum unburdened himself and with a big grin, somewhat ceremoniously sat opposite the circle from Horace. Drum told Horace it looked like a place Annie's Quakers might meet.

"Or a council of the Old People," Horace suggested.

"Who are the Old People?"

"The people of the First Nation, who were in this place before our ancestors came along to slay the forests and hunt the inhabitants to extinction. This land still belongs to the Old Ones, because they still belong to the land, whatever money and lawyers might say to the contrary."

"The Old People still meet here?" The notion appealed to Drum considerably. He wasn't sure why.

"Somebody does, Drum; it may be them, or wanderers like us, or hunting parties, maybe loggers plotting which mountain they will lay to waste next, maybe even the birds and animals who live on these mountains."

"Animals have councils." Drum knew he'd forgotten something about the raven who kept calling them along their way. Something important. He wanted to remember, but Horace kept talking.

"The old stories say they do, Drum, and sometimes humans and animals in past days even counciled together to learn from one another."

"I reckon animals might teach us a lot."

"Ways older than our own kind, Drum; how to save our souls, even."

"My dad said we have to trust Jesus to save our souls."

"If people really trusted Jesus, they might act a lot more like him."

"Horace, do you think Annie trusts Jesus?"

"Does she tell you she does?"

"She says she is always listening for God."

"From the little I know about it, Drum, that sounds a lot like Jesus to me."

#

Nancy stood placidly beside Horace's Model T while Walt Coggins fitted her load to her back. When everything was secure, they plodded away from Annie's house and up the road past her cornfield. The creek was not high and Nancy didn't hesitate to cross it. When they reached the Shining Rocks, she said to Walt, "We'd better keep moving, Coggins, The day is awfully thin right now, don't you know?"

Walt was not surprised. He, too, felt the tingle of power emanating from the rocks. Nancy never spoke to him unless there were spirits in the air. Her voice sounded something like his mother's voice when he was a child. Nancy didn't move her mouth when she spoke. Walt heard her in his head, but it was not like thinking. He heard sound when his mule talked to him. Walt glanced around furtively, afraid of what he might see without having any idea of what that might be, "Let's get out of here, then"

After they left the Shining Rocks behind and below, Nancy fell silent . Walter felt no movement in the air other than an occasional breeze sifting through the trees. He heard no voices but the susurrant conversations of the forest. Oftentimes when he was alone in the woods, Walt began to feel that the forest was not so much a congregation of creatures and plants as it was an intelligent entity, a living being with a sentience and will of its own, manifesting the soul of the mountain. Walt could not have found words to say this, but he felt it, as he felt himself drawn in, felt his own soul melding with the soul of the trees and the creatures and the land itself.

Even had Walt been able to put his sense into words, he could never have explained it to anyone who lived in a city, surrounded by structures made by human hands, following patterns laid out by human minds, in a world ordered in every way to human measure, where even night and the stars were banished. Walt assumed that when God expelled Adam and Eve from the Eden Garden, they went somewhere and built a town, having no place on earth to belong to anymore.

#

They left the circle behind and began picking their way down the gullied trail deeper into the nameless gap. Horace pointed with his stick toward the rounded summit ahead, bald except for a single tree and weathered outcrops of mottled stone thrusting up from tall coppery grasses, "That's where we're headed, Drum."

Drum could make out near the tree the straight line of a roof ridge, barely visible from their vantage. Whatever shelter there was built low on the land. As they crossed the gap, even the tip of the tree sank from view behind the bulk of the mountain.

For the better part of an hour they followed a narrow brush-bound path twisting up the farther slope, detouring around an occasional cluster of boulders, pushing their way through copses of briars and berry bushes too broad to pass, the tall ruddy grass ever weaving and whispering all around. In every direction, blue mountains rose up wave upon wave in the distance, some higher than the ground they traversed now. As they neared the crest of their knob, the solitary spruce inched upward into view again, and then they were there and Horace said, "We're home."

Home was a low log structure, two rooms, with a dogtrot between, all roofed with wooden shakes. Several days' supply of firewood was cut and neatly stacked under the dogtrot. Horace went straight to the door and opened it.

Drum recalled that Annie didn't lock her doors, either. "Don't you lock your door, Horace?"

"Wouldn't do any good, Drum. Away off up here, there's none to see. Anybody who wanted in would be in. Besides, somebody might get caught out in weather and need some shelter."

"Do you come up here much?"

"I've been up a few times, whenever I could, but I plan to hang out here most of the summer. Martin McMinn built this years ago when he was grazing sheep and cattle on the bald. He doesn't use it anymore and gives me squatter's rights when I need to get away from towns and people. Martin owns most of the land we've been walking on today since we passed the Shining Rocks. Pigeon Timber and Pulp have been after him to sell it to them for years, but Martin loves his land more than money. Martin is land poor, though. Eventually he'll have to sell or lose it for taxes, or he'll die and his boys will have a check in their pockets before the funeral. I'm glad I can share this with you before it's all gone to stumps and mud."

#

After Nancy ushered Walt away up the mountain, Annie continued working on her wall. She found a sapling growing up between stones she laid the summer before, whacked it off with her brush knife, then cut it to length for a staff. It would serve her just fine until Drum came home with her stick. She continued laying up stone on stone until her empty stomach reminded her she had missed her lunch. As she stepped across the low wall toward home and nourishment, Annie felt a stab of hot pain in her leg. She was not angry at the snake, although she set aside her peace testimony to promptly dispatch her attacker with her staff, but her lack of watchfulness peeved her mightily with herself; she had not been aware of the copperhead until it struck. A timber rattler might have warned her first.

Annie pulled off her boot to examine the wound in her calf. A half-inch lower, and the stout leather might have spared her. Only one fang had punctured. That much was good. Useless to yell for Walt. He would be up on the ridge by now, half-way to Martin's old herder cabin. She would have to tend to this herself.

A week later, Annie still hobbled about her yard, leaning heavily into her staff. After the first day, she knew she would live, though a fortnight later, the ugly open ulcer where the snake had bitten, she was still treating with teas and poultices. By the time Horace and Drum returned home and she told them about her adventure, she still limped but no longer needed her stick to walk. However the leg would never again seem to her quite whole. It hurt whenever she was much on her feet. Walking long distances for pleasure became something she used to do, although whenever word came of a need for her presence and skills somewhere in the cove, she went without excuse or complaint.

When Walt Coggins, showed up in her yard sooner than she expected, Annie hid from him, for she knew Drum and Horace would come straight away if they heard what had happened to her. She wanted them to have their time on the mountain, where they would be undistracted by the peopled world and available to the working of Spirit.

MURA

Kitamura was glad the rocky and rutted road ran fairly level as the wagon lurched and lumbered along it. A ferocious sun glared down on him. He wished he had a hat. The beard driving the wagon was saying something to him. Kitamura, still dazed by his sudden and drastic transference, tried to pay attention. The wagoneer spat over the side into the dirt. Kitamura noticed he did that frequently, talking like his mouth was full, which made his weird brand of English even more difficult to comprehend.

"I'm Dan Hoots. Most just call me Hop." He held out his hand. Kitamura gripped it as his was gripped, managed to resist the temptation to bow. He suspected he might be better off if his origins remained a matter of speculation.

Hop paused barely long enough to spit again and continued, "I come from just acrost that mountain yonder," Hop wagged his head in a generally southerly direction, where a high dark wave of mountains loomed over the nearest range of hills. "My Brother Evan looked the wrong way and let a tree fall on him; got broke up pretty bad. Don't know that he'll ever be good for much again. I'm just here for a wee spell to help Marthy and the boys catch up the place. Headed out of a morning, and I can drop you off at the Post Office in Walnut. Somebody there is bound to be set for Asheton, and would let you sideby into town. Myself, I try to steer clear of towns as much as I'm allowed. What's your name, Picture Man, if I be not too pokey to ask?"

Kitamura wasn't sure what manners were expected on introductions here, so he offered his hand as Hop had done. Hop hesitated, shook it, looking mildly surprised. Kitamura said, "Tad... Ted. Ted Mura."

"Don't know many Teds around here. I bet you are some kind of foreigner. I bet you are from New York City."

"San Francisco," Mura had been there once.

"Lord have mercy on you then. I reckon you'd rather be here on Deep Laurel."

Mura wanted to steer the conversation away from where he had come from, "I like mountains."

Hop seemed unable to decide whether to spit or laugh, finally settled on a laugh, oblivious to the brown drool down his chin. As he threw back his head, Mura noted the yellow stains on his teeth and beard. "Well, Mr. Mura, sir, you've come to the right place. Mountains is most of what's here." Mura wished he had some film in his camera.

Jouncing and jarring along on Hop's decrepit wagon, Mura felt weary to exhaustion. Every muscle and joint in his body screamed in protest whenever a wheel jolted against a large stone. Stones abounded in the road as it uncoiled down the valley, through laughing singing creeks and across rickety rattly bridges, past cornfields, some tall and green, some scraggly and yellowed and beset with grass and weeds, by homesteads whose barns were larger than the houses, built of logs, or clad with riven boards, weathered to the hue of the shadows in the forests around them, The smell of the sweaty mule, and of the human driver, the rustle of the corn ears piled in the wagon bed behind, the conversations of crows and jays, and from time to time, the wild pure cry of a hawk circling high above the valley, wove Mura into the fabric of the day as if he belonged to it, had always been a child of this place, not hurtled here by some power beyond his knowing. Unreasoned recognition tempered his alarm. As Hop's wagon left the minutes behind them in the road, a feeling grew that wherever Mura had come to, he had come round right.

Mura's brain seethed, a confusion of half-thoughts and fugitive memories. He glanced at Hop, ceaselessly talking in his nigh incomprehensible version of English. Mura could detect no wariness in this stranger, who apparently found no surprise in finding a gaijin in the middle of his home environs. Hop seemed to regard his passenger with benevolent curiosity, apparently intent on educating him on all things local without delay. There was seldom a space in Hop's discourse for Mura to respond or question. The words went on and on, and Mura was content to let them wash over him like a warm, welcoming stream.

In spite of the rattling rumbling jolting jostling progress of the wagon, Mura kept nodding off, jerking awake on the brink of unbalance. Hop didn't appear to take notice, hardly altering the stream of his discourse, until he observed, "If you don't collect yourself here, Mister Mura sir, I'll have to tie you to that seat for fear of losing you down the side."

#

Martha Hoots greeted the two men at her door, wiping her floured hands on her apron as she scanned Mura with an appraising eye while Hop made introduction. Martha was used to the men in her clan bringing home stray companions without notice. Hospitality was a religious duty among the hill folk, living as they did where roads were steep and long and shelter often scarce. To them the second greatest sin was to withhold hospitality from a traveling stranger. The greatest sin was to abuse any welcome that was offered.

"Youns might need to sleep in the loft tonight," she informed them. "Evan'll have to keep his bed to oblige his frailty. I'll put the boys on the floor."

"Oh, let them boys stay put, Marthy," twanged Hop. "We can tide just fine in the barn. Besides, we'll need to be off for home before light. Ganny I'll drop Mister Mura off at Walnut on the way. There's no need to rouse the house on our account."

"Well, you'll need to eat before you go," protested Martha, loath to miss an opportunity to interrogate at her table a stranger from away.

"Wrap us biscuit and cure, then. That will keep us to Walnut."

"If that suits you, but I'll feed ye good tonight."

"Marthy, you never do less."

It was a sincere complement, and Martha's mouth twitched on the verge of a smile before she reined it in. "We'll supper as soon as the boys are in," she said, as Hop led Mura away toward the barn.

#

The inside of Martin McMinn's cabin, dark as a coal mine, smelled rank and musty. Horace threw back the shutters on the unglazed window, and a million tiny motes of dust and chaff swirled in the golden light. "Well, Drum, Looks like we've got some housekeeping to do here. Last who came by weren't much for cleaning up after themselves. At least they gathered more wood than they burnt."

Two makeshift beds made of poles laced with ropes

105

ran along one wall. Horace eased his pack onto one; when it didn't collapse, motioned Drum to the other. A wobbly table with a bench either side filled most of the room. At the end opposite the door, a small wood-fired cook stove crowded hard against a stone fireplace. Shelves beside the single window held a few pots, pans and chipped dishes. Several cast iron skillets and pans hung from the low rafters in front of the stove. If the cook were a tall man, he would have to be careful as he worked not to bump his head on them. Horace, a little below average in height, had bare clearance.

Drum saw things could get a little tight, "What's in the other room, Horace?"

"That will be Nancy's. This is a herder cabin, Drum; one room for two-leggeds, and one for four."

"Where's Walt going to sleep?"

"Walt likes to sleep on the floor by the fire. If the mice get to bothering him, he'll roll up on the table. If I start snoring too loud, he'll go across the dogtrot and bed down with Nancy."

Horace hefted a cedar bucket from the corner and handed it to Drum. The bucket was half full of stagnant water. A drowned mouse lay in the bottom. "There's a spring a little ways down past the cabin, Drum. You'll see the path. Would you take this and wash it out good and fill it clean for us, while I get started on readying up this place for civilized habitation?"

Drum took the bucket, tried to estimate how long since the mouse had drowned, and started for the door.

"Oh, Drum, watch out for bears."

Drum thought Horace was joking about bears until several days later, when he was on his way to the spring to fill their bucket for the morning, he came face to face with a yearling bear who had just been for a drink himself and was running out to meet his day. Drum yelped, threw his bucket into the air, and hightailed it for the cabin. The startled bear wheeled and ran full tilt in the opposite direction.

Horace stood in the dogtrot, coffee in hand, laughing as he watched. He assumed a solemn face as Drum charged up to him, "I think you dropped something back there Drum." Drum looked back. The bear was out of sight but they could still hear him tearing through the brush below. Then they both laughed.

But this first trip to the spring, when Drum returned with the filled bucket, he'd encountered no bears, saw much along the way that invited closer inspection, extending the duration of his circuit somewhat beyond adult necessity. Horace put some dried beans and several strips of beef jerky into a pot of water to soak. When they had the cabin cleaned to a degree Horace considered livable, he took from his pack a few simple provisions, meal, salt, sugar, coffee, a tin of tea, and hung them in a bag from one of the rafters. Then he clapped Drum on the shoulder, "Let's go forage some."

Forage turned out to be Horace's code word for what Walt Coggins would describe as gandering about. They met their neighbors, crows and sparrows, a couple of harmless snakes, a gray fox Horace said probably had a den among the trees lower down the mountain, and had come up here to the bald looking for slow or careless mice or young rabbits to feed her kits. If rabbits were about, they did not show themselves to the humans. Perhaps they knew that Horace was packing a pistol and might be tempted to risk a shot at one of them to add to his supper that night.

A red squirrel scolded the trespassers when they wandered through his maze of scrubby laurel. Horace called a halt and sat down on a handy boulder, patted the stone for Drum to join him. The squirrel became invisible and silent. Horace pulled a small bag of roasted peanuts from his pocket. Drum helped him shell them out and eat a few. Most they set down between them until they had a small heap, then Horace put them at the base of the little tree where they had seen the squirrel, and sat back down beside Drum.

They waited, still as two stones on a stone, quiet as flowers. The wind sighed. Away off somewhere crows discussed common interests, and far above them a hawk prayed for prey. Drum thought this was a Meeting as much as the times he sat in expectation with Annie. After a short while that seemed shorter than it was, the squirrel manifest again, and after giving them a cursory glance began very methodically making the nuts disappear. Once or twice he left with stuffed cheeks to carry a few off to secrete in his hidden larder.

When Squirrel had downed the last nut, Horace opened his little bag and very slowly shelled three more nuts which he placed on the stone between him and Drum. As Horace moved, the wee rodent jumped up onto a lower branch of his laurel, and watched the whole operation intently. A few minutes after the humans turned into stone again, Red, as Horace named him later, leaped down, scampered directly to their perch, hopped up on the boulder and snatched the nuts, then disappeared off into the thicket behind them.

Drum looked at Horace with a boy's big grin, "Do you two know one another?"

Horace looked like a boy very pleased with himself,

"I'm acquainted with his family."

#

Daniel Hoots halted his wagon at the Walnut general store/barbershop/tavern/post office, and tied his horse to a tree beside the building, "Well look at that thing! How do you reckon he got it away out here?" In front of the store, several men were gathered around a Lippard Stewart express truck. The driver was enthusiastically extolling the virtues of his machine to a somewhat skeptical audience. Hop and Mura walked over to take in the show.

Hop prefaced his query with a precisely directed cud, "You come all the way from Asheton in that?"

Before he answered, Oren Shorts stepped sideways to put a little distance between himself and Hop's apparent target, "Yes sir, I'm supposed to pick up three gentlemen who signed on to work at our new hotel, but none of them have showed yet."

Mura had never seen a vintage vehicle in such pristine condition. Setting aside caution, he spoke, "This looks new."

"Indeed it is. We had it shipped down all the way from Buffalo." Oren's cheerful proclamation made it sound like he and his employer were partners.

Hop looked at Mura, "Maybe this fine gentleman will take you back to Asheton with him."

Oren seized on Mura as an opportunity to redeem what was turning out to be a wasted day. He held out his hand, "Oren Shorts."

Mura shook it, tried to seem American, although these people were not exactly like any Americans he remembered, "Ted Mura."

Oren looked at Mura's camera, "You a photographer Mr. Mura?"

"Before I came here."

"Looking for a job right now? Not photography, maybe, but regular pay."

"I need a job, and a place to live."

"Then we're both in luck. Ride in with me, and I can give you one of each."

Hop delivered another round within an inch of the last, "I'm gone now, Mura, if I'm home before morning. Looks like I'm leaving you in good hands." Mura, grateful, forgot himself and bowed. Hop looked puzzled and amused. Nobody else let on they noticed.

#

Horace and Drum reconnoitered their bald for the rest of the afternoon. When an owl somewhere down the mountain announced it was time to start cooking their supper, they had cleaned the spring and located enough windfalls and ice-broken limbs down along the forest verge to feed Horace's fires for the season.

Horace explained his firewood strategy. "If Walt can persuade Nancy to drag some handy pieces up by the cabin, we won't have to carry so far what we cut and split. More time for watching and wandering."

As they started back up the slope to the camp, the heat of the day rode away on the wind. The sun hung low over a purple undulation of mountains away to the southwest. Horace pointed, "Those are the High Balsams, Drum." We might just get across there for a couple of days before the summer's done. It would be worth the walk."

Horace's mention of the High Balsams stirred something akin to remembrance in Drum. He couldn't recall when he had ever seen them before, yet some essence of the far heights called him out of himself, spoke to him of home and friendship. When they reached the cabin at last, the Balsams were still visible against the fading face of day. As night began to well up and pool at the mountains' feet, Drum paused at the door and looked on the High Balsams long and longing before he went in to help Horace with their supper.

Horace built a quick fire. Kindling was already at hand, left for them by some previous visitor. Horace put the beans on to cook, measured out meal for cornbread, had Drum dice the softened jerky. Horace planned to add the salty bits to the cornbread batter, "That will taste like we killed something today."

Nancy's bray not far off interrupted their cheffing. Horace waved a spoon toward the door, "Drum, I can carry on here. Maybe you could fetch a couple of buckets of water for old Nancy to drink tonight, and Walt might be glad for some help unloading. If I know his ways, he's brought something along to contribute to our table tonight."

Walt poked his head through the doorway as Drum started out, "Shame on you Drum, walking that poor old Horace to death all day, then making him cook your supper."

Horace didn't look up, kept pouring his batter into a hot frying pan, "Talk like that, young feller, and you'll cook your own tonight."

Walt clearly enjoyed the banter, having no one but Nancy to talk to all day. With a twinkle, he slapped Drum on the back, "Come with me. I brought stuff that might taste up his grub enough so we can eat it."

Somewhere along his day's route, Walt had come upon a patch of ramps. He pulled a bunch of the pungent leeks from one of Nancy's bags and handed them to Drum, "Take these in to Horace. He knows how to fix them right."

Drum held the ramps at arm's length, "Man, Walt, they sure have a smell."

"Yup, they're a tad strong, gone a bit past season, but Horace'll butter them up and they'll still be good, and a good dose of ramp will cover up our own smell for a few days."

#

Horace acquitted himself well as a field cook. While the beans simmered he sautéed the ramps. Walt had brought along a side of cured bacon and half a ham. Horace put a cut of bacon in the beans and sliced ham to fry. He seemed to relish his kitchen duties, and by the time Drum and Walt had unburdened and provisioned Nancy and put her away snug across the dogtrot, Horace had their supper about ready.

While they ate, Walt expounded and queried on the latest news, "Horace, where's Germany?"

"In Europe, Walt,"

"Must be near France."

"That's so; what's happening in Germany?"

"Germany and France are having a turn-to; the paper says England is about to jump into the fight."

"Yup, Unfortunately; I heard about that."

"Wilson has enough sense to keep us out of it, I ganny,"

"He may try, Walt, but there's a lot of money to be made by waging war, and money generally gets its way. In the end, he'll give in to those who bought him the votes to rule, and we'll be into the mess along with everybody else."

"You might be right, Horace. It's hard to have a free country where everything's for sale, but if I had a young'n, I'd break his leg or hide him in the woods afore I let him go off to kill folk he don't know or have quarrel with."

"The people who get this country into war generally don't send their own sons to fight in it, Walt. If they have sons, they send them to Harvard while other men's sons go off to get shot at."

Drum, who had been listening mute to this conversation, found his voice at that, "Nobody can make me fight if I don't want to."

Walt threw back his head and laughed, "Well, Drum, Eldon said he had a smart little tussle with you at the Warwoman's school."

"That was different, Walt."

"What be different about it? A fight's a fight, be it between two or two thousand."

"But we were still friends when we were done. We never wanted to kill each other."

Horace leaned across the table, looking serious, "Men don't want to kill each other in a war, Drum. They fight because rich men stand to get richer from their striving, and fool them into thinking there is some good cause for their dying. I hope you will stick to your word, Drum, and never raise your hand to strike down a blameless life."

"Annie told me the same thing."

Horace's face went from serious to sad, "I wish somebody had taught me that when I was your age. I'd sleep a lot better nights than I do now."

#

By the time his truck sputtered and clattered into Asheton, Oren Shorts decided he liked this strange little man with the beat-up camera who had ridden up to the Walnut post office on a farmer's wagon. Mura wasn't much of a talker, but answered all questions with a child-like directness. He looked like a worker, was open about his skills or lack of them, and a few days after Mura settled in with Doug Bradley's woodworkers who were rushing to finish the interior trim in some of the rooms at the newly opened Oak Forest Hotel, Oren felt his initial judgment more than justified. As Mura promised, he proved a capable woodworker, worked well on a team, and when Bradley finished his project, Oren had no qualms about signing Mura on with the hotel staff as a bell-hop and valet.

The staff liked Mura. His helpful and gentle manner caught on with the patrons, and when Oren invited him home for supper, and his guest insisted on helping wash the dishes, Oren had no trouble convincing his wife, Allie, to take in a border for their spare room off the porch.

Over the seasons that followed, The Shorts clan discovered Mura to be a fine gardener, passable cook, as well as a carpenter and photographer. He created imaginative games and costumes for the three juvenile Shorts, who worshiped him, introducing him to visitors as *our Mura*. Before winter set in, Ted Mura was regarded by the entire household as one of the family.

When he had put by enough savings to purchase some chemicals and equipment, Mura converted an unused toolshed in the back yard into a little darkroom, and soon was developing and printing film for guests at the hotel. When Fred Elliott heard about this, he offered his competition a job in his own establishment, and never had cause to regret it when Mura accepted.

Mura continued to live with the Shorts, generally blessing and enriching their lives with his generous and considerate presence for years, until Fred retired and sold his photography business to Mura, who finally moved out from the Shorts amid many hugs, tears, handshakes and bows, to set up housekeeping upstairs over his own shop, which he named High Country Photography. Mura never showed Fred his beat-up Eastman view camera, which, except for the wear, looked identical to the one in Elliott's studio.

A born entrepreneur, Mura quickly struck a deal with a printer in town to make postcards to sell at the hotels. Mura's images went beyond the usual fare, and soon the cards were being sold in shops all over Asheton and beyond, not only to tourists, but to locals who took their favorite scenes back home to tack on their cabin walls. As the postcard business flourished, Mura had more cause to trek the back-country coves and ridges stalking new images, and his attraction for the land became his passion.

#

Horace laid out simple but hearty fare for their supper, cornbread with cracklins, pinto beans seasoned with pork fat and onions, and big slices of cured ham, fried with Walt's ramps. Walt had also packed in a jar of honey for sweet; it was still too early for apples.

After they ate and cleared the table and washed the plates and pans and put all away, for Horace kept an exceeding tidy camp, Walt sat by the fire and began to sip occasionally from his flask. He offered none to Horace who eschewed all spirits when he was on the mountain. Horace nursed cup after cup of his strong coffee, fearless of caffeine, and Drum imbibed the hot cider Horace made for him. Barely hardened, the heat had driven off the alcohol, but left a flavorful twang, as Walt observed.

Walt's corn squeezings began to free his imagination and loosen his tongue, and he reeled out for them one after another tales he had learned from his grandmother,

"She was one of the Old Nation, don't you know. What she couldn't read in books she wrote on her heart to remember, and as I growed from a boy, she told near all of it to me."

Drum was spelled, as Walt would say, by the stories tumbling forth from the old man, tales improbable and impossible , yet so real and familiar to a boy's ears that he felt he might have lived them all himself, how Maker raised the Shining Rocks from Earth's heart, and brought Ju and his wife Min out of the unformed Gray into the world, where full of the darkness they came from, they were slowly cleansed and changed by Earthlight into the first people, how their daughter, whose name meant Dragon's Breath, had tried to murder the young Rider because she was afraid he would grow powerful enough to send her back into the Gray, how Li, the fiddler woman had played a song that spun out all the creatures and plants on the mountain. Drum listened deep to Walt's telling, and his heart said *yes* to each and every tale. Carried along on Walt's narratives, a tired boy drifted into sleep, and asleep, was carried by his dreams farther up and deeper in.

Night fell over the circle where Horace and Drum had rested at the height of the day. In the center of the circle the dark stirred and became Li, whose true name can only be spoken in the One Tongue, but if it could be shaped in human speech, would resemble *Wasam Willbe*. She sat with her legs crossed, head bowed, her fiddle in her lap, looking more like a shadow than a young woman. Wasam Willbe had many names and many forms beside the ones she wore presently.

When it was full dark Li stood, flowing upward like a growing corn stalk, her dress falling down all green

116

around her like the slopes of a summer mountain. As she rose, the moon slipped from behind a cloud and silvered her hair woven with scarlet and golden flowers. The bare earth of the circle greened with grass and pale trillium blossomed, turning their pearly faces to the moon as if it were the sun. Li pulled from somewhere among the strands of her hair a silver bow, which she stroked across the strings of her fiddle as gently and softly as a wind in May.

She played and played her music into the night, soft and strong, slow and swift, rising and falling and swirling and plunging like a stream on a mountain or a bird in the air. The music drew fireflies up from the grass and out of the trees around the circle. The fireflies looped and spun about her head then lifted away and above until they mingled with the stars wheeling across the darkling sky. The music wakened innumerable rustlings and stirrings from the shadows, brought owls to voice among the dark trees, roused a symphony of frogs and crickets and stirred the night wind to sibilant whisper and mimetic murmur. All these voices blended with the fiddle into one melody in manifold variation as the mountain sang Drum's dreaming into the sleeping world.

Then in an instant, all the voices ceased. Even the wind fell silent and still. Drum heard only the slow beating of his heart and the coursing of his blood within his skull. Li held her fiddle by the neck in front of her with one hand and dangled her silver bow from the other. She began to sing as she looked at Drum, a high clear note that rose in pitch until it wavered, then surged higher still until the very air was screaming and Drum was awake in his chair and Horace was taking the kettle from the stove to warm a basin for Drum to wash before bed.

#

Breakfast came early next morning, pancakes and bacon, and the stout black coffee that fueled Horace through his days *on the wagon*, as he termed it. Soon after sunrise, with Horace and Drum helping, Walt and Nancy dragged a number of large limbs up to the cabin for firewood, then before noon, plodded off down the winding trail northward along the ridge toward the circle grove and home. Walt had not been able to bring up Horace's entire stash in one trip. They agreed he would return within a week or so with Nancy and the rest of the supplies for the summer, and Drum would go with them then back to Annie. Meanwhile, Drum and Horace belonged to the mountain. Horace would roam the heights and gaps to find the peace and calm that eluded him in the peopled world, and Drum would go with him, an explorer in search of a place of belonging he only glimpsed in dreams almost become memories and memories almost become dreams.

Horace and Drum spent the rest of the day cutting the wood they'd gathered. Horace was insistent, "Best to get ahead of it now, then we won't have to fret rainy days, and we'll have some sunny ones free to wander in." A part of every day they spent cleaning the cabin and washing their clothes. Drum judged Horace a pernickety housekeeper, but they never had to waste time looking for a mislaid tool or a clean shirt. Their simple chores, timely done, bought their freedom to carelessly enjoy the bulk of their days on the mountain. For all his years, Drum would remember the lesson Horace taught him here, and promptly attend to the necessary maintenance that enabled his life.

Among the necessities for life in camp that Nancy

carried up the mountain was a stack of little hard-bound black notebooks with unlined creamy pages. Horace divided them equally with Drum. Horace wrote in his. Drum mostly drew in his. From time to time, Horace would ask permission to look at the drawings, occasionally requesting, "Might I use this one for an illustration in an article?" Sometimes, he would ask Drum to draw a particular scene or plant or creature. "Next time, we need to bring a camera with us. There's a Kodak thing out now that folds up to drop in a pocket. We maybe need one of those." Drum recalled vaguely that in his former life, his grandfather had owned such a camera. He didn't mention any of that to Horace. Somebody a long time ago, Drum couldn't quire remember who or where, had told him, "One life at a time is quite enough."

Except for a day spent repairing their roof after a violent thunderstorm, their domestic chores were typically done in an hour or two, and they invested the rest of their time under the sun communing with the mountain. During long evenings after supper they would sit around the fire spinning tales, or Horace would read aloud to them from one of the books he brought along. Drum's encounter with the bear at the spring provided conversational fodder for weeks of evenings, the tale expanding and transforming with each remembering and retelling until it assumed mythic proportions.

#

For most of the day, Mura had been rooted to this slab of stone, his view camera set on the tripod before him, now covered with the rain poncho he had thrown over it when a brief shower came across the mountain an hour past. At first light he had begun walking up from Deep Laurel where he had spent the night with Evan and Martha

Hoots and their four children. Hospitable as most highlanders were to strangers afoot, they had taken him in simply because Evan's brother Hop had thought him worthy of a ride on his wagon. When Mura returned to visit on his own, he brought with him simple gifts of cheese and raisins that marked him as generous and grateful, and not inclined to be totally beholden, all traits of character admired and cultivated by mountain folk.

Five hours after he left Evan's porch, Mura set down his burden on the rocky bald of Myrtle Mountain, over six thousand feet above sea level, and three thousand feet higher than Deep Laurel Creek where it ran behind Evan's barn. A fairly passable road took Mura along the stream up through Raven Gap, where hunters and a few hardy foot travelers crossed the mountain into Tennessee. From the saddle of the gap, a less defined trail led most of the way to the summit, where Mura sat now. Hunters came up top occasionally to listen for their hounds, and a few mad souls simply sought this high place because it was apart. Mura had come for the view and for the light.

He wanted a photograph of the High Balsams on the far side of Deep Laurel Cove thrusting dark against a cloud-crowded sky, and the floor of the valley lit by the sun as if by a spotlight in a theater. If he had to wait much longer, the sun would be lowering and the valley would be in shadow until the next day. At that point, Mura would have to settle for a lesser shot, or come back some other day and try again, or spend the night on the mountain and hope toward the morning. But the clouds had mercy, drifting over the balsams, shadowing them black against the billowing white cumulus beyond and admitting a shaft of sunlight into the cove which transformed the bottomland along Deep Laurel Creek into a field of glory.

Mura pulled the cover from his Eastman, removed the cap from the lens and exposed his sheet of film. In quick succession he inserted and exposed three more before the clouds closed overhead and the valley below receded into deep shadow. He knew he had the image he was after. He would carry back to Asheton something of the soul of this place. People who saw his photograph would embrace it like a memory, and would long to make the experience present in their lives.

Carefully Mura packed his exposed film away in his bag, and began to enjoy his deferred lunch of fried eggs and biscuits and blackberry turnovers that Martha Hoots had made for him. Before the summer was out, Evan and Martha would have a print of his photograph tacked above their mantel, and postcards picturing *The View East from Myrtle Mountain Summit* would be on sale at Oak Forest Hotel and other tourist gathering spots around Asheton. But Mura did not sit all day alone on a mountain so he could make postcards to sell. He sold postcards so he could spend whole days alone atop a mountain. Mura pondered now about this one in particular, as he gazed off toward the dark range of rounded summits to the south, knowing the woman who would be his wife was a child now somewhere just beyond them. Would she ever stand on this spot, and whom might she bring with her? Had his imposed presence here already altered the future as he remembered it? Mura vowed to keep vigilant lest he unwittingly interrupt all that should be or not.

In spite of the ache in his back and hips, as he packed his gear and started back down his trail, Mura felt he'd had a good day. He also wished he carried the sort of camera slung across his shoulder the morning he met his wife. Where other photographers might get a dozen or more pictures in a day, Mura was content with three or four, or even one or two images that were more than pictures, true reflections of the Spirit of the high and solitary ground he walked. Mura loved these mountains the way he might once have loved a woman, or a deity. Every photograph he made was an act of adoration, of worship and communion.

#

Summer left before it had well begun, and Drum thought he had spent far too little of it on the mountain with Horace. He did not begrudge his time helping Annie, though. Her leg continued to ail her, and she counted on Drum for more than she liked. They brought in a good crop of corn. The garden was bountiful and late summer was full of gathering and drying and canning all manner of edibles for the winter ahead.

Drum made drawings of everything that did not move too fast for observation. By the time Horace came down from the herder cabin at the end of the season, both their stacks of little black books were full. Horace confided that he had begun work on a novel. Fiction was something new for him. He was full of plans to invite his publisher down to look at these mountains that had inspired him, so he could pitch the book in situ.

In August, several men and a lady drove out from Asheton to look at Annie's school. When classes began, Annie informed her students that this would be their last year under her tutelage. Marshall County planned to build a school in the cove, and Zeb Pounder's niece Marjorie would be the teacher. Annie did not tell the class that she had offered herself for the position, and political and familial connections had won out over academic qualifications.

Drum caught Horace's craving for the high lonesome, and as often as he could be spared from work around the farm, he would steal time from his studies and trek off alone up Sorrow Creek, or away into the forest above the Shining Rocks. Autumn came on gradually and mild, and several times he persuaded Annie to let him camp alone overnight on the mountain. When he realized how much she worried about him during these solo expeditions, he resolved to keep them to a minimum. Still, now and again he would go, drawn by a movement in the air or transient quality of light or a wind-borne cry of some wild thing. The looming peaks and ridges spoke to him continually in languages that were just beyond the threshold of understanding. Drum was certain that if he could get away by himself and be still enough, and quiet enough and attentive enough, the Truth the mountain was trying to tell him would come to him unbidden the way the red squirrel had visited him and Horace in the laurel tangle on Haynes Knob.

#

Oren Shorts looked forward all day to Ted Mura's fine venison stew. The aroma enticed Oren to taste as he came through his kitchen door after work. He also attempted to stick his finger into the apple cobbler Allie had set on the counter to cool, but she rapped his hand smartly with the big ladle she was using to stir Mura's stew. Oren put his insulted paw to his mouth, licking off the sweet residue, "That hurts!"

Allie leaned over and gave him a lover's kiss, "I'll tend to your hurts when you've helped me clean the kitchen after supper, old man." Mura, who stood across the kitchen mashing sweet potatoes to go with his stew, smiled to himself and pretended to be unaware.

Besides the Shorts clan, who all agreed included Mura, Horace Kellett would share their table. He had asked if he might bring along his publisher from New York, Jason Lentz. The other guests included John Huffman and his wife, Laura. John owned a large tract of forest above Deep Laurel Cove, which included Myrtle Mountain and several lesser summits in the area. The brand new state governor, an Asheton native, Craig Keys would also be joining them, along with William Souther. Of all the guests, Souther seemed the most unlikely; He had made his money laying rails for the timber companies to haul their logs out of the mountains to be milled. Souther was a forward looking man, though, and he realized the timber boom could not be sustained much longer as most of the old growth trees had already been cut. If he were to make any money as a railroad man in the years ahead, he needed a steady supply of passengers, tourists who came to Asheton to see mountains and forests, not gullied slopes and muddied streams that would be left behind if all the timber were cut and hauled away.

All Oren's guests were committed to preserving some sizable remnant of their mountains intact and undisturbed for future generations. But there were also powerful and moneyed interests in Asheton, and in the capital, who argued that the mountains should be kept in private hands, managed in a sustainable way to remain commercially viable sources of timber into the future. The conflict between preservationists and conservationists was deep and pervasive. While they argued and debated, the timber barons raced to strip the mountains of everything that could be turned into lumber or pulp before there were any legal impediments to their pillage.

#

Horace never spent another summer in Martin McMinn's old herder shack. Martin died the winter after Drum met the bear at the spring. Martin got religion during his final illness, and with his sister's encouragement, left with her a hand-written will stating that he bequeathed all his worldly goods, other than his house and fields, to the Lord. William and Wallace had little desire to become farmers, but felt the hundreds of mountain acres Martin held title to were of more profit to them than to the Methodist church.

They gained an audience with Zeb Pounder, sheriff and uncrowned king of Marshall County. Zeb and a deputy spent a day exploring his domain, and he filed a report with the clerk of probate that the Lord was not to be found in Marshall County. When word of the deal got to Asheton, some agreed the report was likely true.

The Lord not appearing before the probate judge to defend His claim, Wallace and William inherited Martin's mountain, and before the spring of nineteen fifteen, Pigeon Pulp and Paper set about harassing Annie to sell them her forty acres to give them direct access to the road, so they could conveniently haul away their newly acquired timber. Her steadfast refusal to do so eliminated any chance she might have to ever teach at the Sorrow Cove school. When the school expanded to two teachers, a young woman from Asheton was hired for the job. When she couldn't find a place to live in the cove, Annie offered her lodgings.

Judy Waldrup proved a good fit in Annie and Drum's household. A quiet, sensitive young woman, she preferred sitting in Meeting to attending worship at the Methodist Church. The pastor there wrote a letter to her parents, whom he knew, expressing his dismay at their child's abandonment of her religious tradition.

Judy had a passion for the wild woods and mountains equal to Drum's. Although she was seven years older, they became frequent companions on expeditions into what remained of Sorrow Cove's forests.

#

"It looks like the wreck of the world, Drum." Judy Waldrop shook her head in disbelief. They stood above the Shining Rocks on the ridge Drum first visited with Horace as his guide. Now he'd brought his teacher to show her first hand that the predations of the timber companies she had been reading about in the Asheton Citizen were all too real and present.

The machines had moved further south along the ridge, leaving behind a tilted devastation of raw and fissured rock and earth, shattered stumps and the remains of equipment broken and left to rust. Deep in the ruined valley below, a silted river, writhing like a wounded snake around the base of the mountain, glinted dully, like tarnished copper in the light.

Drum had resisted showing Judy this place. Now he wished he hadn't let her talk him into it. "Horace says it is the wreck of the world, Judy. He says none of us alive now will ever see it made whole again."

Judy just stood, not answering a word. Her eyes were luminous. Drum thought she was about to cry. "But look over there," he said, pointing back the way they had come, "We have all this left."

Judy turned toward the green mountains and dark valleys falling away like waves in the sea until they blued with distance. For a long moment they just stood together and saw what was good beyond words. Finally, Judy whispered, "But can we keep it?"

Drum had more doubts than he wanted her to see, "People like Horace are trying awfully hard to keep it. There are a lot of folks who want to save our place. If enough people could see it just like we do, I don't think they'd give this up for any kind of money."

The sun got lost in a cloud for a minute and although it had been a warm day, a chill wind stirred, made Judy shiver suddenly. Drum noticed, "You all right?"

Back to herself, Judy laughed, "Someone stepped on my grave, my granny would say. We'd best get started back. Annie will think I've seduced my student."

"Teachers don't do that sort of thing, except maybe in books, do they Judy?"

"Only in France, Drum," and they began retracing their path back down the mountain to help Annie with supper.

#

In the spring of his sixteenth year, Drum still coddled a strong fancy for the new teacher at Sorrow Cove School, but when Horace proposed to Annie that he pay Drum's room and board with Oren Shorts and his family, so Drum could attend the high school in Asheton, Drum never looked back. The idea of living in what was to him a real city overrode any qualms he felt about leaving Annie to manage without him for most of the year.

They all agreed it was time for Drum to move on to the next phase of his life. When he unveiled the big plan to Judy Waldrup, she clapped her hands delightedly, "You're on your way now Drum. One day back in our little cove, we'll be hearing wondrous words about you."

Drum made himself immediately at home in the Shorts household. The children adopted him right away as their surrogate big brother, a role he filled gladly and more than adequately, unhindered by any of the complications of sibling rivalry. Drum also struck up a friendship with his fellow boarder, Ted Mura. Within a year, he was spending more time in Ted's darkroom than with his classwork. Neither Annie nor Horace seemed much surprised when they asked him if he had thought about the prospect of university, and he informed them that he had decided to pursue photography as a career rather than academics.

When Mura bought out Elliot's photography business, he hired Drum as his assistant. Mura confided to Horace, "Drum already has a better eye as a photographer than I do."

Working alongside Mura, the young photographer learned not just the technical skills of handling a camera and manipulating negatives in the darkroom, but the more spiritual discipline of capturing a revealing image. For Mura, seeing involved waiting for the subject to disclose its essence in its own way and time.

"Many pictures will not suffice for the right picture," he preached. "Never rush things. Be a waiter and a watcher. Always patient. Ever ready. Stay open to the instant you never see coming until it is upon you."

Jason Lentz came down from New York to do a camping expedition with Horace and Mura. He wanted to publish a book about the mountains with photographs by Mura and text by Horace. As they were sorting through some images in Mura's studio one afternoon, Jason mistakenly picked up several of Drum's photographs, thinking they were Mura's. The publisher was sufficiently impressed to purchase several of Drum's pictures, paying money for them even though Drum tried to make them gifts.

Later, Mura, took Drum aside and said, "Your images are worthy and should cost something to those who have them. That is how you teach them to value what you treasure."

The following winter, a letter came from a magazine in Washington, DC offering Drum a job as a photographer on their staff. The editor had seen Drum's prints in Jason's office and said, "They make you feel like you are there in the middle of it. That is what we need."

Drum told Mura, "I don't think I'm ready."

Mura responded with his usual enigmatic smile, "Youth is never quite ready, but they are ready for you. I think you should go."

When Drum had left his mentor alone with his regrets, Mura sat down in a chair and allowed himself tears. He wept not for the life and love he had lost, but for his future past, for the awful wound he would inflict upon this soul he now loved like a son.

#

Annie insisted Drum graduate from Asheton School before he went traipsing off to the big city. Jason and Horace put in their word for him with the editors of American Scenes Magazine, who informed Drum at the end of the term that there was still a position for him on their staff as two of their photographers had not returned from the Great War. They promised to hold the position until the fall, to give him time to arrange an orderly departure from his present employer. He and Mura actually spent most of that summer walking on the mountains with Horace, where, under Mura's tutelage, Drum made a multitude of photographs and honed his skills as an image maker considerably.

Horace's family lived in Washington, and he persuaded his wife Eleanor to take in Drum as a boarder. So late in August of nineteen-twenty, Annie, Horace, Ted Mura, Judy Waldrup and the entire Shorts tribe stood on the platform at the Asheton station as Drum prepared to board his train. They shared fond tears and brave laughter and heartrending goodbyes as the conductor yelled his last call.

Annie hugged Drum as he gathered his baggage. "Our love travels with thee, Friend Drum," she whispered.

"I'd hoped Emmalou would be here," he murmured, gazing somewhere past Annie's right shoulder, afraid he might cry if he met her eyes.

"She wanted to," Annie said, "but she had to be at Berea College to start her classes this week."

Drum nodded mutely, kissed Annie on her forehead, a rare sort of gesture for him, then picked up his bags and turned toward the train. When he found his seat and stowed his bags, he looked out the window to see his friends waving as the world of his youthful becoming slid past and out of sight behind him.

A week later, Drum was standing before Howard Ridgeworth's desk, portfolio under his arm, reporting for duty. Howard pulled his glasses down almost to the tip of his nose and scrutinized his new photographer intently, "You look younger than I was led to believe. You're just a boy."

Without a word, Drum loosed the tie on his portfolio, opened it, and laid it on the desk in front of Howard, who adjusted his specs, and silently perused them one by one. When he was half way through, he looked up suddenly, "You take these?"

Drum barely suppressed a smile, "All by myself."

"You do the processing?"

"All but three. Ted Mura wanted to show me a couple of his tricks."

Howard leaned back in his chair, folded his pudgy hands over his ample belly and lifted the corners of his wide mouth into a pleased grin, "Welcome to American Scenes, Benjamin; I'll just call you Drum, if you don't mind."

"Everybody who knows me calls me Drum, Mr. Ridgeworth."

"Howard. Let me show you around, Drum, introduce you to the rest of the staff. Then I'll buy you lunch at Kelsey's and tell you how things work around here."

DRUM

By the summer of 1960, most in Asheton believe that Benjamin Drum is lost and dead, just as Horace Kellett was lost decades before. The High Balsams have a way of devouring souls whole, the locals say. Stories of disappearances get told and repeated, evolving with each retelling. When known tales no longer suffice to satisfy a mountaineer's appetite for mystery, tellers invent new variations. Drum and Horace have become the stock of Appalachian legends.

Millicent Robbins knows better, though she has never tried to convince anyone. Drum is not lost. She has seen the place where he's gone. The way is not at all difficult to those who know it. If need be, she could go there now.

This whole day has teetered on the brink of rain. Most of her guests have kept to their rooms or sat rocking on the porch playing cards or gossiping through the day, abandoning their chairs only to go search for lunch. It is the kind of day when young couples conceive babies, her father remarked earlier. He says many calculatedly atrocious things, which, true or not, all sound true. He delights in declaring an inconvenient verity to the unwary, even if he must invent one.

A half hour before Myrtle Mountain eclipses it, the sun drops below the overcast and gilds the range of hills and peaks beyond the town. A puddle of blue gathers in a corner of the sky. The blue will spread and deepen during the night. Stars will rise to its surface and before morning the whole sky will be flooded with sparkling dark.

Millicent expects she will likely have only one seating in her dining room tonight. Having been cooped up all day, the tourists and travelers will scatter into town seeking some novelty to close their evening. A severe cold plagues her. She won't risk sneezing or coughing in proximity to startled guests. Alice and the staff can handle things. Soon, she thinks, she will join Drum in that vast wherever, and Alice will likely be the innkeeper herself. Alice has always been as much friend as employee. It would be fitting.

Millicent looks at the bundle of old letters in her lap. She wants to hold the man rather than his mail. From behind her chair, her father's voice startles her,

"You should read those. You really should."

She hadn't smelled his cigarette. She realizes she has not seen him smoking since the wedding, is glad though surprised somehow that he has stayed on with her. "These weren't written to me," she says to the wavering form in front of her now.

"They will tell you things you need to know, things Drum would have told you himself if there'd been time."

"You seem to know a lot about things for a dead man," she retorts, returning the smile her father flashes at her, wishing she might reach up and touch his hand as he fades into the wallpaper.

Alone again, Millicent shuffles through the sheaf of letters, most written by folk she has known or at least heard of. A few envelopes are addressed in Drum's hand to one or another of his correspondents. Scanning the names, she wonders why these missives were saved and kept, and who had brought them eventually back to the writer.

"Nothing is really lost, ever," her father likes to say, "though everything comes back to you changed."

She looks at the postmarks, thinking the old stamps rather quaint, opens the envelope that appears to be the earliest, and begins to read.

\#

Friday, September 10, 1920
Dear Annie,

Washington is a mad place compared to Asheton, but I am well situated in Georgetown now with the Kelletts. They are very kind and welcoming to me, and I think I shall like it here, but they are not at all like the salty old Horace we know back in our mountains. It is hard to imagine him being at home in these stiff and formal surroundings. It is evident, though, that he is much loved and respected by his family, who speak of him fondly and often and are full of tales of his visits, and maintain a seemingly constant stream of correspondence with him. I will endeavor to follow their good example and keep all of you informed of my misadventures in the Capital as long as any are interested.

I seem to be the junior member of the photographic staff at American Scenes, in terms of both age and status. My job was left vacant by a brave guy who went off to France to photograph the War and is buried there now with some of the airmen whose exploits he meant to picture. He went up with one of the pilots to get some photographs of the fight aloft, and they were shot down on their return only a few kilometers from their aerodrome.

Howard Ridgeworth, my immediate superior on the staff, seems a likeable and competent sort. He knows photography and likes my work and I think we will get along in harness together. He was pleased that I am capable to do my own dark room work when required, as prints transport more safely than undeveloped negatives. Mura has been a thorough teacher, and I will have reason to thank him many times over, I am sure.

Ridgeworth tells me we are to be in New York next Thursday to shoot some pictures for a series of articles on American Finance. Life comes on suddenly and fast in this business. I suppose in time one gets used to it.

I miss you and Horace and Mura and of course Oren and Allie and the children. Tell Judy I will soon send her pictures from this big city.

Give my love and greetings to everyone-

Drum.

#

Ninth Month, Sixteenth Day 1920
Sorrow Cove, North Carolina
My Dearest Drum,

I read thy letter to Judy. She misses thy walks with her on the mountain. The dear girl (or should I say woman?) seems quite sweet on young James Coggins, and he appears to regard her with some fondness of his own. So we may have a romance budding among us here.

Horace and Mura were by last week. They were on their way to photograph the logging work past the Shining Rocks. Horace feels there is real hope now the state may establish a Park before all our mountains are hauled away to mill.

I give thanks daily that the horrible War is done, and that thee will not be off over the water to picture death and destruction. No good can come of all that suffering, I fear. Thy Horace is convinced the struggle has merely planted the seed for a more dire conflict in the next generation. I pray he's wrong.

I am without a mule now. Johnny was down with a colic when I went out day before yesterday. Horace brought out a vet, but Johnny died before they got here. Johnny was a good and faithful soul, of more comfort and support than some of the humans I have met along my way.

I think it is today thee is to be in New York with thy camera, making pictures of banks and bankers. I told Horace about thy assignment. He said to be certain to get some clear portraits, as they will likely be displayed in post offices across the country sooner or later. He blames the War on the bankers and the industrial tycoons, believes they pushed Wilson into it because there was profit to be made from the war effort. He says we will face another major war in twenty or so years because of the greed of these men, and Mura agrees with him. One cannot argue with thy friends; they are convinced. I listen and pray they prove mistaken. Horace carries a deep anger toward society, and I think that is why he hides himself away in our mountains. He cannot rest before anything he regards as injustice.

There are no words, Drum, to express how proud we all are of thee. Mura is convinced thy pictures will outlive us all. "Drum will hold a mirror to our times," he says of thee.

I have no news to compare to the excitement in thy life, so I will close now not to weary thee with trivia. Night and day, I who love thee am holding thee in the Light.
Under the Mercy,
Thy Annie

#

Saturday, September 19th, 1920
Georgetown
Mura, good Friend,

I am back in Washington now, bruised but unbroken, and have a couple of days off to rest from my adventure in New York. Please reassure everyone that I am all right up here. My first assignment, as you must know by now, was everything but the expected.

Howard Ridgeworth went with me, as he wanted to do the interviews himself. We arrived at the Corner around lunchtime. The streets were a thronged rush, so we left our driver by Trinity Church and walked back a block to Broad and Wall. We found where we were to do the photographing, and I left Ridgeworth talking to a young broker he knew named Joe Kennedy, and went back out to fetch in the equipment.

As I crossed the street toward the Sub Treasury, a sad old bay horse pulling a loaded freight wagon stopped right in front of me. I stepped around to the curb and the driver jumped down and ran past, nearly knocking me over. He never looked back or apologized. I thought, *New York manners,* and headed back toward the church. The bells at Trinity rang noon. Ahead of me a handsome young couple were walking in the same direction, dressed for an occasion. The father was carrying their little girl, maybe two or three years, on his arm. She giggled and waved at me shyly.

At that moment, Mura, the world ended. The explosion was huge. I was walking past an express truck parked at the curb. It shielded me some from the blast, which took me off my feet and leveled me to the pavement. When I could breathe, I raised my head to see the truck toppled next to me, the top inches from my face. The happy family ahead of me were not so lucky. The father was lying face down about a dozen paces ahead. His left arm had been torn off. The mother's headless body was sprawled just beyond him. Their baby sat in the street between them, covered with her parents' blood, but crying lustily, apparently not seriously hurt.

I stumbled to my feet and picked up the child and started with some other survivors toward the church. I glanced to my right and saw the head of the child's mother, still wearing her hat, stuck against the wall of the sub treasury. Everyone walking seemed to be bleeding or burnt. All around us on the street lay the mangled dead. Pieces of people, body parts, were strewn across the pavement. Could war produce any worse horror?

I was blooded myself from shards and debris flung out by the explosion. Nothing serious, the worst being a nasty contusion on my forehead and a deep burn across the back of my right hand. I didn't feel any of this until later. By the time I reached Trinity steps, I could not see clearly for the blood that kept dripping into my eyes. A large, dark skinned woman appeared in front of me as suddenly as if she had stepped out of the stone of the building.

She held out her hands in my direction and said with a strange pitying smile, "Let me take her, Ryder." My knees were trembling. I was afraid I might fall down, and handed over the poor babe into her ample arms.

Just then, Ridgeworth called from behind me, "Drum! Thank God! Are you sound?" He had been inside the Morgan offices talking to Kennedy. Though shaken, they had not been hurt.

As he came up to me, I looked back around and the

woman and the child were gone. "Where's the dark woman with the child?" I asked him.

He answered, "I didn't see who you mean."

"But she thought she knew me; she called me 'Ryder'," I told him.

Ridgeworth just stared at me and repeated, "I didn't see her, Drum. Let's get you to the car."

We returned to our driver then, and I sat in the car until I steadied a bit, and then, before Ridgeworth hauled me away to the hospital to get checked and patched, I got out the camera and made a few pictures, not of the Captains of Finance, as we had intended, but of the innocent victims of their unceasing war to own the world. The bankers, though, are no worse than those who covet the power they represent. They are all ruled by the same greed. Horace, I think, is right in everything he says about such men.

I wish today that I had never seen the terrors I have photographed this week, and that I was with you now, seeking the faces of mountains. Give my regards to the Shorts. Witness to all there that I am still in one piece, and loving and missing every one of you.

Ever your student and friend-

Drum

#

Thursday 30 September 1920
Asheton, North Carolina
Esteemed Drum,

Nights are getting cooler now, hinting at the autumn to come. More than there are any words to say, we are all gratified that you are not seriously hurt from the unseemly assault in New York. Some souls are not

139

granted to be children of their own time, but are swept by unruly tides into strange scenes and alien places to witness the mysterious afflictions and exaltations that occur.

For reasons we may discuss one day, perhaps you and I might be considered among that number. The world is stranger than humans can know, and there are currents and waves moving beneath the surface of all things that order history according to a plan too vast for mind to grasp. In years to come you will witness events that some have forgotten, and we will be reminded again by your images. Perhaps this appears nonsensical to you, but the universe excels at humor. Almost always, the joke is on us, though we forget to laugh.

Allie Shorts is elated that she will be voting in the next election. Oren teases her that she doesn't need to vote for he has always voted just the way she commanded him. But most of those we know agree that this is a good thing and a right thing. Of course, I will not be voting as I have no proof of citizenship. I could apply, but that would require explanations of the inexplicable. My history eludes even me. My past is no more real to me than my future. It would be quite beyond me to account for my life in any logical way to be understood or believed.

Dreams have come on several nights concerning your account of the bombing. I believe with certainty that you were not there by accident, or even merely as a witness, but to deliver that child from harm. You will perhaps see the Dark Woman again. If my dreams are informative, as they have sometimes been in the past, she is perhaps familiar to you, although you may have forgotten her now. When you come here again, we should perhaps talk at length about these things.

Besides photography, your friend Mura has become a path-finder. I helped John Huffman lay out a couple of trails on his mountain. More and more people are coming from away to Asheton, wanting to walk on the high peaks and ridges. Huffman seems determined so far to preserve his holdings from the timber companies. He has set up a camp for tourists on top of Myrtle Mountain and is talking about building a permanent lodge up there.

Our friend Horace is hiding out somewhere in Deep Laurel right now. I haven't seen him in about a week. He misses you, as do all of us your friends.

Please keep us informed of your life, as we are all very interested. One of your photographs of the bombing aftermath appeared in the newspaper here. Did they pay the photographer for that, or the magazine?
Be well,
Mura

#

Monday, July 11th, 1921
Washington, DC
Dear Judy,

What a thrill, though not a surprise to hear that you and James have made the Grand Announcement. Unfortunately, I will be out of the country (in France) in August on my first foreign assignment for National Geographic. Ridgeworth was sorry to see me go, but his budget at American Scenes did not allow for an increase, and N.G. offered substantially more in salary as well as a chance to travel regularly beyond our borders. I have left the Kelletts, and have rooms now closer in to our offices. I will miss them, although we will visit occasionally, I am sure.

My first foray for my new employer turned out to be interesting. Duncan Phillips has opened his art collection to public view, and they sent me out to get some pictures. In one of the galleries there were a couple of incredible little paintings, not much larger than this sheet of letter paper, by Albert Pinkham Ryder, who died four or five years ago. They were dark and mysterious things, one of a fishing village by the sea, and the other of a ship under full sail against a sunset, called "Homeward Bound."

Phillips was quite taken with the marine painting. My favorite, though is the other one, of the little village, just two houses, actually, before an expanse of moonlit water which could be the sea or a broad river. The moon strikes a silver wake across the surface that made me recall a recurrent dream I have had from time to time since childhood. Always the same. I am high above a wide river at night, whether suspended or flying I cannot tell. The moon above me sets the water beneath asparkle like cold fire. And suddenly I am falling toward the water. I am not afraid; it feels like coming home. But I always awake when I am still far above it.

Give my regards to James. He is a good man and a fine craftsman. He will do well by you. Tell Annie hello and give her my love, and Horace if you see him. I heard from him recently that Mura is not very well. I wish you and James the very best for your future. I will send you a wedding gift from over the water. I still miss our walks on the mountain.

Ever your friend,

Drum

P.S. News has just come in that the British are to sign a truce with the Irish today. I remember Horace saying there will always be fighting over there, that the Irish will fight one another if there is no one else to draw their wrath. I hope life remains peaceful in our Cove. The entire world seems to be always itching for a row.

#

Thursday, May fourth, 1922
Dear Drum,

Our son was born at 2:14 last Tuesday morning. We are well. You will be pleased, I hope, that James wanted to name him after you (as did I). He said we couldn't give him a Coggins name or the rest of the clan would feel slighted and be mad at us. Benjamin has your far wandering gaze already. We shall have to keep a close eye on him.

So where are you wandering now? It seems an age since we last heard from you. Annie worries, but Annie worries about us all. If you won't come visit us, at least write now and then and tell us we are not forgotten.

Annie and James send their love. Ted Mura was by here with Horace this afternoon to meet our Ben, and asked of you.
Ever your friend,
Judy Coggins

#

Sunday, May 14th 1922
Washington DC
Dear Judy,

What great news, and an undeserved honor for me. I hope your Benjamin carries the name better than I have done. Because you haven't seen me doesn't mean that I don't think daily of you all.

143

The magazine owns me, it seems. I hurry around and away to every place except the one I really want to go to. I just got in last night from riding on trains for weeks making photographs of large steam locomotives toiling up majestic mountains. To my mind, the mountains would look better without the railways, but my editors say the people want to see trains, and the railway companies are no doubt paying under the table for them to be seen. It is advertizing pure and simple, but none dare call it that. The readers will see whatever the magazines show them, and be convinced by clever words that it was what they wanted to behold.

Later this week, I'll be packed off down to Mexico to photograph the remains of dead civilizations razed by the germs and steel of greedy foreigners. In some ways, it resembles the history of our own green coves and mountains, though our kind have been as much among the oppressors as the oppressed, and have kept our place with more success. Some few, like me, are driven on the wind to places not our own, recording scenes that amaze the eye without opening the heart. At times I don't think I've photographed a true image since I left Mura.

Believe I do miss all of you dreadfully. I'm too tired to write more now.

Your friend,

Drum

#

First Day, Fifth Month, 30th, 1926

Sorrow Creek, North Carolina

Dearest Drum,

What a delight to see thy pictures of the fine Shackleford horses in the issue of National Geographic that arrived this week. Unfortunately, we are at the opposite end of the state from the Outer Banks. Perhaps one day soon, thy editors will need some photographs from the Carolina mountains, and thee will be near enough for awhile to visit thy old friends who miss thee here on the Creek.

I need to tell thee I have decided to sell my place here to Judy and James. With another Coggins on the way now, they will be needing a larger house, and I am needing a smaller one. Young Ben is turning out to be a wanderer like his namesake. A few days ago, he somehow managed to slip out the door, and Judy was frantic until she found him hiding among the squash in the garden.

Last week, there was a huge fire on the ridge above Shining Rocks. It stayed above the creek, but burned along the entire south face of the ridge all the way over by Haynes Knob to Martin's old cabin, which was consumed. Horace walked through just after and said nothing at all is left up there but scorched earth and blackened stumps. The little shelter he put up down on Hazel Fork was also lost. Horace says he is planning to look for a new hideout over on the High Balsams. The fire burned for days before they finally got it out. Men came over from Tennessee to help fight the flames. The sky glowed red night after night. The air still reeks of smoke and burning.

Emmalou Truelight will be home for the summer in a few days, and will be going off to Providence in the fall for her post-graduate studies. She has been following thy career. She asks about thee as often as she writes. I feel fortunate in my brief sojourn as a teacher to have learned with so many fine students, several of whom have gone on to inhabit larger worlds. I am proud of each one of thee, and hold all in the Light day by day.

145

Horace is worried about thy friend Ted Mura. He says Mura has an angry cough that will not go away, that he spends too many nights sleeping on wet cold ground. Thee are all three restless and rootless at heart, for all thy love of the good Earth, and seem to this old woman's mind like lost boys seeking thy way home. I love thee all. Always thy Annie.

#

Sunday September 9th, 1928
Mura, Old Friend,

I will treasure the copy of "Smoke on the Mountains" you sent, with your splendid photographs and Horace's finely honed text, pithy and insightful as his speech. Your images make me homesick. While I look at them, I am there, reliving our days and nights on the ridges and balds, and in the deep woods and shadowed laurel, tasting Horace's cooking, breathing the balsamed air, listening to Walt's fantastic stories. Every time I make a photograph, the lessons you taught me in those places come back to guide me, so that my images have some chance to answer the truth of a place rather than the readers' expectations of what they are supposed to see.

I'm writing from Cleveland tonight, where I've been making pictures for an article on the recent acquisitions in the Wade Collection. The project has reacquainted me with Albert Ryder, whose paintings have fascinated me, as you know, since I first saw some of them in Duncan Phillip's collection in Washington.

One of Ryder's paintings here, "The Race Track," particularly haunts. Very small, as is most of his work, it depicts a pale gray death figure on a galloping horse. Supposedly Ryder painted this after a friend, a waiter at the hotel his brother managed, bet his savings on a race, and killed himself when the horse he had picked lost.

The painting is weird enough in itself, but the strangest aspect is the effect it had on me when I saw it. You no doubt remember me telling you about the dark woman who took the little girl from my arms after the Morgan bombing in New York. I've wondered ever since why she called me "Ryder," who she thought I was. Perhaps the incident is partly to blame for my keen interest in A. P. Ryder's paintings, although they manifest the same quality of distance and atmosphere one encounters in your photographs of our mountains.

But as I was looking at "the Race Track," I felt a certainty, I don't know why, that the Dark Woman did not mean "Ryder;" she was calling me "Rider." Now what do you suppose that means, if it is indeed anything more than a fanciful notion?

Tomorrow, I catch the train back to Washington. N.G. is threatening to send me off over the water to Ireland to photograph some angry poet. I recall Horace saying on occasion that the Irish are always angry.

Give my love to all there. Tell them I will be in Asheton before spring to stoke the home fires and swap all our tales of the between times.

Still your pupil,

Drum.

#

Monday 31 August 1931

Drum, Respected Colleague and Cherished Friend,

The past month has been dry and poplars are already shedding their leaves, conserving their juices for what seems likely to be an arid autumn.

You may have read in the papers that Horace Kellett is lost. Three weeks ago, Oren Shorts and I drove him up to Big Tom Bald, wherefrom he meant to walk westerly across the High Balsams and find a good campsite to stay through the change of season.

We agreed to meet at the road there the next day with some supplies and Walt Coggins, who would go with him to his camp and help carry things. When we returned, we waited overnight, but Horace didn't appear. Oren and this writer had to return to Asheton, but Walt insisted on going by himself to try and locate our friend. When we returned in three days, Walt said he'd located Horace's camp. He said it looked like Horace had slept there the night before and built a fire for breakfast that morning, and that all looked neat and orderly as Horace usually keeps his camp, but Walt could find no sign of the man himself in any nearby place.

Since, search parties have been raised and forayed, dogs set to track, but there is as yet no trace of Horace. Personally, I do not think that Horace would disappear so thoroughly unless he meant to do it, and I still expect him to show up at my door one day soon as suddenly and mysteriously as he vanished, to unload some grand tale of adventure. That is all our hope.

So all of us here desire that you keep yourself fit and safe in whatever far regions you inhabit at the moment. We have too few friends left to lose another right now. Perhaps your long and winding road will lead you back to us for a visit soon.

Regretfully to report, the photography studio is not thriving, which can be said now for every business in town. Some around Asheton who are positioned to know these things are saying it will take thirty years for the city government to pay off the town's debt. All our prosperity was written on paper that is now not worth the ink on its face. The whole country will be a long time coming through this crisis. Meanwhile, everyone continues to work as we are able until happy days return.

With no better news to write, I remain your unworthy friend.

Mura

\#

Sunday, November 20, 1932
Asheton, N.C.
Dear Drum,

I'm sorry to be writing such bad news so soon after losing Horace. Ted Mura died last night. Influenza, according to the doctor, although his lungs were already weakened by all the problems he had with his breathing the past several years. Horace's loss weighed on him. He fell into a depression over the decline of his business, which he had worked so hard to make prosper. I don't believe he had the will left to resist a serious illness.

He was sick for weeks and refused to see a doctor. Finally, I had Dr. Nichols come by and check him out. Nichols put Mura in hospital immediately, but things were already too far along to do him much good at that stage. I feel guilty now I did not take Mura's situation in hand sooner. You know how stubborn he could be once his mind was set.

He was a kind and gentle soul, and a faithful friend to our family. Mura deserved to end his life in better circumstance. It is ironic that he and Horace Kellett would both be gone so suddenly now, when all their labors to preserve these noble mountains for our grandchildren are about to bear full fruit.

I am executor for Mura's estate, such as remains. His funds are about gone, as the studio had not made a profit in the last two years, but we have a couple of people here interested in buying and continuing the business. He told me on several occasions he wanted you to have all his prints and negatives. We will need to arrange at some point to transfer these materials to you.

It would be a good thing if you could find time to spend a few days in Asheton. Annie Starling is still living in the house on Sorrow Creek with James and Judy Coggins, who bought the place from her. James is building her a smaller house farther down the Creek where it meets the Long Broad. It is nearer the county road, and will be easier for her to get out in the winter. James says he has arranged a young man, Ronan - I forget the last name - to help her keep the place up, and James will drive her into town as she needs. She is still a right energetic old woman, but not so spry as she once was. She would like very much to see you, as would we all.

You and Mura were good and close friends. I am sorry to be the one to give you this news. He was very proud of you. Insisted that you are the better photographer.
With sympathy and shared sorrow-
Oren Shorts

ELIZABETH

Horace woke before light from a dream of a fiddle playing. He couldn't recall the fiddler, but retained a dim impression of a green woman. While he waited for enough light to cook by, he performed his morning duties, then picked up his coffee pot and walked down through crowded spruce to a little brook. Moonlight filtering though the branches above limned his path without revealing the anonymous shapes populating the night around him.

Nearing the brook, he thought he picked up cadences of the fiddle again, but when he stopped to listen for a tune, he only heard water chuckling to stones about their secret joke on him. He sat for awhile, damped his bottom on a mossy stone, and though he never learned the jest, could not suppress a smile for the sheer joy of being an aware member of the living mountain.

When dawn glinted the dancing water and he could see outlines of boulders in the stream, Horace stood, brushed away the trash clinging to his soggy backside, filled his pot from a little pool, and started back up the slope toward his camp. As the brook's giggling faded behind, he fancied he heard more fiddle music, but when he concentrated on the sound, there was only the slough of the breeze, and faint and far away, the croak of a raven.

Back at camp, he stirred his fire to life, added some fuel, set on the pot for coffee. Carefully, he unfolded a towel from his haversack, pleased when he found the four eggs inside still intact, and broke two of them into his pan. As he stirred his eggs, he thought about where he might stretch his tarp for shelter. The night before, he'd spread it on the ground and slept upon it, silver stars and butter moon lighting him into his dreaming. He thought that in the peopled world humans were as likely to suffer from too much shelter as from the lack of it.

After breakfast, he rigged a line and stretched his tarp like a lean-to between two red spruce, rolled his bedding and stowed it undercover with his haversack, poured the coffee left from breakfast into his canteen, carried his cooking gear down to the brook, washed it clean, scouring it with sand from the streambed. Still tired, though he had slept well and deep, and his dreams had been peaceful, as soon as he put his camp to order, he lay down on a stony ledge to soak up the morning sun while his cooking fire died to ash.

Almost drifting off to sleep when he heard again, still faint but carried to him clearly on the wind, the singing fiddle. Oren wouldn't be up the mountain with Mura and Walt until afternoon. Horace decided he had time for a walk. He threw a line over a high limb of a dead spruce, he made it on his second toss, hauled up his haversack with all his edibles, except for a bag of nuts and dried figs that he put in his jacket pocket, and tied off the line. He thought bears not likely, but he was not minded to encourage them.

Horace slung the canteen over his shoulder. If he drank all his coffee, he would look for water. Meanwhile, he would be glad for the caffeine to stimulate his weary body and brain. The high it gave would keep him from missing alcohol quite so much as he adjusted to abstinence. He scanned the campsite one more time, to make sure all was in its place, then waded off through the tall grass across the curve of the bald, negotiating his way around occasional clusters of briars or blueberries, and down the farther slope into a broad stand of spruce and fir in the general direction of the music he'd heard.

Once among the trees, Horace found nothing resembling a path, but the ground beneath the canopy was more or less open, littered with past seasons' cones and needles. Sun and shadow wove a matrix of warm and cool between the trees, and he unconsciously fell into step with the shifting patterns. The wind whispered its slow poem, and his mind followed it, slipping free of time, forgetting even why he had started his walk. He moved in the rhythm of the day and the mountain, and his soul rested in it.

He came upon a small clearing, sat on a sun-washed boulder and sipped his coffee, still almost hot. The sun had climbed well past noon and already slid down toward evening. He should start back to meet his friends. Then on the wind, he heard the fiddle again, nearer and clearer now, soaring and falling like the tumble of a stream.

"They can wait," The sound of his own voice startled him. He crossed a small creek, wider and more tumultuous than the little brook by camp. Rocks were handy for stepping and he reached the opposite bank with shoes still dry. Once across the stream, the music seemed quite near, then faded as the conifers gave way to hardwoods, oak and hickory, maple and poplar. Sometimes he heard no music at all, then when he thought he'd followed the wrong direction, it came again, each time near and ahead, sad and glad at once, so pure and deep his heart ached to hear it.

Hungry, Horace reached for his bag of figs and nuts,

decided he wasn't, dropped them back into his pocket. He stopped finally beside a large creek, rowdy and insistent in its plunge toward the valley. The fiddle raged louder than the water, wild and compelling. The trees shivered in the sound like in a wind. Horace wished Eleanor was here to dance to it. When he was done with this, he would go back home to her. He had written and she had told him to come. He had never meant to be so far from those he loved for so long. His children had grown while he was gone. Always next year, always one more thing to do, one more place he had to go. But Eleanor had waited down the years until nobody had any need at all for his skills or labors.

Suddenly, Horace wept for those seasons that slipped away while he hid from his life. The music demanded now he dance on their grave, but after walking and climbing all day, he was spent. He wanted nothing but to be with Eleanor, but he was afraid she would not be pleased to see him, afraid his long and wearying road would leave him diminished in her sight.

When had the sun gone down? How long since the woods went dark? Horace thought he glimpsed through the trees across the creek the flicker of a lantern, or was it the reflection of moon on leaf? Over the howling music, he caught a hint of sound, familiar, like a woman singing; perhaps it was only the wind. The sudden pain in his chest impaled him like a spear, staggered him, took his breath. Horace pitched forward into the creek, felt sharp stones cut his cheek, icy water swirling about his head and shoulders, but found no strength to lift himself. One clear thought as the stream carried away his mind - *She waits*. He heard the water roaring in his ears, the tortured laboring of his failing heart. Then he heard only the music.

As consciousness wavered, reflex ruled, and he took one deep breath.

#

Drum sat at a table with Kent Rockwell in a dim corner where Kent could watch the ebb and flow of the patrons without being prominent in their scenery. The two had spent the day photographing Kent in his studio, in his garden, in his barn, in his favorite trout stream, and in just about any other locale that Kent thought might speak to his unique mode of existence. Now, thank God, there was no camera and Drum wasn't being required to photograph Kent in his favorite pub.

Kent was a gifted artist; since arriving, Drum had seen ample proof of the man's talent, and was duly impressed. Kent was also arrogant, opinionated and overbearing, although he could be kind and charming to anyone he liked. He apparently liked Drum. After a couple of servings of bangers and mash, Kent had concentrated on nursing successive beers while he regaled Drum with an endless stream of tales and gossip about the locals, many of whom seemed to have a high regard for Kent Rockwell. By this stage of his assignment, Drum had experience to know there were also some in this corner of the parish who did not think so well of the famous painter in their midst.

Most of Kent's banter Drum found genuinely interesting. He politely pretended to listen to the rest. From time to time, he had respite to attend to his own drink as one or another of Kent's acquaintances stopped at his table to chat or argue. Those who liked the painter and those who didn't regarded him as a colorful character of genuine reputation, who by his alighting here had brought a little notice to this otherwise obscure rural district. It was suggested on infrequent occasions that the community might be improved slightly by the absence of their famous resident and the publicity he generated.

When he lost count of his beers, Kent began downing whiskeys. About midway through the second, when Kent was beginning to have a little difficulty maintaining the thread of his narrative, the room suddenly quieted. One of the musicians who had been playing through the evening, cradled her fiddle in her arms, closed her eyes and lifted her face to the amber light, and began to sing,

I need to go awhile away
upon a snowy mountain,
where silence fills the blessed day
like water from a fountain,
and there to stay a spell alone
among the spruce and heather,
as calm and patient as a stone
beneath the winter's weather
until my restless mind is still
and all my cares forsaken
and in the space they used to fill
I feel my soul awaken.

As he listened, Drum fell under a spell deep and pervasive as he felt when a boy with Horace and Walt Coggins at Martin McMinn's cabin, as Walt told his fantastical tales of Li the fiddler woman whose song had raised the mountain. Horace, lost and surely dead by now, was alive and present while the fiddler's pure voice filled the space. Drum glanced toward the bar, half expecting to see Horace there leaning against it, glass forgotten in his hand, as he was lifted with all of them away into the song.

Other verses, other songs followed, and Drum was away from time until the voice was silent and the other musicians took up the music, and people moved and talked and laughed and the world began to flow again.

The young fiddler, a vision of raven hair bound back by a scarlet ribbon, creamy skin and a blouse the color of an new risen moon over a long green skirt that matched her eyes, walked straight to their table and spoke to Kent while she looked appraisingly at Drum, "Well then, Kent, what specimen of artistic Yankee male have you presented us here tonight?"

Kent answered, surly voiced, "This is Ben Drum. He isn't an artist. He's a photographer come to take pictures of an artist. In fact, he isn't even a real Yankee. He's a good old southern boy from the wilds of Appalachia. He isn't worldly like you and me. I doubt his performance would be to your standards."

The fiddler laughed, still fixing her frank gaze on Drum, "If I want a performance, Kent, I know where to find you. Actually, I was hoping to find an open mind tonight." She reached across the table to shake Drum's hand. He noted the strength in her grip. "Since Kent won't introduce me, I'll tell you I'm Liza Charon and bid you a hearty welcome to our wee pub, Benjamin Drum. I'm betting your friends all just call you Drum."

For no reason he knew, Liza's insight didn't surprise him, "Then you've won your bet, Liza. You seem familiar, but I don't recall our meeting before."

"It was probably some time and place so far off we don't remember. I hope you'll be around long enough for us to get reacquainted."

Kent mumbled a barely audible "Shit!" Then lurched to his feet, knocking over his half-empty whiskey glass, and stumbled toward the door.

Liza's laughing eyes locked to Drum's as she nodded

toward the retreating painter, "Your friend is sick, I think. You'd better take him home and put him to bed.

"He isn't a friend, Liza, just a man I'm paid to take pictures of, but I'll take care of him."

As Drum started after Kent, he heard Liza behind him, "I'm done here after eleven. If you can't sleep tonight, come back and have a drink with me before I'm gone."

Drum stopped and turned to meet her eyes still on him, "If I can have coffee, I might take you up on it."

Outside, Drum caught up with Kent, who stood at the curb, bent over with his hands on his knees, emptying his stomach into the street. Drum reached out a hand to steady the older man, and when Kent could bring up no more from his belly, guided him toward their car, "You should have stuck to the beer, Kent; spirits don't mix well with brew."

"Stick to your camera, Picture Man, and spare me your diagnosis," Kent snarled. By the time Drum sat him in the car, fished the keys from his pocket and started the engine, Kent Rockwell was a famous artist fast asleep.

#

Barnabas Andrew Ronan Darner pulled his skiff ashore near the mouth of Sorrow Creek and set to work in Annie Starling's garden, weeding her corn rows. Small for a human male, Ronan looked younger than he was. His unwieldy name remembranced his father's three brothers. After an hour he was done. He pulled off his muddy shirt and trousers and put on some clean ones that he'd wrapped together with a light blanket, a tin of matches and his two books in his waterproof poncho. He washed out his gardening duds at the river's edge and hung them on a line stretched between two sycamore trees. He dropped his hat on top of the matches, wrapped them carefully in the poncho in case of a shower, and set the package on the seat of his skiff. Then, with his books under his arm he headed up the hill past the garden for another two hours with Annie studying math and grammar, two subjects he was not especially inclined toward, although he was a great reader and a good history student, being fond of tales of any sort that managed to contain a surprise for the reader.

He raised his fist to knock on Annie's door when she opened it, having seen him from her kitchen window, "Come in, Ronan, and sit thee down. I'll give thee a bit of bread and honey and some mint tea before we turn to books, and thee can tell me about thy week."

Ronan's week had been fairly satisfactory, he thought. He'd managed to get through school without getting into any noteworthy trouble, which he had a talent for. He made a feed trough for the family's milk cow, and his father, who was generally stingy with praise, said it was good. Ronan's ambition was to become a carpenter, maybe even make real furniture. When Annie told James Coggins about her student's gifted hands, James said if Ronan could get his father's permission, he could work with his crew as a part-time helper and begin to learn the trade. Ronan's father, Steve said he should take James up on it if he wanted to be a carpenter, because James Coggins was maybe the best builder in Carolina. James built houses for rich people who wanted to spend their summers in the mountains. He'd learned working wood from his father Houston, who Steve said could turn a tree into a rocking chair with not much more than a bow saw and a froe.

When Ronan thought he had about as much math and grammar as he could carry with him, he thanked Annie for her tutoring, and promised to come back in a few days and stake her tomatoes. It was already dark and fog rolled up from the river as he came out her door. Ronan hurried down past the garden, pausing to get his clothes from the line, was surprised to find them still wet, then saw that, although they were about the same size and similar material, they weren't the shirt and trousers he'd left. He looked toward the water and was surprised again.

Annie still sat on her steps watching the fireflies when she saw Ronan walking through her yard with his books under his arm going back up toward the road, "Ronan, did thee not come down the river today?"

"I did so, Miss Annie, but I reckon I'm walking back home. Somebody took papa's skiff."

#

It was nearly midnight when Drum got Kent Rockwell home and handed him over to his wife, and Drum was too tired to fancy drinking with a strange woman in a pub, however compelling she might be. He went back to his hotel, packed up his exposed film from the day's shooting, and got ready for bed.

Drum doubted Liza Charon's invitation was meant seriously, in any case. He had just provided her with a handy excuse to needle her friend Kent. She obviously enjoyed deflating male egos. Drum thought it might be fun to risk being her target when he wasn't so tired. He lay on his bed, opened a volume of Yeats he'd found in his room, fell asleep in the middle of the second page, woke about two in the morning with the light in his eyes, set his book on the table, turned out the lamp and was asleep again before he took three breaths.

Below him, the river flowed and flickered like a ghost under the moon. He could hear dark wind whispering to water, and hear the water's sibilant answer. He fell slowly toward the river, waves and ripples on its surface drawing up moonfire from the depths. A dark shape on the water gradually expanded, became a boat. Sitting in the boat, a woman with hair black as the night, but like the water, shot through with moonsilver. Her green dress in the moonlight looked almost as dark as her hair. Drum was seated in the boat with her and she fixed her deep shadowy eyes on him and lifted her fiddle from her lap and began to play. They weren't in the boat any more but in a dark room where she stood in front of a large hearth where a fire burned and flared as she played. The flames soared and danced to the music, and the music was in his head and he was trying to remember who the fiddler was.

"Are you Liza?" Drum asked, not certain if he spoke aloud or only thought the question.

Without pausing in her playing, the green fiddler laughed, then began to sing.

Liza is me
and I am Li
Wasam Willbe
has sent to thee.

She sang more but Drum did not hear it. He was suddenly wide awake and wondering why he was afraid. He got up then, dressed, and took a walk through deserted streets, thinking about Horace Kellett and Walt Coggins and Mura and Annie and Emmalou Truelight and the little girl he picked up from the pavement after the bomb exploded on Wall Street. When the sky finally began to brighten, he went back to the hotel to find his breakfast, a scrap of a fiddle tune running through his mind.

#

Horace opened his eyes with an effort; his lids were as heavy on his face as wet leaves. He was too tired to turn his head, but he could see a curtainless window past the foot of his bed, sunlight streaming in. His chest hurt. He took a breath, gathered himself before he took another. His ribs felt broken. The green woman flowed into his field of vision the way a vine grows into the light. He knew without asking that she was the fiddler whose music he had heard before he fell into the creek and darkness. But where was he now, and how had she brought him here? Horace thought the question without strength to voice it.

She smiled, "I had help. Now rest."

Horace didn't know if she had guessed his query or read his mind, but before he could wonder about it he was taken in again by deep and dreamless sleep.

Light returned. When Horace managed to focus his vision, an exceedingly narrow face peered down at him over a frayed flannel shirt and a pair of faded overalls. When he saw Horace was awake, the thin man cackled in delight, "Well look at you, and who has she brought us now?"

Where was the Green Woman? Horace saw her like the Fiddler in Walt Coggins' tales. She had fiddled him into the world again the way Li fiddled the creatures into the mountain. He tried to ask the thin man where she had gone. All he could get out was her name, "Li?"

The thin man misunderstood. "Well, Mr. Lee, Welcome to the Laurel. A good dose of this stuff will bring you to yourself in a rush."

Thin Man put a hand under Horace's head and lifted it gently as he brought up what looked like a whiskey bottle with a sop stuck in the mouth. Horace glimpsed a greenish liquid inside and caught a pungent aroma from the sop.

"Open up and draw on this," Thin Man commanded, turning up the bottle and grinning broadly as Horace took the sop between his lips and sucked greedily. It did not taste especially good, nor bad, merely peculiar, like pine oil and sorrel and mint and chives all mixed together with other tastes beyond his experience. It was wet and answered his raging thirst. It was soothing in his throat and warm in his belly and after a couple of swallows his ribs quit throbbing and he was sleepy again as the Thin Man faded to black.

#

Two days later Drum had more photographs documenting Kent Rockwell and his doings than would ever find a page in the magazine. He sent off all his film with Roland Alston who was writing the text for their article. Drum wanted to be off his leash here for a couple of days and capture some images of the tumbling green countryside for his own fulfillment.

Kent was right. Drum didn't think of himself as an artist, creating stunning images that would impress people with his skill. As Mura had told him more than seldom, "The picture is not to convince the viewer you were there, but to convince them they are there."

When Alston's train pulled away from the station, Drum walked back to the pub, ordered shepherd's pie and a pint of dark beer. He ate at the bar with only two other patrons, an old man nursing his ale alone, and a younger in a business suit intent on his newspaper. While the bartender wiped his glasses for the third time, lifting each one and holding it to the light as if it were a marvel before replacing it on the tray, Drum asked him if he knew where within walking distance he might get some good photographs of rocks and water.

The bartender, a red-haired man named Dogie, as well as Drum could make out, responded as if this were a request he heard every day, gave him directions to several places within two hours walk, then asked, "Are you the Yank Liza fancied the other night?"

Drum was surprised, and a bit flattered to hear he'd made any impression at all. "I talked to her briefly. We'd never met before."

"She left you a note." Dogie fished an envelope from behind the bar, handed it to Drum, then leaned on his elbows, grinning expectantly while Drum opened the envelope and read his note.

"She's gone to London," he informed Dogie.

"I reckon you'll be off then yourself."

"In a few days, on my way home. I'm going to get my pictures first." And he did. Later, back in Washington, when he'd processed and printed his images, Drum thought they might be the best he'd ever done. Looking at them made him homesick for the Creek. He sat down and wrote Annie Starling a long letter, promised to come for a visit before fall.

#

Drum fastened the leather straps on his suitcase, slipped the envelope with his train ticket into his jacket pocket. Eighteen years after he rode a train out of Asheton, Drum was actually on his way back to the nearest place to home in this life. He left there expecting to return for a visit before a year was out, but there was always something. New jobs, new assignments, pictures to be gleaned from some spot in the world he had never expected to go. He had promised and he had planned, but something always turned up that must be done first.

Horace and Mura and Walt were gone now. Most of the souls he knew there were dead or scattered. Judy and James remained, and their four, Ben almost grown by now. Judy told him Annie was getting frail. It was for Annie that he was going back. Annie had always believed in him, had suffered his absence without blame or complaint, never begged him to return, although it was plain from her letters that she longed for it. Drum had few clear recollections of his mother, who, as near as he could reckon, would be about twenty-five now, carrying her first child, who would be named after her husband's eldest brother. When Drum thought mother, though, he usually thought Annie.

Drum picked up his suitcase, slung his bag of gear over his shoulder, and started for the door. As he turned to lock it behind him, his phone rang. Probably Eric announcing some wondrous new brainstorm that would require Drum to spend a week or a month among people whose language he did not know. Drum hesitated, then locked the door. This time, he would keep his promise to Annie.

#

Drum had only returned to Washington three days before. He was still travel weary and fell asleep before the train was clear of the city. When he woke it was nearly dark and he could barely make out the rounded upheavals of the Blue Ridge against the fading light to west. The train huffed and rattled into night between the hills toward Roanoke. Sometime during the morning, he would be in Asheton.

Drum enjoyed his breakfast. Eating on a train always called up in his memory a breakfast he ate on a train to

Baltimore with his mother to see his father off to war. He had slept that night in an unheated room, weighted down by quilts riddled by moth holes with the batting poking through. He had been busy pulling out as much cotton as he could get between his fingers when his mother had opened the door briefly, slapped his hand lightly, and told him to go to sleep.

"Aren't you going to sleep with me?" he queried petulantly as she turned out the light.

"Not tonight. I'm going to sleep with your father." Drum hadn't said anything more, but wondered why his father didn't want to sleep in the same room with him. That was when he began to suspect that his father didn't like him very much. The next morning, when he stood with his mother at the railway station, waiting for his father to appear at the window of the passenger coach, a sailor threw his still-lit cigarette out onto the platform. It bounced and rolled right up to Drum's feet. He watched the smoke curl up like a forlorn spirit, then stooped and reached down for it, and burned his fingers. He yelped and stood up, looked to his mother for comfort.

"Don't touch that, Benjamin," she admonished, "It's nasty." Drum burst into tears. His mother bent to pick him up. At that moment, his father looked out the window of the rail car, smiling and waving. The last glimpse the father had of his family before he was carried off to fight was of an angry little boy crying, distracting his mother from bidding goodbye to the man she loved. It was about to happen all over again, Drum thought, the boy with the curious fingers already kicking in his mother's womb. Then the conductor came through.

"Next stop, Asheton," he sang, as if announcing their approach to Heaven.

When Drum stepped down from the pullman, he found James and Judy waiting on the platform. He recognized them, although he thought, *Dear God, do I look that old?* They also looked somber. He walked up to them, set down his suitcase to adjust his gear bag, "You two don't look glad to see me after all this time."

Tears welled up in Judy's eyes; her voice trembled, "I tried to phone you. You must have already left. Ronan found Annie in her garden. The doctor thinks it was a stroke. She died this morning."

#

On the drive out from Asheton, once beyond the city limits, Drum tried to take his bearings. Where he had known pastures and gardens and cornfields and woodlots, were now stores and small factories and houses. But once through McMinn Gap, when the road began to drop down into the cove toward Sorrow Creek, the years fell away behind them and Drum believed he was coming home.

Except for the paved road, the scenery endured much as Drum recalled it. A few more houses perched along the hillsides. Big houses. Money had come into the cove since Drum had left, most of it in the pockets of people whose families had grown up in other places. Now they came riding in on the tail of hard times to buy beautiful land on the cheap from people who could no longer afford to pay their taxes on it, and must sell it or lose it. As James drove, Judy pointed out the houses her husband had built, invariably more solid and at home than their neighbors, fitted to the land rather than pasted against the scenery. When they turned off onto the gravel road that wound along the Creek, Drum felt as if he'd never been away. He was surprised, though, when James brought his Willis up the hill to Annie's house.

"What happened to the logs?" Drum asked.

James shook his head. "Every builder in the county was coming by, badgering me to sell the house, so they could tear it down for the chestnut, so I covered it all up."

"Bear was wrong, then." Drum bit his tongue.

James glanced in his mirror, "Who's Bear."

Drum tried to laugh, "Just remembering out loud, James. Somebody I used to know a long time ago."

Judy pointed at the house, "There are the girls all out on the porch, waiting for us." Annie was fourteen and serious. Ruth, twelve, had red hair and a ready smile. Elizabeth, nine, with a tooth missing in front, took an immediate shine to Drum. She gazed with fascination at his photography gear, "I know where you can get some great pictures," she piped.

Judy shook her head, tried to look serious, "Let him get settled before you launch a tour, Lizbet."

James picked up Drum's suitcase and started up the stair, "We'll put you upstairs in your old room tonight."

Drum whispered to Lizbet, "Maybe you can show me around in the morning while the old folks are all asleep," hoisted his gear bag and started up the stair after James.

When they reached the room at the end of the hall, James put the suitcase on the bed, pointed to a door, "Bath's in there. This is Ben's room, but he's off on a gander with his school class. They won't be back until the weekend." He took an envelope from his pocket and handed it to Drum. Across the front, in handwriting he recognized immediately, Annie had written, *For Drum*.

James held on to the envelope until he finished speaking, "Annie knew she wasn't well. For the last several months, she kept this on her mantel in case she returned to earth before you came home." Drum thought he saw accusation in James' face, but the voice was pleasant and neutral, so he wrote it off to his own feelings of more than a little guilt and regret.

James smiled before he went out the door, "We'll have some supper in a little while. Come on down when you've settled in."

Drum sat on the bed and held his letter in his hand, remembering what had been and grieving for what might have been. Finally, he opened the envelope and unfolded the paper inside, expecting some last words from Annie. The paper was blank, but as he unfolded it, a key fell out into his palm.

#

When Drum went downstairs to supper, he found Judy setting dishes around the table while James stood at the stove frying pork chops. Lizbet was ferrying knives and forks to the various places. Drum asked Judy about the key. She looked at him as if he were one of her students slow to catch on to his lesson, "It's to Annie's house down by the river. She left the place to you. Annie said you would need somewhere to come home to."

"I don't have a right to it," it was less a protest than an admission.

Judy turned from the table and laid a hand on Drum's arm, "Love is the only right any of us ever has. Annie loved you as her own. Don't refuse her gift until you're certain you don't need it."

James glanced over his shoulder as he turned the chops, "I'll take you down there tomorrow, if you like."

Drum winked at Lizbet, "Maybe after the funeral. I have an appointment in the morning." Lizbet clapped her hands and lifted on her toes to slap her heels on the floor, as she informed them with a delighted shrill, "In the morning, I'm going to show him the Rocks, and he's going to take pictures of the Other Side."

Drum lifted his eyebrows at her, "The Other Side?"

Judy laughed and shook her head, "For months now, Lizbet has been talking about her imaginary place where all the people who have died in the cove are still living."

"It isn't imaginary," protested Lizbet, "The most real places in all the world, you can't see when you're not there."

"In the morning, you can show me, Lizbet," Drum promised.

"Will you take pictures?"

"I will try, but cameras are not very good at picturing real places. The really real places, you can only see in the heart."

Drum looked up to catch Judy smiling at him. "Well," she said, "You haven't forgotten everything Annie taught you."

"Annie was a good teacher," affirmed Drum, "Her lessons stick with you."

James turned the pork chops onto a platter. "Meat's ready. Lizbet, go fetch your sisters before supper gets cold."

#

That night, Drum slept poorly, unused to his bed, and woke several time from dreams of a moonlit river. He was up before dawn, and at first light slipped out of the house into the chill morning. Lizbet was sitting on the porch steps waiting for him.

Drum reached down and tousled her hair, "You're an early bird."

Lizbet shook out her locks and grinned up at him in

the dimness. "I like to be awake when the world comes back. First there's the wind, and then the birds, and finally the light, when everything is alive again. Besides, I was waiting for you."

"Are you going to show me your Rocks?"

"Sure thing. It's how we get to the Other Side. Bring your camera?"

"Sure thing." Drum lifted the strap from his shoulder and held up his Leica D in its case between them. "We are inseparable."

Lizbet bounded across the yard, expecting Drum to follow. When she reached the trees behind the house, she stopped and waited for him to catch up. Drum could hear the creek tumbling away through the dark wood below and to his left. He suddenly had a vivid memory of Jonas, and it occurred to him that another Drum might breathe in the world by now, not on the Other Side anymore, but here in this time.

Lizbet took him by the hand and led him up the road that was so familiar to him in times past and times to come. Corn no longer crowded the field just right of the road where he first saw Annie and Johnny. It was populated with saplings and well on its way to merging back into woods. In another ten or twelve years it would be the same overgrown patch he had seen the first time he had walked up this road with Jonas. The day was rising about them now, and from somewhere beyond the trees he heard the remembered hoarse and guttural call alerting them they had been noticed.

"That's old Raven," Lizbet told him, "He watches all the time so he can tell those on the Other Side what we are about over here."

Drum smiled, recalling a transference his adult mind

171

insisted was a boy's fantasy, though in his deepest heart, he still knew to be real. "How do you know so much about the Other Side, Lizbet?"

"Raven told me how to get there, don't you know? All you have to do is slip through the Shining Rocks. It's as easy as crawling under a bed."

Drum stopped in the road, listening to the creek as it tumbled across their way just ahead. The music of the water struck his ears like the echo of an old fiddle tune. He could almost remember where he'd heard it before.

Lizbet looked up at him, concern on her face, "Don't be afraid, Drum."

"I'm not afraid, Lizbet. This time I'm with someone who knows the way."

When they came clear of the trees, and the Rocks hulked before them, surrounded by the mouldering stumps of the murdered forest, Lizbet jumped atop one of the stumps, stretched her arms wide and compassed about, "I am getting lighter and lighter. Before I am grown up, I will be able to fly away."

Drum's years away had not rendered him entirely immune to the power of the place. The Shining Rocks, with the dark bald behind them, gathered light from the brightening sky and seemed to glow faintly from within. Still, he did not feel the tension in the air he felt when he first came here with Jonas. Perhaps it was because the time between his departure and his present had diminished. Perhaps he had just grown up and magic had a weaker hold on him now.

Lizbet ran on up the hill toward the Rocks, "Come on, Drum; It's this way!" She ran behind the Shining Rocks. Drum followed her. She pointed at a crevice between the rocks where they emerged from the mountain, "The Other

Side is through there, Drum!"

"I think I'm too big to fit through there, Lizbet."

"But I'm not!" and before he could stay her, Lizbet dove into the dark opening and disappeared.

Drum knelt down in the dewy grass and peered after her. He could see light filtering in from the far opening, but Lizbet had vanished.

"Lizbet. Are you in there?" His voice sounded mildly ridiculous to him. No response from Lizbet. Drum stood and walked around the boulders to the other side. No sign of the girl. He knelt again and peered into the opening. Because the fissure turned along its course, Drum could not see through, only reflected light from the far side. He still could not see Lizbet.

Drum stood, called a few times. The only answer came from the crows in the trees down by the creek. Lizbet was obviously hiding from him; he would let her enjoy her game. He made a few photographs of the Shining Rocks, the looming bald beyond, the blossoming sky, the tiny farmstead below, the forked roads winding off up the slope above. He realized he had never followed the left fork . Did it actually lead to some definable place, or did it just wander off to fade away in grass or trees?

At length, Drum concluded that Lizbet had gone back to the house without him. She might have gone to the Other Side, but he felt it safer and saner to expect she would greet him with a laughing dance on Judy's porch, pleased with her mighty joke on the visitor. He started back down toward the creek.

"Drum! you've been there, too! This is yours!" Lizbet's voice startled him as if she'd hit him with a stone. He turned, and the child was standing atop the Shining Rocks, waving something bright over her head. Drum turned back to meet her as she clambered down from the boulders and came running toward him.

Her clothes and hair hung wet and heavy. Droplets of water sparkled on her face and arms as she thrust the bedraggled and sodden pad into his hands. "You left this on the Other Side. It has your name on it."

"Judy will kill me, Lizbet. How did you get soaking wet?"

"There was an awful storm on the Other Side. Look! It says *Drum*." Lizbet pointed to the word on the front of the pad. It was in pencil and still readable, though the paper was soaked through.

Very carefully, Drum peeled back the first few pages. He recognized the drawings. His adult mind decided his deepest heart was right. He denied the tears he wanted to release. Then he handed the pad back to Lizbet, "No, you found it. This is yours to keep."

Drum turned to walk away, but Lizbet caught his sleeve, "But when were you on the Other Side, Drum? I never saw you there."

Drum laid his hand lightly on Lizbet's head, like a gesture of blessing, looked sad and hopeless as he smiled down at her, "The Drum who drew in that pad was a finer boy than me, Lizbet."

#

The next morning, Drum rode with James into Asheton to fetch Annie's ashes at Wolf's Funeral Home. On the drive back, Drum held the cedar box containing the ashes in his lap. Neither he nor James were inclined toward conversation, but eventually James spoke to logistics, "Ben will be home tomorrow, but we can put you up on the sofa in my office for as long as you can stand us."

"Would it be all right if I stayed down at Annie's house

for a couple of days?"

"I don't see why not; it's your place now. I can run you over there whenever you're ready."

"How far is it?"

"Nothoisted his load more than two miles."

"If you can stash my suitcase for me, I might just walk."

"No problem at all. Just follow Sorrow Creek Road until you're almost at the river. You'll see her name on her mailbox to the left. There's plenty in the garden now, so you won't get hungry. I'll come check on you in a day or so."

Grateful that James assigned him no fault for not coming back to visit Annie in spite of all his promises and pledges over the years, Drum could not prevent his own conscience from leveling enough accusations to keep his mind occupied. The two men rode the rest of the way in silence.

#

They met for Annie's memorial service down by the creek at the place where Drum had rescued Emmalou Truelight just before the flood delivered him to Horace Kellett and Walt Coggins. Emmalou could not attend but sent apologies, Judy said. Polly Coggins was there, shy as a wren, and Willard Hoots, who taught mathematics at the Asheton Campus of the state university.

When Drum shook his hand, habit betrayed, and he addressed Willard as "Owly," apologized in the same breath, "Sorry. Willard."

Owly laughed, "Don't be sorry, Drum. Nowadays only my students call me Owly. I'm glad to be reminded I have a few friends left above ground who have earned the right."

The girls brought quilts and blankets and spread them in the shade by the stream. As the party gathered round, Judy carefully and gently placed the cedar box atop a small boulder in their midst. They began settling to the earth when Eldon Hoots came down the path with his plump little wife, Edith.

"Late as usual," James whispered good naturedly to Judy, who laid her finger across his lips, as everyone stood up again. Hands were clasped, greetings spoken around.

When Eldon shook hands with Drum, he winked, leaned close, and whispered, "I should have whipped you when I had the chance; now I'm too old," then hugged him like a brother.

When they all sat and stilled, Judy laid a flower from her garden beside the cedar box. Polly took from her bag an apple, pale and green, the color of a spring leaf, and laid it next to the flower. James had already made his offering, the cedar box that held the ashes. Young Annie read a short poem she had written on a sheet of blue paper, her voice as whispery and fleeting as the breeze in the trees. When she had read, she left it beside the apple, weighted it with her mother's golden iris, lest a stray gust catch it away. Owly presented his old algebra book, still bearing notations in Annie's clear hand. Eldon fumbled in his pocket, finally produced the battered pen knife that Annie had confiscated more than once when he was whittling in class rather than writing answers to his test questions.

"I was just sharpening my pencil," he would protest every such occasion.

Annie, refusing to confront him with his obvious lie, had always answered, "Better thee be sharpening thy wits, Eldon."

Drum was astonished to see tears in Eldon's eyes as he sat back down, and thought about his own tenderness of heart, which he habitually kept hidden away even from himself in order to navigate less painfully among the hurts and losses of his life.

Ruth and Lizbet had nothing in hand to give to their remembering, but sang a hymn that Annie had taught them.

Elijah went for forty days,
Without a friend and raven fed,
Along the desert's stony ways
Up to a mountain where God led,
To find a cave where he could hide
And safe from injury, abide,
Therein to wait through fire and wind,
While mountains fell and rocks were rent
Until at last there was an end
And in the silence God had sent,
Elijah heard then, quiet and low,
The Word that only God can know.
Lord, lead me as I sojourn now
Amid the noise and clamor here,
That I may find the grace somehow
To still my soul and tune my ear
To catch the silence where You dwell,
The Word that only You can tell.

Their clear young voices lifted to the air like birds in flight. Drum heard it as Annie had sung it to God and him in meeting, and the tears he suppressed the day before at the Shining Rocks now coursed soundlessly down his cheeks.

When the girls had sung and were silent, and the creek

carried the ghost of their music down the mountain, Drum propped against the cedar box his own gift, a photograph Mura had made of Annie Starling's log house. The Shining Rocks gleamed like a beacon above the dark trees beyond the house. Before the shadowed porch stood Annie, one hand raised to shade her face against the bright morning sun, and either side of her, Horace Kellett, hat in hand, and the homeless boy, Drum, squinting against the light. Two lost souls come to her for refuge.

Offerings made, they descended together into Silence, which wasn't silent at all. Sorrow Creek murmured and chortled and chattered past in endless conversation with the stones. A mocking bird in a poplar overhead sang his entire repertoire in praise to the day. A light breeze sighed among the treetops and the spring sunlight dappled shoulders and heads and Annie's love altar, falling down gentle and warm like a blessing upon the gathered souls. Annie was present to her friends there in the quiet ongoing of Creation, as they waited with her, for how long, none of them could have said.

Drum heard the music before he was aware of it, blending perfectly as it did into the song of the day. At first, he thought it was the rattle and clatter of pebbles in the creek, but gradually the cadences became louder and clearer until he made out the unmistakable tattoo of a bodhran. Drum glanced about him at the others. They sat as if oblivious, sleepers waiting to be wakened from a spell.

The music drifted to them from toward the house, along the path they had all just walked through Judy's garden. Louder now, Drum could make out a tune riding on the drumming. A fiddle? No. Highland pipes skirling out Amazing Grace. Faces lifted and eyes opened, more in expectation than surprise, as Benjamin Coggins and Ronan Darner strode into their little clearing and circled about the wee congregation, filling the forest with their wild, praiseful lament.

Donald Cameron, the music teacher at Asheton School, had started a pipe and drum club, funding the project from his own sparse salary. Between them, Ben and Ronan made up half the band, the best half, according to Don's estimate. The old sounds spoke to them, and they answered with hours of practice. Ben's chanter often sang out from the shining rocks on summer nights. Even James, the least musical man on the Creek, would sit with Lizbet on the porch after supper, listening until Ben got tired and came down to the house to study subjects he deemed less important.

The boys compassed the assembly, intent in their music. The pipes wailed and cried like a flight of raptors; the bodhran throbbed like the beating of a great heart, the sound transcending the small size of the instrument, seeming to be amplified in the pounding heartsong of the Mountain herself. As the boys walked, their progress too slow and dreamlike to describe as a march, their kilts whispered like grass in a morning breeze. The sound was faint and nearly lost underneath all the music and movement, but Drum could hear it, a still small voice that stirred deeper than any loudness could touch.

The Circle completed, the players stood with their backs to the Creek. Ronan shifted the pattern of his drumming and Ben began to play the Quaker hymn his sisters sang to the gathering before. All stood and began to sing it again together. Everyone but Drum seemed to remember the words.

As the last note was sung, Ronan beat out a faster

tempo with a more complex rhythm, and Ben's pipes wailed out into *Sally Morgan's Field*. The mourners looked from one to another. Lizbet and Polly began to clap their hands to the music. James looked down at Judy with a broad questioning smile on his face, and they reeled away after the tune. Hulking Eldon and his round little Edith followed them, and Annie Coggins forgot her seriousness when Ruth grabbed her hand and the sisters were off as well. Owly whispered to Polly, "Don't let me bump into anyone," and they whirled after the rest.

Drum stood on a boulder by the creek, out of the way and forgotten, entranced by the driving drum and soaring pipes and the flight of the dancers. He wished for his camera, when a clear high voice that somehow sounded to him like Annie Starling's made him look down.

Lizbet held both her hands up to him. "Drum, will thee dance with me now? I'm all who's left."

"I'm not a dancer, Lizbet"

"Then we'll just have to fly."

Drum laughed, stepped down from his perch, grabbed her hands and swung her around off her feet. Then they flew away after the other dancers, borne aloft on Annie's love.

LIZA

Horace handed Li a basket of ruddy faced biscuits he'd baked for their breakfast. He put a platter of eggs scrambled with sweet peppers and chives on the table between them and sat down. Li helped herself to the eggs, then, as Horace lifted his cup toward her, reached across the table to pour him tea.

"You're a good cook, Horace. Such skills will win you hearts in Laurel."

"I was a good cook where I came from, and was appreciated for it by a few. I need to get back there."

Li launched a wry smile, "Go back now and you're dead in a creek. Better to make yourself useful while you wait for your friends here."

Horace asked the question nobody in Laurel seemed willing to answer, "And where exactly is here?"

Li looked sympathetic, but answered in a riddle as she always did when he broached the subject, "Here? Laurel is a space apart, Horace, out of any moment. Your world might think of it as something like a singularity enfolding all times, all places. The reality is more like the center of a flower, where all the petals join and become one with the others. The truth is that you haven't gone any place you have not been before. It is your awareness that has shifted. You are still Horace, and Creation is still what it ever is. But you relate differently now."

She spread her napkin on the table, "Think of it this way, Horace." She laid her hand flat on the napkin, "This is Creation," Li picked up a biscuit, broke off a piece, and placed it on the napkin. 'This is you." She folded the napkin over, covering the biscuit. "You are still the soul you were before the folding, but now your awareness and being is directed toward the Other Side. Do you follow me at all here?"

"I follow your words, Li, but they lead me to a place my mind finds unacceptable. No matter how you fold the napkin, I'm still stuck here. I can't just walk back the way I came."

"Trust me now, Horace; you would never want to. None of us can ever go back, for Creation cannot undo its endless becoming. But we can always go onward as way opens."

"You sound a little bit like someone I used to know, Li."

"Annie Starling?"

"You know Annie?"

"I knew Annie before you did, Horace. She is as close to me as you are."

"The more you tell me, Li, the deeper the mystery."

Li tossed back her long black hair. Among the dark, strands of silver glinted in the morning light. She took a sip of her tea and laughed, before she spoke in a voice that sounded to Horace for all the world just like Annie Starling's, "Horace Kellett, thee is the only mystery. Know that, and thee will know all thee would learn."

#

His last night with the Coggins clan, Drum slept on the sofa in James' office, so Ben could share his room with Ronan, who was also staying overnight. The evening was warm, the windows all left open to the dark. After he turned in, Drum heard the boys up on the Shining Rocks practicing to please Don Cameron. The sound of their playing drifted down on the still air like a Jacobite ghost until the wee hours. Underneath the music Drum sensed a single tone, high and pure and constant, as pervasive as the heat that seemed to rise up from the earth itself. *Tinnitus,* Drum thought to himself, *You're getting old.*

He was still awake when the two came in, laughing quietly. Already they sounded more like men than boys, he thought. *Two handsome ones there, and smart. They'll break some hearts in their time, and likely make some trouble for themselves in the bargain.*

Drum responded to masculine beauty, found it easier to photograph men than women. Their character was more visible, he explained his preference. But Drum never took a fancy to one of his own sex. It was the otherness of women that captured his erotic imagination. Once, when propositioned by a male colleague who preferred men to women, Drum told him simply, "I'm flattered, but no thanks. It would be too much like having sex with myself."

Actually, Drum seldom hungered for sex at all, though he often longed for the sort of relationship it might express. But whenever the possibility of a deeper personal involvement with a woman presented, he usually fled the opportunity, as he had made it a point not to accept Liza Charon's invitation to return to the bar. His parents had taught him that any relationship aspiring toward love was doomed to disappointment. Drum ever expected to be disappointed and ever feared to disappoint. As a result, he led a life that most would consider lonely and solitary. He was a watcher, detached observer of the world's movement, who seldom joined in except with little girls who had no expectations of him beyond the dance.

Still, when Drum dreamed, he dreamed of women. Strong, wise and nurturing women had been the anchors of his life. Jonas, Horace and Mura had been friends and mentors and he loved them. Mary and Annie and Judy had been the companions of his heart, and he worshiped them. Yet it always seemed he wound up worshiping from afar. Friendship, for as long as it lasted, had the advantage of proximity.

Finally the house and the night beyond fell quiet and still. Drum slept, and dreamed that Lizbet was pulling him by the hand away up above the rooftop and Creek and Shining Rocks toward the High Balsams.

"See, you can do it!" she shouted over the wind. Then she turned loose his hand. The river below sparkled in the sun, and once more he began the long slow fall toward water and light.

#

Drum woke in the dark while the rest of the house still slept. He packed all his photographic equipment into his suitcase, except for his Leica, an extra lens, and several rolls of film. This left room in his gear bag for essential toiletries and enough clothes for two days, and the cedar box with Annie's ashes. After the memorial service, Judy had held out the box to him, "She wanted her ashes scattered in her garden. She wanted you to do it." Then she turned away, leaving the box weighing heavy as blame in his hands.

Drum dressed, hoisted his load, slipped out the door, and crossed the yard. A waxing moon slid momentarily from behind gathering clouds to light his way down to the road. He did not take his footing for granted on the loose stones of the steep drive. At the mailbox, he turned right, following the road along Sorrow Creek toward the river.

The creek voiced louder as he walked, until Drum could hardly hear his crunching footfalls on the gravel road. As dawn began to spread like a pale stain up into the overcast sky, he met neither car nor walker.

After the first mile, he passed now and again a light from an occasional house among the trees crowding the road. The new day leaked into the landscape in a wash of gray light, muting colors, diminishing contrast. Drum felt as if he were walking through one of Mura's old photographs. Abruptly the road began a rising turn and Drum glimpsed through the tops of trees below the road the dull glint of a muddy river. A fine rain began to sprinkle down. Then he saw the mailbox to his left, *A. Starling* stenciled neatly on the side. A graveled drive grown grassy in the middle meandered down in the direction of the river through a stand of poplars and beeches that shielded Drum from the rain as he came in sight of the house, small and tight and neat, at one with its place. James put his hand to every house he built with the thought and care he would give to his own dwelling.

As Drum crossed the yard, rain began coming down steadily, making creekish sound as it drummed the forest. He stepped up onto the porch, glad for the shelter, found the key in his pocket. It turned easily in the lock, and when he pushed the door, it swung open soundlessly. Annie's presence poured out of the darkened house and enveloped him, brought a rush of tears to his eyes.

Drum could only manage a hoarse whisper, "Annie, I'm sorry I'm so late."

Well, thee is here now, Drum heard her voice clearly in his mind, felt her forgiveness falling down upon him like the gentle rain. He had come finally home.

Drum stepped inside. When his eyes adjusted to the

glauming, he closed the door behind him. Light filtered through uncurtained windows at the far side of the room. Annie never liked curtains, said they were frivolous and fussy and kept out the light. Here, the forest on three sides and the river beyond the garden below rendered curtains unnecessary. On a small table beside the door, a kerosene lantern and a box of Diamond Strike Anywhere matches. Mountain Power had run electricity to the Coggins homestead the year before, but the lines did not yet extend this far down the road.

An oak rocker, stained dark, with green corduroy cushions, sat in the center of the room. Drum dropped his gear bag on the seat of the rocker, and looked around him as morning began eating up the night. He walked to the windows and looked down into the garden, rows of vegetables and grape vines nodding and bobbing in the rain. A rush of déjà vu dizzied him for a moment as remembrance of another garden, green among misty hills, flooded his mind. He never allowed himself to think about going back there. The people he'd loved in Jonas Gap would not be there now and when they were, would not know him if he came; the boy they had loved was grown away into another life. Ethan might be there already, but would not meet Mary's summer boy for years to come. Without Mary, what welcome would there be for Drum in Jonas Gap? Whatever meager belonging left to him resided here, in this life, where Annie had waited for him last.

Past Annie's garden a few old pines and sycamores screened the river. It lay flat, opaque like old pewter under the gray morning. Drum stood at the window, watching the rain, his hand resting on the back of a craftsman style arm chair with a green cushion of its own.

Another small table like the one beside the door companioned the chair. Several books were stacked on the shelf beneath. A big stone fireplace with raised hearth filled the entire wall right of the windows. A split half of a walnut log served as a mantel. The log had been barked and planed and polished, and even in the gray light, shone with a luster imparted by patient and loving hands, a simple thing fashioned with care and artful grace.

In the near corner to the left, a jumble of papers spilled out of the half-opened tambour of a roll top desk, stained dark like the rest of the furniture. Drum thought it was not Annie's way to leave any mess behind. Left of the desk, centered in the wall, a wide doorway, and left of the door, a simple coat rack, pegs affixed to a board attached to the wall. Annie's green wool coat and a shawl hung from one of the pegs. A pair of galoshes sat on the floor beneath. Propped in the far corner, Annie's staff and a black umbrella. Either side of the door where he entered, bookshelves floor to ceiling, filled with volumes and stacks of papers or magazines.

Through the open door by the desk, Drum could see the landing of a stair, the corner of a table, and glimpse a farther door which appeared to open into a kitchen beyond. He felt unsettled, estranged from himself. He wondered if there were a calendar tacked to the back of a door somewhere in this house, and what date it might show. He suddenly felt tired and frail, like an old man. A high pitched tone on the verge of hearing slowly loudened until it rang in his head like the drawn out peal of a vast bell. He shook his head, but the ringing didn't stop or waver. He sat down in the chair, and stayed there for an indeterminate time.

#

Elizabeth was up early; she wanted to quiz Drum on the sketchpad she had found with his name in it before the real adults were up and about. She peeked into her father's office and saw Drum's suitcase beside the folded bedding on the sofa. Irritated that Drum had absconded when they had explorations to discuss, she went out onto the porch in her nightgown, thinking about slipping away to the Shining Rocks before her parents were up to nay her, but it was raining. She sat on the steps, watching drops falling from the wide eaves of the house to land just beyond her feet, splattering her bare toes with heaven's cool sweet tears, making a music like a little waterfall or a stone thronged brook, voicing somewhere between a whisper and a song.

She listened to the rhythmic splashing until she heard within it the creak and sigh of the rocker behind her on the porch, arcing from rest to rest on the wide boards. Lizbet looked over her shoulder, saw the rocker quite still. Annie sat in it, smiling at her. Lizbet was not surprised; she had been to the Other Side, after all.

"You're dead now, Annie," Lizbet knew she was stating the obvious, but felt a need to speak clarity to the situation.

Annie didn't move, simply sat smiling, as still as her chair, but Lizbet could hear her voice quite clearly, "Yes, Child, I'm dead to this world, but I'm not gone from it. I'm as much here as thee, as the grass, the mountain, the weather."

Lizbet had wondered about something for much of her short life, and finally, she was with somebody who would surely know, "Annie, where do we go when we die?"

Annie laughed and flickered in her chair, like a candle flame when somebody opens a door suddenly. "We don't go anywhere, Elizabeth. We are still here where we always are. The living go on, though, into the future. Soon they cannot see us who remain present."

"But I can see you, Annie."

Annie's form settled and steadied again, but as the dawn brightened, Lizbet could see through her like a cloud, the rocker dimly visible behind her shape, "That is because you have been to the Other Side, like your friend Drum."

It pleased Lizbet to be compared to the photographer, "I want to be like Drum when I'm grown, and see things, and make others see what I've seen."

Lizbet thought she saw the chair move a bit as Annie, fading now, leaned toward her, "Thee has a seer's soul, Elizabeth Coggins, and the artist's gift, but thee will not grow up to be like Drum. There's no other soul in creation with the gift to be thee."

The empty chair rocked slightly as the blossoming morning raised a breeze, and Judy opened the screen to look out, "What are you doing, sitting out here in the rain, Lizbet? Come in and get dressed. You can help me with breakfast."

#

Drum was on the river. Not high above it, but in the skiff, rocking and slowly turning in the current. He looked for a paddle, but except for him, the little boat was empty. He felt the low morning sun behind him, bright and hot; he could see his shadow riding along on the water ahead. Rounded boulders protruded all around from the slow, wide, shallow river. He thought he likely could wade his way to shore.

While Drum pondered the need, he heard far away yet drawing nearer, rhythmic pounding like a railway locomotive. A spindly iron trestle spanned the river downstream, but it wasn't a train he heard; somebody was knocking at his door. Drum opened his eyes and sunshine spilled across the room from the window behind him. Dust motes danced like fireflies against his shadow on the floor. His head hurt. How long had he been sitting here in a stupor? What time was it? Judging by the sun, it was still morning. Drum groaned, pushed himself up from the chair, as the knocking resumed. He crossed the room and opened the door.

"Judy sent you some eggs." Ronan Darner held out a brown craft bag toward him, "Man, you look terrible. Are you alright?"

Drum took the bag, stepped aside, "Too much travel. It catches up after awhile. Come on in, Ronan."

Ronan looked around the room as if he expected it to be somehow different without Annie. Drum stood silent, recognizing in him now the man who would become Mary's husband, wondering for a moment if Ronan would remember, after the boy was a man and a soldier brushed by death and married and a father to girls, that before all that, he had delivered some eggs to a man who shared his nephew's name. Shaken by the flood of memories unleashed, memories he kept steadfastly hidden away, even from himself, Drum wondered what had he been doing while Annie and Judy and James had lived their lives without him. What had been so important that it had kept him apart from the only lives that connected him to the world? He had spent two decades watching the dance when he could have been in it, touching and moving and being moved by the ebb and flow of the music of kindred souls. As it was, Drum wasn't sure if his life had been for any purpose at all, or, if it had, what that purpose might be.

He started for what he thought was the kitchen, and Ronan followed him. Drum set the eggs on a table there and turned back to Ronan, "You walk all the way down here?"

Ronan grinned, "Not hardly. James is starting a new house down by the river. He wanted to go take a look at the site. He dropped me off, so I could get the skiff and head home."

"Skiff? You have a boat here?"

"It's pulled up down below Annie's garden. It's quicker just to cross the river in it than walk around the road by the bridge."

"Well, Ronan, do you have time to stay for breakfast? I don't know my way in this house, but you've brought some eggs. We ought to be able to rustle up something to nourish us."

Ronan seemed in no hurry to leave, "I can help you find stuff."

Drum scanned the kitchen, "There's no fridge."

Ronan looked sympathetic, "We don't have one either, no electricity, but James says there will be line run down to the river by next year. He expects there will be more houses going up in the lower Cove after that."

Ronan pointed out the pantry. Drum found a jar of beef sausages. "Ronan, any onions in the garden?"

"For the eggs? Maybe some chives."

"Chives are even better." Before the words were out, Ronan was through the door.

Drum found a frying pan, and in a covered keeper, some butter. He swiped it with his finger, tasted, not stale, someone had put it here for him. He broke a half-dozen eggs into a green glazed pitcher with the potter's name scribed into the bottom. Salt. Pepper. Ronan was back with a clutch of green chives, two red sweet peppers and a cantaloupe.

Without asking, he washed them at the sink, "There's a spring up the hill aways. James piped water down from there so at least Annie could have indoor plumbing. Even a bathroom, just like in Asheton. You won't have to hit the trail after dark."

This elicited an appreciative nod.

Ronan pulled a knife from a drawer, diced the chives, and when Drum held the green bowl toward him, dropped them in. "You want one of these peppers, too?"

"You read my mind. I think we learned from the same cook."

"Annie tutored me awhile. We'd study at this table, and I'd stay for supper sometimes."

"James says you helped her a lot."

"With the garden, mostly. She kept me in school. I owe her a lot more than I did."

"I owe her a lot more than you do, Ronan, and did less for it, I'm afraid. If I try to hang on to this place, can I pay you to watch after it when I'm not here?"

"For as long as I'm here, I'd be glad to. As soon as school is done, David and me plan to join up."

"Military?" Drum asked the question knowing the answer, wanting to say *Don't* and spare the boy his hurt. But to spare him that, might also be to deny him Mary. What else could it change? Drum kept his silence and listened.

"Army. Pa says we're about to be in the war. I don't mean to wait to be conscripted."

Drum stared at the eggs while he stirred in the peppers Ronan had chopped as they talked, "Strange."

"That I want to join the army?"

"No, in your place, Ronan, I'd likely do the same. When I first came to Annie, the country was on the verge of war. I was too young to soldier then, and now it's about to happen again and I'm maybe too old, although if there's a fight, I'll probably get packed off to photograph it."

"Being a photographer sounds exciting, traveling all over the world, seeing strange places that most folks don't even know exist."

"Travel wonderfully narrows the mind, Ronan."

"That's what Annie used to say."

By the time they finished their brunch, the sun was lost in clouds again and a misty rain damped upon them as they walked down through the garden to the riverbank, where Ronan's overturned skiff was waiting, pulled up next to a tree and secured with a padlocked chain around the trunk.

Ronan fished a key from his pocket and loosed the chain, with a rueful explanation, "Lost this once, when Annie was still here. Just disappeared one day, then a few days later, it showed up again, just like I left it, but without the paddle and the stuff I had in it. Never knew who took it or why."

Drum helped him right his little craft, and as Ronan settled in the stern, pushed it away into the water, Ronan slipped into his poncho, which had been tied into a bundle and stowed with the paddle underneath the skiff. Taking up the paddle, Ronan waved, then turned the skiff toward the far shore.

Drum watched the boy dissolve into the fog shrouding the river, stood for a while then, looking at the dripping garden and the house on the hill above. By the time he was getting thoroughly wet, the rain tapered and the fog thinned above to reveal a vague ghost of sun.

Drum raised his arms to the side, then let his palms fall to slap his thighs. "Well, Annie, what do I do now?"

Annie was silent, but the fog continued to lift and he could barely make out Ronan, almost across the river. Somewhere out over the water, a hawk cried an answer. Unfortunately, Drum could not understand. He began a slow traverse of the garden, wondering where in it Annie would want him to scatter her ashes.

Annie's presence was everywhere, in the soil underfoot, in the twining bean vines, in the tall stalks of fruiting okra that made him think of Mary, in the trees all around, in the windows of the house on the slope beyond, watching, welcoming, inviting. Drum fancied he could almost hear Annie speak to him in this place, but the quiet of woods and water held neither counsel nor summons. Life murmured on gently around him as the sun brightened and the last of the fog melted away into boundless blue.

At this moment, no imperative burdened Drum to go anywhere, do anything. Time pooled in abundance. Just past the squash vines crouched a weathered, rustic chair, built from barked saplings woven and fastened together. Drum rubbed his fingers over the *B. A. R. D.* incised into the back, smiled at the proprietary notice, sat down somewhat tentatively. The chair took his weight with scarcely a creak. "You did good, Mister Ronan," Drum said to the chair.

He leaned back and closed his eyes and listened to the morning transmuting into afternoon. He would sit right here for now. This was as good a place as any to wait for the rest of his life to show itself.

Too close to sleep to open his eyes and too near wakefulness to dream, Drum sat in Annie's chair while the sun arced slowly above the treetops and the earth turned him from sun to leafy shadow and back to light and warmth again. Finally, Drum squinted against the glare and looked up the hill toward the house and remembered the cedar box in his bag, "You have a big garden, Annie; where in it do you want your ashes."

Annie kept her Quaker silence, but the trees sighed, *Not yet, not yet*, and a whip-poor-will intoned, *You will see; we'll show thee.*

"I'll keep my eyes open," Drum said aloud to the day.

He stood then, pushing himself upright with his hands pressed against the twiggy arms of the chair. His joints were stiff and sore. He thought he might be a tad feverish. He started walking again, aimlessly through the garden, up a row between Blue Lake beans and Cherokee tomatoes and back down another bounded by sweet corn and okra.

Drum remembered working with Annie in her corn, the feel of dark loam warm between his fingers, the earth dried crumbly in the sun, the memory so vivid now he could smell the dirt. Drum bent and scooped up a fistful of soil at his feet. *If I hold on to this place, I might have a little garden here when I get old,* He mused. His handful of dirt was too soggy from the rain to crumble finely as he remembered, but fell stickily between his fingers in cakes and clumps. *Pipe dreams,* Drum rebuked himself; still, the notion held him.

As he started again toward the house, he glanced down and saw a white glimmering where he had pulled up his soil sample. Drum squatted down and fingered the bit of bright stone loose from the wet earth and laid it in his palm. He'd turned up an arrowhead, flaked from the same sort of white quartzite as the Shining Rocks. Still sharp, as if made the day before, with rounded shoulders. A hunter's point.

Drum stared at it in wonderment. How long had it lain here? Had it found its target or fallen away lost? What sort of man had sent it to this ground? How many lives crossed a place, knew it as their own and called it home, yet never touched, leaving only the detritus of their days to bear witness of their passing there to those who might follow long after?

Drum dropped the point into the pocket of his shirt. He felt lightheaded for a moment as he stood. On his way to the house, he stopped twice to look behind. Drum did not feel threatened, but had an uncanny sense that he was being watched.

Back in Annie's kitchen, he washed up the dishes from his late breakfast with Ronan. Without really thinking about it, Drum already knew he would keep the place. Annie was right when she told Judy he would need somewhere to come home to, but Drum would always think of it as Annie's house. As often as he might return to it, he would be coming home to her.

Dishes cleaned and put away as best as he could find their places, Drum went back to the living room, grabbed his bag and climbed the stair. His light-headedness returned as he reached the upper landing. To his left was a bathroom under a dormer, and to right a bedroom, where two large windows framed the garden. One end of the room opened like a balcony overlooking the living room below. In a couple of her letters, Annie had referred to her aerie. So this was what she meant.

The room's simple furnishings included a bed, a small

sofa, a wardrobe, a tall chest and another oak rocker, this one plain and armless, with a woven cane seat. A small table with a mirror hung on the wall behind served as a dresser. No curtains occluded the windows. The only adornment in the room, a surprise to Drum, framed pictures on the wall, a couple of his boyhood drawings and several of his photographs.

He dropped his bag on Annie's bed. He would sleep tonight on the sofa, he thought. For now, meant to leave as little trace of his own presence as possible in the house while he gathered Annie's echo. He could feel her around him now, close and strong and forgiving. He needed to nurture that sense of her nearness, her forgiveness, especially.

Drum stood leaning with his hands on the window sill and peered down at the garden as he waited for another spell of vertigo to pass. He'd forgotten how changeable the weather could be in the cove. The sun was gone again and a thick fog had rolled up across the garden from the river. Drum thought he saw a figure standing where he had found the arrowhead, looking up at the house. He wiped the condensation from the glass to gain a clearer view, but if anyone had been down there, they were gone when he looked again.

#

Talks To Trees was out hunting when he stumbled into the gray man's garden. Talks To Trees had not always been his name. When the Labyrinth folded him into their time, bereft of all remembrance of who he was or how he came to be there, the People had taken him in, cared for him, given him family and fraternity and purpose. Old Owl, their shaman had used his herbs and trances to guide Talks To Trees back to his memories, bit by bit. It took a long time for him to know again he was the Rider, and to recollect Millicent, his Flyer. He remembered Gates, and though he could no longer pass through them, he could sense their presence, and something of what lay beyond them.

The People lived in a thin stream of being, neither in Laurel nor Shadow, but somewhere between times. Gates abounded in their place, embodied in stones and trees and waterfalls, some opening to Laurel and some into Shadow, and some into realms so alien to the Rider that he could not comprehend what he sensed from them.

He missed Millicent. Hers was among the first memories to reclaim him. He wondered if she were near or far or sooner or later. Without her proximity, he remained incomplete. Millicent could carry him back to wholeness with his life. He was standing before a Gate manifest in an ancient Beech, attempting for the thousandth time to summon her, when one of the People observed him. When the tale spread over the village, the People named him Talks To Trees. Because he was good with a bow, he was elected a hunter. He knew guilt whenever his arrow took a blooded life, but that was better than seeing hungry children when a long winter emptied the village storehouse.

Talks To Trees rarely missed his mark during a hunt, but on this day, he was distracted, released his arrow hastily, wounded when he should have killed. The buck vanished into the laurel thicket across Drowning Man Creek, and Talks To Trees listened until he could no longer hear the wounded animal thrashing through the brush. Then he gathered himself, and followed his arrow. A track here, moss scraped from a stone there, branches broken, blood smeared on leaves or scarlet against the dark wet earth, left an easy trace. Though as he moved after the buck, the feeling that had broken his concentration grew stronger, almost oppressive, the urgent awareness of a Gate, which Talks To Trees could not quite locate. It seemed not to emanate from any particular object but hung in the air like the fog that thickened around him as he went.

The deer outran all expectations, but after an hour, the fresher blood shone brighter. The buck was weakening, slowing. Talks To Trees breathed thanks to the dying buck and to the living Mountain for allowing the mercy of food for his People, in spite of his carelessness.

The fog rolling in off the nearby river became so dense that Talks To Trees had to bend close to the ground to see where the buck had left the creek and followed the river bank upstream. Judging from the sign, the buck must be very near now. He expected to find more laurel and dog-hobble ahead, but instead came out into a cleared space. Somebody had planted a large garden on the sloping ground up from the river's edge. Faintly through the fog beyond the garden, he saw the shape of a house. It looked like one of the houses in the gray towns. In the garden below the house stood a gray man. He was apparently unaware of Talks to Tree's approach. The buck was gone, but as he came near to the man, he saw that the gray man held the quartz point from the arrow.

Talks to Trees spoke quietly, so as not to startle the man, who had still not noticed him, "That is mine."

The gray man didn't react. He looked right into Talks to Trees' face as if seeing only the trees and the river behind. Looking at the gray man was like looking at his own reflection in water, like facing himself. He reached out to touch the man's shoulder and his fingers passed right through him as easily as through the foggy air.

Talks to Trees understood then. The Gate was not in a tree or a stone. The Gate resided within himself. If he could learn now to touch it with his mind, open it, he could travel between times and beyond place. By some power beyond his comprehension, Talks To Trees was becoming like Millicent, the Flyer, in that space between raindrops, neither quite present nor absent but both, and the gray man was undoubtedly the boy with his face, whose staff had sent him down the timeless length of the Labyrinth, now grown and restored to his place of belonging.

As the gray man walked away toward his house, Talks to Trees stood watching for a long time, wondering. If, indeed, he stood in Shadow, and he was almost certain of that, the Flyer must have brought him to himself. Where was she now? What form did she assume here? Would he recognize her if ever he found her?

#

Drum went back to the bathroom and threw up his breakfast. *I'm really sick here,* he assured himself. Then he crossed the landing again to Annie's room, lay down on the sofa and fell immediately into a dark and dreamless sleep.

He woke to blackness as deep and featureless as his sleep, closed his eyes, uncertain if he were really awake, or if this still knowing was itself a dreaming. When nothing happened to confirm his state one way or another, he opened his eyes again, and as they adjusted to the dark, he could barely perceive a gray rectangle of window, the outline of a chair before it, and the contour of head and shoulders belonging to a figure sitting in the chair.

"Annie?" Drum inquired of the dark.

He sensed the figure watching him before she spoke, "Not your Annie, Drum. I knew you before Annie, and now you know me when she is gone."

A familiar presence flooded the room, but Drum could not identify this soul whose proximity comforted him, even while his unknowing made him afraid. "I know you, but I don't know who you are," thinking as he spoke that he sounded childish and nonsensical.

The light from the window fluttered as if wings had passed before it, then brightened slightly. In the silence after, Drum thought he was alone, until the voice spoke one more time, very quietly, almost a whisper, intimate and familiar, "You will have plenty of time to find out who I am, dear Drum, but you have love to lose before you find mine."

Drum could see the rocker clearly now against the dawning. It was empty and still. Then all was dark again and he slept like the dead. When Drum woke, it was morning and the sun was shining and he felt full of light and health, also hungry. He went downstairs and put on a pot of water, made some tea, scrambled two of Ronan's eggs for breakfast, ate them from the pan. Before Drum left the house, he found flour, yeast and salt, and kneaded a clutch of bread dough. He left it in a blue bowl with a chipped rim, covered by a towel, to rise until his return.

Then he went out to find the new day. It never occurred to him to lock Annie's door behind him.

#

Days became weeks and weeks accumulated into a month and Drum still lodged in the house by the river. Eric fumed in Washington, but when Drum complained that he had never taken a vacation in all his years with the magazine, the editor relented and gave him the summer. Eric ended the conversation quietly but firmly, "But you do have a contract with us, you know. Come September, we'll expect you to honor it." Drum promised that he would.

So Drum was in the audience when Ben Coggins and Ronan Darner graduated from high school. Ronan went off to the army and Ben went to the state university to study forestry. Drum was there to comfort when Judy learned she had cancer, and Drum sat with James in the hospital during her surgery. James helped Drum find an old pickup to buy, in which he rattled around the cove, often with Lizbet as his passenger and accomplice, making photographs of rocks and clouds and trees and animals and people. Drum gardened and cleared brush. He drove up the creek to cook for the family while Judy was recuperating. James sent one of his young employees, a carpenter's helper, Caleb Two Trees, who agreed to look after Annie's homestead when Drum returned to his job in the fall.

In September, it was a changed Drum who dawdled over his breakfast on a train to Washington, as the mountains slid past the windows and the sun crested the hills to east. For the first time in his life he had friends it pained him to leave, people in his life he thought of as family, a place in his heart that he meant to return to as soon and as often as he could manage.

When he shook hands with Caleb the day before he left, Drum said, "I'll be back to see what you've done with this old place."

Caleb smiled, and in the soft musical speech unique to the boy's family as far as Drum knew, "Sure then you will be. The cove has rooted in you deep now. You'll have to come back to it."

Drum smiled to himself, as he remembered the conversation, savored the truth of it, and he held out his cup gratefully when the waiter in the dining car gestured with his carafe. The waiter made Drum set his cup on the table before he poured. Watching the man move on to the next table, Drum tasted from his coffee, thinking he'd never been served bad coffee on a train. Then he went back to the newspaper left by the young soldier who shared his table earlier. He felt very far from home as he read the headline, *Nazis Invade Poland*.

#

The next year passed in a blur. First Drum was in Newfoundland freezing his fingers making photographs of rocky shores and grizzled fishermen. By the time word got to him there that Annie and Ruth Coggins had drowned along with one other student when their chartered bus slid off an icy road and toppled into Beaver Lake, the funeral was done and the girls buried. Lizbet had the flu and missed the trip. Before Drum could mourn for his friends or think about going home, Eric sent him off to the northwest freezing his fingers making pictures for a National Parks issue. Drum photographed mountains and rivers and large, potentially dangerous wildlife. The landscape there thrilled and awed him, but he felt like a tourist the whole time. The sharp towering mountains and raging rivers did not inspire any sense of belonging in him, and Drum rode the train back to Washington homesick for Annie's little house by the river where the land was greener and gentler, and the mountains were tall and rough enough to make him feel small, but not so stark and fierce as to make him feel diminished.

Eric grumbled when Drum took time off and spent Christmas and New Year's in the Cove with the Coggins clan. All present tried to set aside their mourning for Drum's visit, and made a valiant attempt at good spirits, though Judy obviously didn't feel well, and when he boarded the train north on his way to photograph Adirondack waterfalls frozen in the snow, Drum had no doubts about the location of home.

Through the summer, Drum was continually on the road, photographing tall buildings in big cities, and herds of humans milling about without any of the purpose and intention of wild creatures. Drum considered cities as a truly barren sort of wilderness, lacking any of the spiritual comforts of unregulated nature.

Back in Washington, he sat listening to Ed Murrow on the radio describing the German bombs falling on London when the phone rang. Drum chewed a bite of his ham sandwich, swallowed, and picked up the receiver on the third ring, "Hello, this is Drum."

"Drum, it's James Coggins. Afraid I have some more bad news."

"How bad, James? Is everybody all right down there?"

"Judy's back in the hospital. They're running more tests, but the doctor isn't encouraging us any."

"James, I just got back from an assignment, Give me a few days to get grounded here, and I'll head home if you need me."

"There's nothing you can do, Drum. Wait and pray is all any of us can do, but Judy would like to see you."

"Keep me posted, James. I'll let you know as soon as I can get away from here."

"I'll do that. Take care of yourself."

"I'm just fine, James. All of you take care of one

another. I'll see you soon."

"Soon, then," James said and hung up.

Drum had barely finished his sandwich when the phone rang again, "Drum, this is Eric. Have you unpacked yet?"

"I'm afraid to ask why you're asking, Eric."

"We have you on a flight with an AFO ferry pilot out of Gander tomorrow night. You're going to London to photograph the bombing. Richard Holford is already there."

"How long?"

"Two weeks at most. We need to get this along quick."

"As soon as I'm back, Eric, We need to sit down and talk."

"I'll buy you a steak, Drum. Our driver will pick you up in an hour."

Drum hung up the phone without waiting to hear if Eric had more to tell him. "Shit," he shouted to the indifferent air.

#

Horace thought if he had to be stranded out of his life and time he could not have landed in a better place. The Laurel would do nicely until Heaven came along. He looked into his basket more than half full of tomatoes from Li's garden and decided he had enough room left to cut some basil. The Laurel summer was already slipping away into a golden autumn and this would likely be their last cutting for the season. When Horace came through the kitchen door with his aromatic burden, Li was sitting at the table stirring her tea. He could tell by her dress she was about to be away on a mission.

She looked up as Horace set the brimming basket in a chair opposite her at the table. Li rewarded his labors with the smile that always made him peacefully content to remain in his present state for a little while longer, "And what have you brought me, kind Horace? Is that basil I smell?"

"Some tomatoes for ketchup, and basil, yes. I thought I would make some pesto for you."

"You know the way to a woman's heart, my friend."

"Your heart is open to every lost soul you meet, Li. You have on your gray dress. Are you going any place I remember?"

"Only to a bombing. They're having another war over there."

"Do you enjoy getting blown up?"

"I won't get blown up. Whatever happens, I'll hurry right back here where I can savor your pesto."

"You'll be back soon, in any case, I hope."

"We always come back. That's the rule. It will be like I never left. While I'm yonder, Ernest wants to take you out toward Poplar Spring where he's found a place you might like for your own. It has good water, and the river at hand, and enough bottomland to do a little farming. If you like it, he'll take you down to Beaverdam to work out a trade. He wants to introduce you to his people in the Guilds. They're looking for somebody to take things in hand and he told them about how you saved your place from the grays."

"I didn't save anything, Li. My friends and I just raised enough ruckus to worry some people in power into doing the right thing."

"You were there to make a difference, Horace, and in spite of yourself, you did. Go with Ernest while I'm gone. It may be that you can make some difference here. I didn't sing you over just for the fun of it."

"No?"

"In your case, Horace, it was also fun."

#

When the transport lifted away from Gander in a flurry of light snow, Drum and a young aircraft mechanic from Ohio were the only passengers. Drum tried to sleep as the ocean spread out below and stars blossomed from the clearing sky ahead. Far and away on the horizon the barest brightening of a coming dawn. The plane bucked and shuddered in the contrary air and Drum dreamed briefly of jolting up a mountain road in Walt Coggins' wagon, before he woke again feeling vaguely sick. He was cold. He had friends who might have need of him and he was headed in the opposite direction at two hundred miles an hour. *The story of my life,* he thought.

Drum had ample time to consider his lonely life before they finally set down at Prestwick, where Richard Holford met him to begin the long rail ride down to London.

"I met someone over here the other day who knows you," Richard said as Scottish hills slid by the window, brown and somber under the overcast.

"Who could that be? It's been awhile since I was in this end of the world."

"Liza Charon. She sings sometimes at a pub just up the street from my lodging. She says she remembers you."

"Liza?"

"Yes, striking woman. Black hair with streaks of silver gray. Eyes that kill. You recall?"

"Oh, yes, I remember her, but I'm surprised she remembers me."

"You must have made an impression, Drum."

Drum didn't answer. He had fallen asleep. Richard let him dream his way into England.

207

HENRY MITCHELL

Over breakfast next morning at the Thorn and Ivy, Richard laid out their drill, "We'll just muck about today, get your bearings, gather a few street shots. I'm out of here in two more days, but they'll keep you up in my place until you're finished. The only rule is that when there's a raid, get to shelter. Nobody wants to see you killed trying to picture an explosion. Aftermath is impressive enough for our readers. This is as good a place to eat as any you'll find. The food is relatively cheap, consistently edible, and once they know you here, they'll look after you. Here comes somebody you know."

Drum looked up to see Liza Charon coming through a door behind the bar. She stepped around it and headed for their booth as if she were keeping an appointment. Liza leaned over their table, patted Richard's hand while fixing Drum with her fiery smile. "Well, if it isn't good old Drum, keeping company with some disreputable character as usual. Why aren't you with people who love you?"

Something in Liza's devastating smile warned Drum that nothing short of absolute honesty would suffice, "Because all my life I've had a talent for being in places I'd rather not be, but it's mighty good to see you again, Liza."

Liza's smile evaporated. She regarded Drum silently for a long moment with an expression of somber concern, "Come back here tonight and I'll sing to you." Her laugh drifted back to them from the open door as she hurried off into the street.

"She still likes you," Richard said.

"She's just bored," replied Drum, pleased that he registered with her on any account.

After they disappeared their breakfast, Richard led Drum on an amble through the neighborhood. London remained London after all, hurt and battered as she was. There was hardly a block without boarded up windows and shattered roofs and toppled walls. As Richard pointed out the city's wounds and recited the tales they bore, Drum made photographs, getting used to his new camera. It occurred to him suddenly that it was exactly like Bear's.

Between photographs, they talked to people walking on the street or clearing rubble or laying new brick. After lunch at another pub that looked to Drum very like the first one, Richard went off on an assignment of his own. "Get your feet under you this afternoon and meet me at the Thorn and Ivy around eight. We'll eat something and then go see what goes on at an anti-aircraft station. With any luck we might have a raid while we're at it."

It wasn't the first time somebody had reminded Drum that as a photographer he was often the guilty bystander who made his living from the misfortune of innocents. A decision that had been building in his mind since the previous summer began to clarify considerably over the next couple of hours as he made more photographs of destruction and resurrection.

Finally, he returned to Richard's flat and took a long nap. If he had dreams, he forgot them on waking. He washed and changed, and as darkness fell down across the city, he stepped out under a sunset that looked like a great fire burning across the town. He started toward the Thorn and Ivy as dusk settled in the streets. There were few lights, and when air raid sirens began their strident wailing, most of those lights promptly extinguished. Drum stopped by an Underground entrance and saw the pub just across the street. A cigarette glowed faintly through the open door, then all was dark inside.

An elderly man wearing a helmet and an armband

reached out and touched his shoulder,

"Down here, Sir."

"What?"

The man pointed to the sign beside the door, "Shelter, sir. Best come along." Drum could see people filing down the steps behind the warden, gestured toward the pub, "I'm meeting someone over there."

"You're more likely to meet them down here tonight, sir. Please." Drum obeyed, felt the warden's hand firmly at his back as he started down the dim stair. He could hear explosions from somewhere just beyond the Thames.

#

When his eyes accustomed to the dim light in the Tube, Drum beheld as surreal a scene as he had ever photographed. Even had he brought his camera along, he thought it would be unseemly to photograph such anonymous and vulnerable intimacy. A double set of rails emerged from the dark and passed by the lighted platform to fade into an opposite blackness. Along the curved walls whole families were huddled together or rolled in blankets, apparently prepared to settle for the night. A very few young children. Some old people. Young couples obviously diverted from parties or concerts. The life of the city hid in the earth like corn at planting while bombs destroyed the structures left behind above ground. Occasionally the muffled detonation of a distant bomb echoed along the tracks.

Drum walked along the rows of recumbent figures feeling like a tourist in Sheol. A middle aged man sat on a bench scribbling in a pad. There was a space beside him. Drum stopped. "May I?" he asked, gesturing at the empty seat.

"Certainly," the man answered pleasantly, looking up

and smiling as he patted the bench beside him and closed his pad. Drum glimpsed a drawing of rows of human forms, sleeping or dead. The man had a kindly inquiring face that made Drum think of a neighborhood druggist.

Drum sat as another bomb fell, this one nearer than the others. People looked up as dust and grit filtered down through the garish light.

"Are you an artist?" Drum hoped his voice didn't betray his nervousness.

"Guilty. Officially, I'm a *war artist*. They've assigned me the task of recording how life goes on in our city, buried but unbowed." The man held out his hand, "I'm Moore, and you're obviously American. I hope the German show doesn't spoil your visit with us."

Drum shook Moore's hand, noted the firm grasp and the calloused palm, like a laborer. He guessed that Moore might be a sculptor.

"Drum here, also guilty and found out. I'm a photographer for an American magazine. Actually I'm here to catch the German show, get some photographs to convince my countrymen that this war is worth getting into."

"And what about you, Drum. Do you believe our little¹ fight is worth getting into?"

"I don't believe in letting someone beat up on your friends without lending a hand."

"My studio has been pretty much wrecked by a bomb. I'm looking at a little place out at Much Hadham. Perhaps when this is over and I'm settled, you'll come out to see me and we'll drink to friendship."

"I'd like that." Drum would have said more but at that instant the earth throbbed around them with an enormous concussion and darkness followed instantaneously. A

211

woman screamed softly. A baby cried. The lights flickered and came on again as flakes and chips of masonry fell audibly onto the tracks. Dust swirled along the tube like fog. Drum could feel the acrid grains and motes in his throat and suppressed an urge to run for the exit.

Everyone waited silently then until the sirens sounded an all-clear and the warden granted absolution. Most stayed where they were, including Moore. Drum and a few others emerged to the surface. When he stepped out onto the street, the pub was no longer there. The three-storey building that housed it had collapsed into a flaming pyre. Firemen were training hoses on the fire. The water pressure seemed insufficient to make much headway. A policeman was trying to herd pedestrians toward safety. Drum asked him, "Did anyone survive this?"

The policeman stared at him blankly, "I don't see how, Sir."

POLLY

Willard Hoots laid his glasses on the table and rubbed his eyes. Noddie had been after him to "read some Dickens," until Willard finally asked, "Where should I start, then?"

"Barnaby Rudge," said Noddie, "The most neglected but the most rewarding novel he wrote."

"Better than *Two Cities*?" Willard asked.

Noddie pulled the book from a shelf and stabbed Willard in the chest with it. "Better than that. I bet you can't read it before I get back from Boston."

Noddie was always baiting Willard into a bet, which invariably Willard lost, forfeiting anything from a meal at Millie Robbins' Hillhaven Inn to a weekend in Highland, the overpriced, and in Willard's opinion overrated, tourist resort about two hours south of Asheton. Noddie, having grown up in a swamp, loved the mountains. Never seemed to get enough. Willard, who had been born just across a ridge from Asheton, had all his life wanted to get away, yet with each escape, had always found a more pressing reason to come back. The first time Willard left the Cove, to go off to college in Wake Forest, he told his father he didn't know if he'd come back home to stay, that he wanted to teach in a real university one day. He was afraid he'd hurt the old man's pride, but Daniel just smiled at his son like they'd shared some secret joke, "Ye got this mountain in ye, boy. Wherever ye run to, ye'll have to come back."

Thinking about it now, Willard admitted to himself

that he'd always returned, not because he had to, but because when the dust settled, he wanted to. Noddie loved the mountains because they were different from anything in an unhappy childhood. Willard loved them because they were home.

Willard taught physics at the Asheton campus of the state university. He'd come back here because he had aging parents who needed some looking after, and because he couldn't find a job in a more prominent school, and because Noddie, who he met during graduate studies at Duke, had landed a place in the English department here.

What a strange pair they were, Willard thought. How unlikely they'd ever have been together at all. Noddie loved English literature, taught it, breathed it, was a voracious reader, even smelled like books. Willard, because of his minimal eyesight, could never regard reading as more than a chore, sometimes a pleasant one for short duration, but always leaving him tired, with sore burning eyes. Reading was not something he would choose purely for pleasure, particularly Dickens, who didn't hesitate to use thirty words when three would do. The flow and rhythms of being that Noddie found revealed in words and stories disclosed themselves to Willard in equations and propositions that he could carry handily in his head with minimal assistance from his damaged vision. When he wrote formulas on a blackboard for his class, he followed the lines behind his eyes, not the ones he traced on the board.

His childhood nickname had stuck, and to this day he was still Owly to all his friends, and behind his back to his students, and even to Noddie, who would hug him close when he made one of his ill-considered pronouncements on the state of the world, and croon softly, "my wise old Owly, How could I ever do without you?"

Today, Willard was on his way to lunch with Paulette Coggins. Growing up together at Annie Starling's school, both were shy and different, mutual comforters and encouragers. They remained pals and confidants as adults. Polly understood him. She knew things about Willard he had told none else but Noddie.

When they last shared lunch up at Hillhaven, Polly read to him from a novel manuscript she had just finished, an account of Annie Starling's adventures in Sorrow Cove, thinly disguised as fiction, Willard took the manuscript home with him and laboriously read the whole thing. He showed it to Noddie then, who had been impressed enough to carry it along to Boston to pitch to a publisher Noddie was meeting with there. Willard planned to surprise Polly with the news when they had lunch today.

#

Paulette Coggins looked in the mirror, sighed, made a valiant attempt to corral her dark hair into a configuration that didn't resemble a summer storm cloud. Her naturally unruly locks got away from her when she was working. She wanted to look decent while she had lunch with Willard, who would likely be himself slightly rumpled, looking like the absent minded professor he really was. He'd phoned a couple of weeks ago to ask if he could show her manuscript to Noddie, who knew people. She was anxious to hear what Noddie thought of it.

They seemed to Polly such an unlikely couple, Noddie and her friend Owly. Willard, short and shy, dark and quiet, very like his nickname. Noddie, tall and fair, never met a stranger, full of words that spilled out in gorgeous array wherever there were souls about to listen. It must be

215

hard for them, she thought, to be so close when there was so much in the world to keep them apart.

Polly stopped by the door, collected her keys and purse, took down a light jacket, just in case, and walked out into the day. She never locked her door. Nobody in Sorrow Cove locked their doors, except the city-bred summer people. Things were changing now, Polly knew, but among her mountains, so far, at least, change came slowly. She still had some time to write about the old ways and life she had been born into, before it was all carried away along paved roads and utility wires. Polly hoped that somebody would read what she was writing, and remember what was being lost while something of it might be saved and preserved.

Her Ford started on the second turn of the key. Polly steered cautiously down her narrow winding drive, eroded and rutted from the past winter's freeze and rain. She meant to ask her brother to come down with his tractor and try to render it more passable. Once on the graveled county road, she rolled up her window against the pale dust boiling up around her car. Passing her brother's place, Polly waved to Lizbet, who had walked down to the road to retrieve their mail.

Another unlikely couple, Polly thought, brother James and his Judy. Judy, a teacher, in love with high thoughts and deep words, James a carpenter, who thought with his hands, a maker of objects that embodied his love and care for the souls in his life, all the things he could seldom bring himself to speak of aloud.

Polly, on the other hand, somehow had never found her match, unlikely or not. She didn't really wonder about it. It was natural enough, in her view. She wanted things in life, and she was ruthless about what she wanted. She knew women with husbands and children who were living the lives of spouses and offspring, without ever having experienced lives of their own. Polly didn't mean to follow that road. She would make her own life before she opened it in any intimate way to another. Romantic relationships had a way of derailing the most carefully planned vocation. She couldn't afford to share her heart until she had accomplished in the world. Then she would be somebody by anyone's measure, and love would not leave her in another's shadow.

Ambition left room for friends, though. Willard was her oldest, maybe her closest friend. There was no danger of emotional entanglement there. Willard also knew people who might help her. He was entertaining company and he was useful to her cause.

#

Willard was so taken with his friend's novel that Noddie had been hard put not to laugh in his face. Noddie never failed to be surprised and amused at Willard's sudden and transient enthusiasms. Normally quiet, bordering on invisibility, Willard would come across something that caught his fancy and be all achatter over it for days on end, until the enamorment faded or Willard's mind was unsettled by some other unanticipated attraction. It was one of several idiosyncrasies Willard exhibited from time to time that Noddie found at once endearing and annoying.

As much to get Willard to shut up about it, as anything, Noddie agreed to read Polly's manuscript. After a few pages it became evident *Warwoman* was a better novel than most, and it required no nagging from Willard to induce Noddie to finish it. When Jon Davis at Boston Harbor Publishers read the pages Noddie sent him from

Warwoman, he phoned straightaway. "Bring it when you come up here," Jon said.

So on a foggy gray New England afternoon, Noddie got off a train in Boston carrying a briefcase containing Polly Coggins' manuscript as well as his own.

#

Noddie stepped from the taxi into a chilling rain, tipped the driver, too generously, Willard would have said, and sought shelter under a doorman's umbrella. Once inside the building, relatively dry and unruffled, while waiting for the elevator, Noddie studied the reflection in the mirrored wall of the lobby. *I'll do,* Noddie mused, *I travel at least as well as fresh produce.* Then the door slid back, releasing the elevator's descended hostages. Noddie waited for clearance, stepped inside and pressed the button for Jon's floor.

Cynthia Carson looked up as Noddie came in, nodded, smiled her well-practiced smile. Thinking Cynthia had aged since the last time, Noddie stood waiting, clutching the briefcase with both hands while Cynthia spoke into an intercom, "Doctor Nodine is here," then she gestured, "Come right in; Jon is waiting for you," stepped briskly ahead to open the door for Noddie and closed it behind.

Jon stood behind his desk as he put down his phone, came around to take Noddie's hand, then administer an enthusiastic but polite hug. Noddie kissed him lightly on the cheek.

Jon pulled out a chair, "Sit and rest yourself, Noddie. Let me pour you a drink, then you can tell about all you've brought me."

"The train didn't do wonders for my stomach, Jon, Maybe just a little tomato juice, if you have it."

Jon delved into his little fridge, fetched the juice,

conjured something stronger for himself, and when both had been suitably fortified, propped against his desk, arms folded, and beamed down expectantly. Noddie set the glass on the corner of Jon's polished desk, dropped the brief case on the carpet, then leaned back in the chair and stretched out long slender legs that some men and a few women had found enormously appealing.

"God, but you're looking good, Noddie." Jon fairly glowed as he said it. "You don't age like the rest of us. Someone has been taking very good care of you, obviously."

Noddie smiled back at Jon, laced fingers together, tightened arms overhead until shoulders shed their tension with an audible crack and pop, then nodded in agreement, "Blame it all on my wise old Owly, he said; Willard keeps me alive. I'd be worthless without him."

#

By the time the train shuddered to a stop at the platform in Washington, Drum knew what he had to do. He handed over his film to the driver who met him, and sent him off to Eric, then found a window and bought another ticket before taking a cab to his apartment. Drum set his bags down inside his door and phoned James. Judy was home from the hospital, James told him, with no plans to return. She meant to die at home and live with her family in the meantime. She was in some pain, but so far they had been able to keep her relatively comfortable.

Drum listened until James waited silent for his excuse, "I'm on the train out of here tonight, James. I'll be in Asheton tomorrow."

"Judy will be glad to see you Drum. She didn't expect you to come." Drum knew James didn't mean it as an indictment, but the words carried a sting all the same.

James went on, "How long will we have you with us down here?"

"I don't know, James. Awhile. I'm coming home."

Next Drum rang Eric at the magazine, told him simply, "I have to go south now."

Eric sounded beyond annoyed, "You can't go right now. We have you booked already for another assignment."

"I have family sick in Carolina, Eric."

"Photographers with this magazine shouldn't have family."

Drum held his breath for a half second, then snapped back, "Eric, you are absolutely right," hung up the phone, then began packing as much stuff as he could carry with him on the train.

So one more time Drum found himself on a train watching the sun rise over Virginia hills as he was carried among mountains and rivers to the one place on earth where people would be glad to see him without any consideration of how much money he might make for them. He knew he would have to leave again. He had to make a living the only way he knew. But he would choose the times and the places. And whatever sorts of photographs he agreed to make, Drum was determined to make no more pictures of wars and desolations. He wouldn't get rich freelancing, but he knew he could make a living at it, and he wouldn't have to live the rest of his life among strangers.

He went to the dining car, sat in a booth by himself. A somber waiter came to take his order. Drum looked up at the man hopefully. "You got any grits on this train?"

The waiter's instant smile revealed a startling display of white teeth, "Sure enough we do. Somebody must have known you were riding today."

#

Caleb Two Trees waited at Asheton in the rain with Drum's battered old pickup. They scrunched into the cab with all Drum's baggage piled around his legs and on his lap. In spite of the gloomy weather and his friend's illness, Drum felt an unaccustomed lightness as they puttered and rattled out of town. His life felt accessible to him in a way it hadn't in a long time.

He watched the wipers herding rain on the windshield, listened to the clack and flap of their cycling, and noted the sound of the engine, "This thing seems to be running a lot better than I recall, Caleb."

Caleb glanced at him, obviously pleased that Drum had noticed, "I done a little work on it, Drum."

"You didn't tell me you were spending money on my account down here. I must owe you some."

"'Twarn't much. If it keeps on running good, we can settle up, if you want. I've been driving it some, don't you know."

Drum asked the question, dreading the answer, "How is everybody?" Caleb kept his eyes on the road, "Miss Judy seems holding her own, I reckon. She's mostly in bed now. Sits out on the porch sometimes. Ronan's off in the army, says there's talk they'll get sent to Ireland for training. David's took a year off from State to help James, he says, but I think it's mostly to be home with his mother. Pa's been down in his back, hasn't been able to work much this year, but I took up some slack by working for James more."

"You keeping up with school?"

"Ma would kill me if I didn't. Judy helps me study when she feels up to it. You want me to drop you off at their place, or you going down to your house first?"

"Let me go down to Annie's house first and get cleaned up. You can take the truck if you need it."

"Why does everybody always call it Annie's house?"

"Because it will always be Annie's house. I don't guess you knew Annie, did you?"

"Don't reckon I did, but I've heard plenty about the Warwoman. Was she your kin?"

"She was my teacher, and the best friend I'll ever know. She would have helped you study."

"Like she did Ronan?"

"Like she did Ronan."

"He told me about that. He talked about that woman like he was in love with her."

"All of us wandering boys loved Annie, Caleb. All of us still do."

#

Caleb deposited Drum at Annie's little house, promised to pick him up again in a couple of hours, and drove off in Drum's old pickup to attend to some errand for James. Once inside the house, Drum lit a lamp. Riding through the cove with Caleb, he had seen new utility lines ranging along the road. If he meant this to be home, he needed to ask James about electricity and a phone.

Drum washed, not bothering to heat water, which, not cruelly cold, restored his travel weary body and brain to a semblance of alertness. He changed into fresh clothes, then walked down through the garden to the river. Caleb had kept the garden in hand, even through winter. Several patches of turned earth anticipated the coming spring. Neat piles of dried weeds, fallen branches and prunings from the grape vines awaited burning.

The river sounded as cold as the air felt. Drum went

back up to the house as a chill mist commenced again‘ swirling on the light wind. He found kindling already laid for him in the fireplace and lit it. As the flames gathered, the heat loosed his muscles, eased his taut thoughts, and Drum dozed, dreaming he was back under London in the underground with bombs thudding above him. He looked up the dark tunnel and saw a light faint and far away. Drum started walking toward it.

Moore said, "This will be over soon. Why don't you stay?"

Drum didn't answer, but walked away into the shadows toward the distant point of light. In the dimness to either side he could sense more than see the endless rows of sleeping figures. Drum walked for what seemed a long time, and eventually the light ahead began to expand as he came nearer. Drum could hear behind him the shuffle and plod of feet following. He was afraid for some reason to look around to see who all the feet belonged to.

As he approached the lighted mouth of the tunnel, the formidable bulk of a figure, backlit by the glare beyond, stood motionless in his way. When Drum stopped before her, the followers passed wordlessly around them into the light. Drum recognized the dark woman who had taken the little girl from his arms outside Trinity Church. He looked his question into her smiling face.

"Welcome home, Rider," she said, and reached out her arms as if to pull him close.

#

Sharp rapping on Annie's door startled Drum awake. The only light in the room came from the coals on the hearth. More knocking. "Drum, are you in there?"

A woman's voice, familiar, but he couldn't place it. Drum opened the door to Polly Coggins, immediately recognizable, but in some indefinable aspect not the shy little woman he remembered. More hawk than wren now.

"Paulette, is that you? I was expecting Caleb."

"Still little Polly to you, Drum. Caleb phoned and asked me to fetch you for supper. He had to go home and see about his dad. He left your truck at my brother's place."

"You look different, Polly."

"Oh, I've been in the big city since you were last down here. You know what that does to a mountain child."

"Nothing good; I have experience to know that much." Drum grinned at her, feeling a little foolish and not knowing why.

Polly laughed, "But nothing we can't get over. Are you ready to go?"

Drum was ready, hooked a jacket over his shoulder and they walked out to Polly's black Ford. The rain ceased a moment for them. Drum had to pick up several books from the passenger's seat to make a place for himself and sat with them in his lap as Polly negotiated his drive, not so well maintained in his absence as his garden. The books he held were identical, the dust jacket bore a reproduction of a rather florid watercolor, a mountain sunset, and over the picture in a bold flowing font, *Warwoman – a novel -by Paulette Coggins*.

Drum held up the book, "Annie?"

"It's fiction, but the heroine, if that's who she is, borrows a lot from Annie. It's really a story about the families in the Cove and the hard rich lives they lead, until people come from beyond the mountain to spoil it all, and how a few people also came from afar to save and restore the Cove. Annie – In the story she becomes Allie – was certainly in the center of it all. She saw the best and the worst of us, the light of our place and the dark of it, and loved us all the same. Most of us left here owe the best parts of our nature to Annie."

Polly kept her eyes fixed on the road ahead as she testified to her mentor's goodness, then glanced at Drum, "Do you think I overstate her case?"

Drum shook his head, "Not at all, Polly. If I could be sure of God, I would say She sent Annie to us."

Polly smiled at Drum's atypical reference to divine gender, turned off the windshield wipers as they squeaked on the drying glass, "Don't worry about it, Drum."

"Don't worry about what?"

"God is sure of you."

Drum had an intense desire to change the subject. He was leery of talking much about God. He had a nagging suspicion God might speak back to him personally one day, while he had no idea of how he might answer for himself. If his Maker had a plan for his life, Drum held a fair certainty he'd not followed it, not so much for any lack of willingness, but out of his pervasive ignorance of his own nature. As Drum saw it, his life just happened to him. He'd fitted himself to the flow of it as best as talent and luck would allow, but he claimed no sense of any abiding purpose to his days. He saw himself as a gray man in a colorful world.

He'd become a photographer because he discovered he had a knack for it, and found a good teacher at hand. Everything that followed had resulted from convenience and opportunity. When someone asked why he made photographs, Drum always made up a convincing answer, but when he asked the question to himself, he couldn't say. Drum didn't quest after goals and ideals. All his life he had been a finder rather than a seeker.

To shake God off his trail, Drum blurted out the first thing that popped into his head, "How have you and Owly – I mean Willard – been getting on?" He wanted to swallow the words the instant he heard them coming out of his mouth.

Polly laughed out loud, "Willard and me? How do you mean, Drum?"

Drum was grateful Polly was intent on her road and didn't see his red face, "I had a foolish notion you and Willard might be an item." Polly laughed again as she down-shifted the Ford to pull up James' hill, "We've been friends since we were children together, but we'd never become an *item*, as you put it. Willard prefers men that way. He has a relationship now. He can't talk about it, obviously, or he'd lose his teaching job at the college."

"I won't speak of it, Polly."

"I didn't think you would, Drum, or I'd never have told you."

Polly braked gently to a stop before the house, cut the engine, and turned in her seat to look at a thoroughly rattled Drum, "Write this question off to a writer's insatiable curiosity, but one foolish question deserves another; I've wondered at times if you shared Willard's sexual proclivity." Drum took his turn to laugh. Polly's gaze held steady, as if her query were serious and important, and she did not blush.

Drum gave her a serious answer, "I prefer women that way, Polly. When I was a teenager, I had an unspoken crush on your brother's wife, but somehow there's just never been a connection with anyone. I guess I never stayed in one place long enough."

"I doubt that made much difference, Drum. I stayed

right here in the cove all these years, and I never made a connection, either."

They stepped out into the soggy yard. Drum stood shivering slightly as a cold drizzle began to damp on him once again. Polly opened the trunk of the Ford and took out a large wicker picnic basket, which she thrust at him, "Carry this for me, please, sir."

Her smile was calculated to inspire meek obedience, and Drum was pleased to oblige. The basket felt warm against his arms and the aroma of fried chicken was indisputable. Polly slammed down the trunk lid with one hand, and with the other held up a cloth bag of greenery vaguely resembling okra leaves. She looked at Drum and nodded toward her bag, "To make some tea for Judy, and there's something in here to stuff her pipe with. It won't fix what ails her, but will make her feel better about it for awhile."

Drum fell in beside her as she started toward the house, "So, Polly the author is a herbalist as well?"

"While you and Emmalou were all off getting rich and famous, I stayed home reading Annie's books and learning her recipes. Somebody in this world has to cultivate useful skills."

"I'm just a picture man, Polly. I wouldn't know much about being useful to anybody."

"Stick around for awhile this time, and you might get your chance yet."

Lizbet had been waiting unseen on the shadowy porch. Now she came bounding toward them through the rain with an umbrella. She handed the umbrella to Polly and reached out to Drum, "Give me that basket and maybe Aunt Polly will let you share her dry." Lizbet took the basket and dashed back toward the house.

"You've gotten bigger, Lizbet," Drum called after her.

The girl stopped there in the rain and turned back to him for a second, "Well, I haven't gotten old yet," and resumed her flight toward shelter, her laughter trailing behind her in the air like the ringing of tiny bells.

Drum took Polly's bag of medicinals and she held the umbrella over them both as they walked close together, sleeves touching, toward the house. Lizbet ran inside and James stood in the glow from the open door waiting for them. In the last light of the day, Drum looked up above and beyond the house toward the Shining Rocks. In the moaning of the gathering wind, he fancied he could hear Ben Coggins' pipes. But he could not see the rocks. The way he had entered this life lay hid in clouds and darkness.

#

"Have you come back to us then?" Judy asked Drum after supper.

Drum looked into the shadows around her eyes, "For awhile, I imagine. Divorced from the magazine, I'm still a photographer. Even working freelance, there will be some travel, but I mean to be here on our Creek more than I'm away. I don't plan to live the rest of my life among strangers."

"Mura made out very well here before the Depression," James put in. "You ought to do ok."

Drum nodded, "I don't expect to get rich, but I'll make a living. I've saved enough money to get along until I get a practice established."

Lizbet brightened, "We can walk on the mountain. I have things up there to show you." Ben, mute until now, listening to the others, burst into a laugh, "Lizbet would live up there in a hollow log if we'd let her."

Lizbet threw a rolled up magazine at his head. He reached up with one quick hand and caught it, handed it back to his sister, who, under her father's stern gaze, returned it to the table where she got it.

"Seriously, Drum," Polly said, "If you're going to be working from here, I'd like to talk with you about collaborating on a book I have in mind, while there is still something left in the Cove to photograph and write about."

Drum spread his hands wide, "At the moment, Polly, I'm open to all proposals." Then he smiled at a remembrance, "This sounds like some conversations I heard between Mura and Horace. They were fearful it would all be spoilt by now, but the mountains are green yet. Sorrow Creek still runs down to the river, and the Long Broad is still carrying it all away to Tennessee."

Judy spoke as if she were out of breath, "And for the time being, at least, we few are left. Love holds us close just a little longer."

All of them read the meaning in Judy's words, but none dared speak to it. James broke their silence, "I'm astounded and grateful that so much of what has blessed our lives is still with us."

Polly got up and started for the kitchen, "I'm going to make Judy's tea now. Anyone else want anything?"

Heads shook. Nobody expressed need or want. Lizbet went along to help. Judy lay back on her sofa and closed her eyes.

Ben looked at Drum, "So you really done with the magazine now?"

"I'm done with being one of Eric's minions, Ben. If they wanted to hire me on contract for a project that interests me, I'd likely do it."

Judy opened her eyes, and asked with teacherly bluntness, "What brought this on, Drum?"

Drum gave her the truth as best he could say it, "I was living my whole life away from anybody I knew or cared about, Judy. It was time to come home." Drum told them about his assignment in London, about the ravages of the war he'd seen there, about renewing his acquaintance with Liza Charon, about discussing art in a subway station while German bombs fell on her.

When he'd said all he could tell, James and Ben sat silent, with their heads down like mourners. Judy reached across Drum's chair to touch his hand, "I'm sorry. It wasn't your fault, you know."

Drum grimaced, squeezed her fingers, "I know that, Judy. Liza would have been there whether I had come along or not, but that's the story of my life. I'm the guilty bystander who walks away after others go down broken. I didn't do anything to cause the suffering, but I couldn't do anything to stay or ease it, either. As I told Polly on the way over here, I'm just a picture man, stealing images from other people's lives."

Polly came in with Judy's tea. Judy drank it down like medicine, and five minutes later was asleep. James picked up his beloved from the sofa as if she were a child and carried her off to bed.

Drum said good night to Lizbet and Ben. Ben handed over the keys to Drum's old pickup. Polly walked Drum out the door into the yard. The rain had stopped, clouds scattered. As Drum got into his pickup, he could see above the house the Shining Rocks gleaming under the moon. He rolled down his window, and Polly leaned her hands on the door as he fumbled his key into the switch.

"Soon as you're settled in, Drum, let me cook for you

and talk to you about the project I mentioned in there."

Drum looked up at her. He could not see her expression in the dark, but the moon behind her haloed her black hair with strands of spun silver. Where had he seen hair like that before? As soon as his mind posed the question, he knew.

"Polly, cook supper for me, and you can talk about anything you like. I'll bring some wine." Drum turned the key in the ignition. Polly stepped back as the engine fired and rumbled. Drum saw her in his mirror as he drove away, her solitary figure receding into the night. When her form was lost in the dark, he could still catch the glint of the moon in her hair.

Along the road to Annie's house, the gibbous moon lit the land well enough for Drum to see cows in their paddocks and cars in the yards of houses along the way. Once he had to slow as three grown does leisurely crossed the road. He was about to pass Polly Coggins' drive when a man stepped out of the trees right into the path of the pickup. He wore a long sleeved shirt and trousers that looked to be sewn of cured hides. He stared through the truck bearing down on him as if it didn't exist.

Drum swerved frantically in a hopeless effort to avoid a collision, caught a flash of the placid face just beyond his windshield as the back of the pickup slid around. He was certain he had hit the man although he heard no impact. After an eternity filling a second or two, the pickup finally halted on the opposite side of the road facing back the way he had come. Drum turned off the ignition, sat listening to the ringing in his ears until the ringing was louder than his thumping heart, then he got out and walked up the road in the shine of his headlights, looking to see who he had killed. Apart from his own long shadow stretching off toward the night, and the skid marks from his tires, he found no human sign beyond a bottle cap and the remains of a cigarette pack.

When he was certain his fear was not there, Drum walked back to the truck, slid under the wheel, closed the door, turned the key. The headlights dimmed, the starter moaned softly, something clicked and all was still.

"Oh, joy." Drum whispered under his breath. He got out, pushed the pickup as far as he dared toward the ditch to get it out of the way of traffic, climbed back in, set the brake, rolled up his window, cursed once, just for effect. His last thought before he fell fast asleep was that he recognized the face he had glimpsed through his windshield. It must have been a reflection. The face he'd seen was his.

Drum ran along the moon drenched road. His feet made no sound although he could feel the gravel biting his bare feet. The stones hurt and stung his tender soles, but Drum was running because there was somewhere he needed to be and he was late. He couldn't remember where or why, but the urgency filled and drove him. Ahead of him, something moved above the road, hurtling toward him out of the night. He stopped and waited for it.

A great dark bird, like a hawk, or a huge owl, glided soundlessly toward him. The broad wings spanned the road. Drum thought it was going to fly right into him. He threw his arms up over his head to ward it away. He could hear the air sigh as it passed close over him.

Drum started running again. Now he could hear his footfalls on the road beneath him. Somebody was knocking on the window of the pickup. There was a light. Drum opened his eyes to see Polly's face.

She looked worried, "Drum, are you all right in there?"

Drum rolled down the window, "I nearly ran over some drunk, and then my truck wouldn't start, Polly."

"You can stay over with me, Drum, and we'll see to your truck in the morning."

"Let me try it once more; It's been awhile now." Drum turned the key, the engine coughed and purred. Polly leaned through the window and planted on his mouth a firm and earnest kiss.

Before a startled Drum could participate, she stepped back and said, "Good night. Drum. Supper is tomorrow at eight."

He watched Polly walk back to her car, get in and drive away. Then he turned the pickup around and headed toward home. Drum felt pretty good. For once his life seemed whole, and he could think of no reason at all to leave it.

#

A shadow within a shadow, Talks To Trees watched the two humans depart the scene. He still lacked solid embodiment in this stream of being, but he was learning. He remained the Rider, after all. He had managed to make himself visible to the man with his face, and that pleased him. He was not too happy that in doing so, he might have killed the Shadow man as he had almost slain the Laurel boy.

In their latest near miss, their minds had touched briefly, and the Rider saw for an instant their common becoming. He would need to be patient and vigilant until Purpose revealed herself to him. Sensing the proximity of a Locus, he lifted his scarred hand over his head, seeking a strand of the Labyrinth and opened his questioning mind. Above him, the Torus flickered for a moment in the foggy air, then faded. *Wait* was all the answer he gleaned from the contact.

Up on her hill, Polly Coggins stood by her door, looking out into the misty dark, thinking about Benjamin Drum, and for a couple of heartbeats, saw the pulsating web of light revolving slowly above the road below. "Will O the Wisp," she whispered as the apparition faded. All her life, she had heard her elders' tales of the ghostly phosphorescencies that hung over the low valleys and creeks when nights were full of mist and mystery, but this was the first time she had seen one for herself.

#

I can give you something to help with that, Doctor Fitzwilliam said, his face and voice laden with fatherly concern. Judy shook her head. She remembered the scene vividly as her pain pulled her to wakefulness. It was the first thing she knew when she rose up out of sleep of a morning, and would be her last sensation before she slept that night. But the drugs left her head dull and her stomach painfully achurn. Thanks to Polly's tea, she could still sleep, and when she woke again, the tea didn't veil her thoughts and cloud her senses. Judy didn't want to spend her last days with her family in a stupor. As long as she could stand the hurt of being alive, the tea and other herbals Polly plied her with would have to suffice.

Judy had never been afraid to live, and now she wasn't afraid to die. Her thoughts dwelt on those she would leave behind. She didn't worry about her children. Ben and Lizbet were centered, grounded in their world, sure of love. They would bow before their loss, then rise up again to embrace the joys that came after. Judy was ready to embrace whatever joy waited her when she left them to their lives and followed her Ruth and Annie into the unknowable, unguessable What Next. She didn't imagine the sort of Heaven that had been pictured to her in church, but she had traveled among mountains all her adult life. She never expected a road to end just because it disappeared around a hill.

She did fret about James. He was strong, stoic, not a man of words, who lived through his hands. He would break before he would bend. What he could never bring himself to speak, Judy knew through his touch and his daily care for all who held his heart. As she looked around the room in the first light of this new day, Judy saw the skill of her husband's loving hands in every carefully wrought detail of door and window trim, in the wide locust boards of the floor, planed and sanded and polished to a honey glow, even in the furniture, all fashioned meticulously by James to please and comfort her.

And so Judy worried for her lover now. James needed touch and sight to maintain resonance and connection. Without her body here to hold and handle and look upon, bearing witness of the soul who shared his days, would James be able to hold to his place? Would he keep his bearings on Creation, or would he be adrift, unmoored, lost?

Judy prayed to the rising light to keep him close to the living, petitioned the fleeing shadows to hide him from grief. She reached over and touched the sleeping man beside her, laying her hand on his hip. Just short of wakefulness, James turned to her and pulled her fingers to his chest. The fingers told him all he needed to sustain his rest. *She is here.*

#

First thing next morning, Drum drove over the gap to Asheton, bought some groceries, a bottle of wine to take to

Polly come suppertime, and some clothes to supplement the few things he'd brought down on the train. He also went by Mountain Power to inquire about electrical service. They gave him a list of electricians who could wire his house. He meant to talk to James first. At the phone company, he learned that he could indeed have a phone installed, although he would be on a party line with three other families. When he passed High Country Photography, astonished to find it still in business, Drum yielded to nostalgic curiosity and went in.

The proprietor, a grizzled old curmudgeon named Henry Thurston, had been an aspiring young photographer when he bought the business through Oren Shorts. He remembered Ted Mura, had seen Drum's photographs in magazines, was impressed when Drum explained that this was where he had learned his craft. Thurston, it turned out, wanted to retire, had no family interested in continuing his enterprise, and was trying to sell.

"This would be a good base for you," he said, when he learned Drum planned to settle back in the area. Drum agreed it was a fine business, that the price was right, promised to consider the possibility, but left with no desire to be a shop-keeper photographer.

At Hyatt's Office Supply, Drum bought a typewriter and a stock of envelopes and paper. While he was in town he made several phone calls to editors he knew, told them he was available for assignments, "No wars," he said. They were glad to hear, promised to get in touch as projects developed. Drum drove back to the Cove with no firm offer of work, but had expected none this soon. He'd planted seed he was certain would bear fruit in due time.

On his way through the Cove, he stopped at the

Coggins place, found Judy sitting on her porch. "One of my better days," she explained. Drum told her he wanted to ask James about an electrician. James came in as Drum was leaving, said he would send somebody around the next week to see what Drum needed.

By the time Drum carried his groceries across his yard, the sun hung well down toward the river. It had been a productive day. He was looking forward to his supper. Arms laden with bags, he leaned back against his door to close it, and whispered to the still house, "I'm home."

#

Elizabeth Coggins walked down along the brook to the road, crossed the gravel track and followed the path through waving grass down to the river. All she saw seemed familiar, as if she remembered it from some time before, but there was nothing she could look on and say with assurance, *I know that.* She decided finally that she did not know this place, but believed it was a place that knew her. For as long as she was here she could claim belonging.

She watched a hawk circling high and lazy, following a thermal out over the river. Clouds gathered over the hills behind her. Thunder muttered, faint and far away. Elizabeth turned and started back toward the spring. As she reached the road following the river, off to her right, an ancient pickup with ricketyrattly side boards came coughing and clattering her way, trailing a dense cloud of gray smoke. The slight breeze lifted the cloud and carried it out across the water. The truck lurched and sighed to a stop and stood before her shuddering and mumbling as a man leaned out the driver's window. She had never seen his face except in photographs, but she recognized him immediately.

"I know you," She said solemnly, "I've seen your picture."

"That must have been a while ago, young lady. Nobody has taken my picture in a long time."

"Mura took it. Drum showed me."

The man looked only mildly surprised, "You know Mura and Drum?"

"I know Drum. Mura's dead, just like you, Mister Horace."

"Even us dead folks have to be alive somewhere. Are you dead, too?"

"No, I'm just looking around. I have to go back home now, but I think my mom might be here soon."

"Well, I have to go to Poplar Spring right now. You be careful. Don't stay here too long or you might forget your way. Look after my boy Drum when you get back."

"Mom says he's a hard one to look after."

"Always was," Horace smiled and waved, engaged his clutch, and the old truck heaved and sputtered on up the road.

Elizabeth followed the brook back to the spring house, drank some of the cool sweet water from her hands, laid her fingers on the fissure in the boulder where the little stream emerged from its rocky womb. She closed her eyes, whispered, "I'll be back," and the stone swallowed her.

#

Polly Coggins studied the image in the mirror before she went back to her kitchen. Makeup? No, not for Drum. He was not some editor or reviewer she needed to impress. Whatever impression she had made on him was made the night before, in the glare of a flashlight, when he'd accepted, or at least, not refused her invitation to supper. She hadn't been prettied up before that, when they spent the evening with James and Judy, and it hadn't put him off. She wasn't looking to impress, for all that. If she wanted anything from this man it was a simple connection. Either it was there already, waiting to be explored, or it wasn't. Tonight, if he showed up at all, she might begin to find out.

In the kitchen, she pulled the shepherd's pie from the oven, stuck it with a fork, judged it ready, and set about gathering a salad. Simple food to sit with whatever wine he brought, and if he forgot, coffee would serve just fine. For after, she had something a little stronger.

In her own opinion, as well as any who knew her, Polly, though not overly pretty, was finely shaped. Neat and small and quick and quiet. She didn't attract attention in a crowd, but stayed in the mind of any who noticed her. She had always been James' little sister. Big Brother was the one people saw. When the other children grew up and went off into the world, shy and thoughtful Polly had followed Emmalou Truelight's example and read stories with Annie. When Emmalou went away to learn the broader world, Polly had stayed in the Cove, content with the lives she knew and the stories in her books. She never read of any place that seemed to her better than the one she was in. She learned all Annie would teach her about words or herbs or deep knowing. All the stories she wanted to hear or tell swirled around her every day, and when she began to write her tales down, Annie's story demanded to be let out first.

Three years and a dozen rewrites later, her little book, as she called it, was in bookstores, and she was making the rounds doing readings and signing copies.

The novel sold well enough that a large house in New York inquired if she were doing anything else. She sent a couple of sample chapters of her current project, and *Sorrow Creek* was set to publish sometime the next year, assuming she could finish it on schedule. She was also pulling threads together for a third book, not fiction, that she had spoken of to nobody beyond family. That was what she meant to talk to Drum about tonight.

But books were not the main reason she had invited him to supper. She was honest with herself about that. She had made him a character in her book, always apart, wearing his aloneness like armor against the world. The real-life Drum was still solitary and strange and oddly compelling and they were no longer children with time to waste.

#

Drum decided to walk the half-mile to Polly's house. The moon, nearly full, cleared the treetops as he came out his door. It would rise to meet the starry dark and light him home. As he shut the door, he shouldered his bag, weighted and aromatic with a loaf of bread, still warm, and two bottles of wine, a chianti and a chardonnay. He hadn't known whether to get red or white, and the man at the store suggested he take one of each. For all his travels, Drum knew little about wine. He doubted Polly would hold his ignorance against him. By the time he passed the mailbox and turned up her drive, the day had faded to the point he could see his faint moonshadow leading him on. Fireflies sparked the dimness among the trees. Drum counted his breaths as he climbed Polly's sloping drive, slowed a bit when he could see the lights from the house lest he arrive at her door gasping, wondered at the same time why she had invited him, and why he was here. She never doubted his acceptance of her invitation, he was sure, for she had not even given him a chance to answer, simply walked away and left him in the dark, as if it were already arranged.

So here he was arriving like a suitor with bread and wine to share table with this strange little woman he barely knew anymore, had never really known much of, even when they were children together at Annie's school. She flittered through his childhood memories like a wee gray bird, as indeed she fluttered now through his present. She was still small and quiet, glimpsed more than seen, but now present with a power that made Drum hesitate before he knocked on her door, wondering if his future might be simpler if he just turned and walked away home.

Drum didn't get a chance to decide. The door opened as he held his fist poised before it, and Polly looked up at him with a smile like sunrise, "Come into my house, Benjamin Drum, and let me nourish you after your long day."

Mute, he held out his bag to her. She took it and looked inside, "Why, thank you sir. A photographer bearing gifts; That's dangerous, perhaps."

Polly stepped aside and waved her free arm in a welcoming arc. Her long pleated skirt swirled dramatically about her sandaled feet. Once inside, it was obvious to Drum that Polly's brother had built this house for her; it evidenced all the signs of his craft. Drum remembered then another house that stood on this very spot one stormy night when Horace Kellett had fished him from the creek and they sheltered here from the deluge with Polly's uncle Walt.

"I've been here before," Drum said, as he followed Polly across to her kitchen.

She handed him a couple of plates, stacked with

napkins and silverware on top, and pointed back at the table, "When was that? Except for family, you're my first visitor here."

While Polly opened the wine, she chose the red, Drum began laying out their places, "A long time ago, when your uncle Walt had an old shack here that he let Horace Kellett use. We spent the night there when everybody thought I'd been drowned in the flood."

"I remember. Poor Emmalou thought you were lost and gone, and that it was all her fault. Do you ever hear from her?"

"Not since a while now, Polly. Last I knew, she was teaching at some college in the Midwest. A photographer I worked with at the magazine, Richard Holford, was quite in love with her. They were planning to be married, I think."

"But you've never married. Surely you must have had your chances."

"I never stayed put in any one place long enough to get to know any woman that well, Polly. I was married to the magazine. You are still on your own, too, I see."

"There was no one in the cove who fancied me or whom I fancied. Until the book came out, I never went out into the world where I could meet anyone I didn't already know."

"And now?"

"Well, I'm looking."

"Good hunting. Any prospects?"

"Hard to say. Still early in the hunt. Timely that you should mention Uncle Walt's hut just now. That's what I want to write about"

Drum was intrigued, "About the old shack?"

Polly laughed, "That was my favorite place to hide out

when I was little. I could tell you tales. But I want to write about my uncle and Horace. Did you know that after he disappeared, Uncle Walt made several trips over to the High Balsam to look for him. Camped out up there for weeks at a time. Said it was the most beautiful country in the world. He had Oren Shorts haul Nancy over there to carry his gear. Claimed he needed her to have somebody to talk to."

Drum shook his head. "I remember that old mule. Walt really did believe Nancy could speak, I think."

Polly handed the salad bowl to Drum to toss the greens, and set the pie between their places, "Uncle Walt believed until his dying day that Horace was still alive back up there someplace. I want to write a book about their friendship, and my uncle's obsession with finding Horace, and about their treks on the High Balsam. You were part of it. And you are able to make true images of that strange wild place. Interested?"

"More than interested. And for once, I have some time to choose my own project. I'd be honored to be your photographer."

They sat down and Polly served their pie, "Collaborator," she corrected. She lifted her glass, "Here's to Uncle Walt, and friendship."

Drum raised his glass to meet hers, "And to Horace Kellett, wherever he is."

After supper, Drum helped wash and stow the dishes. Polly set out a plate of shortbreads, and brought a bottle of single malt from a cupboard. She held the bottle up for Drum to see, "Do you drink this stuff, or would you rather have coffee?"

Drum pointed at the bottle then folded his hands and bowed his thanks. Polly began to think she might like this man a lot, who gave her speech only when it served best. She was adept enough at her craft to know that a word too many dilutes the power of all that are needful. She saw the same economy of expression in the spare uncluttered images of Drum's photographs. He was not someone who needed to be impressed or to impress. He engaged what was before him and embraced the reality. Made the most of what he had to hand. *Just like me*, Polly thought.

They talked for another hour about times past and times to come, by which time their glasses were empty. The shortbreads went untouched. Finally, Drum stood, a bit stiffly, it seemed to Polly, and fetched his jacket. Polly kissed him as he went out the door, and this time he was prepared and participated fully. The kiss went slightly beyond friendly. Drum stepped out into the good night. Polly waved and closed the door behind him, leaned against it thinking there might be more in him than pictures for her book.

Drum walked away among the trees down to the road. Patches of bright moonlight alternated with deep shadow. An owl called. Drum had a sense of something or someone following him. He stopped a couple of times and looked around, listened, but nothing emerged from the darkness under the trees, and none spoke to him except the repetitious owl.

As Drum passed Polly's mailbox, a pool of dark in the middle of the moonwashed road stirred and rose, assumed a canine form. The dog, if that is what it was, looked at him, as if it had been waiting, then trotted down the road ahead of him. From out of the shadows along the drive, two more appeared, and without approaching him, took up stations to either side and kept pace. Some hunter's dogs, Drum thought, who had gotten separated from their master during the chase, and had taken up with the first human they encountered. They walked with him the whole way until he turned down his drive. Then the trio closed ranks, their black shapes merging to resemble one great three-headed wolf, and moved off down the road toward the river.

Drum let himself into his house, not bothering to make a light. He sat for a long time in Annie's big arm chair looking down at the garden and the river under the moon. He thought about the kind of photographs he might make on the High Balsam. More than that, he thought about the photographs he would like to make of Paulette Coggins. Her close company stirred something deep in him that had not been reached before. Her voice and touch had left him profoundly alert and wakeful, and at the same time wholly content and at peace with himself. Was this something like love, then? Not so much an emotion or a desire, but a state of heightened senses and acute awareness of everything? Is that all it took for life to be joined and whole? One person? The right person? Was it Polly's doing that he felt younger, lighter tonight, finally at home in his world? As her uncle Walt might have said, she had spelled him for sure. He wouldn't fight it. It felt good.

Cradled in the big chair, Drum stilled into sleep. He dreamed about three dogs sitting with him in the circle on old man McMinn's mountain, where Drum had dreamed Li his first night in Horace's cabin. The moon was setting over the High Balsams. There were other figures around the circle. Drum could barely make out their forms in the dark. Fireflies traced slow orbits around and above, their strobing lights making a music like wee bells.

A tall figure stood at the center of all. Her form kept

shifting and re-shaping as Drum watched. Frustrated that he couldn't see her face, he thought at first it was Li from his boyhood dream, then she seemed to be Liza Charon, and after that he was certain it was Polly until he realized Polly was seated beside him in the circle. The woman began to hum a tune that Drum remembered Annie singing.

He heard himself asking, "Annie?"

It wasn't Annie. The moon slipped from behind a cloud, revealed the dark woman who had taken the child from him outside Trinity church.

She pointed to Polly, "Give her to me, Rider."

Drum scrambled to his feet and stood between the Dark Woman and Polly. The Woman loomed huge and towering, he no bigger than a child. She could have brushed him aside with one hand. Drum's voice trembled with panic, "No, not yet! I need her now."

#

Drum opened his eyes to bleak wintry light. He'd fallen asleep on the train, slumped against the window. The side of his face hurt. His neck hurt. His head throbbed. His trip had been a disaster. His oldest friend had died right before he left, and while he was gone, her firstborn had carried his name off to war. He'd spent most of January in army hospitals photographing faces he wished he'd never seen for an article the army was determined would never be published.

Out on the platform, gathering his baggage, Drum looked around, saw Henry Thurston across the street, going into his photography studio. Thurston saw him wave, returned the gesture and beckoned before he went in his door. Under the overcast, Asheton lay colorless, forlorn, vaguely diminished, like a town under siege.

Drum found a phone, dialed Polly's number. The phone rang and rang, and he was about to hang up when Lizbet answered.

Wondering as he spoke why people instinctively ask unnecessary questions, "Lizbet, is that you?"

"Drum? Are you all right? Where are you.?"

"I've been better, Lizbet. I just got into Asheton. How are you?"

"I'm staying down here with Aunt Polly now," Lizbet said, as if that were an answer.

Drum thought she sounded old somehow, not like a child at all. "How's your dad?"

"He's still drinking, just like he's been doing since Mom died."

"Is Polly there?"

"She's up checking on Dad. She'll be back in a little."

"How is she?"

"She worries a lot about Dad and me, but her new book's selling, so she's happy. You want her to come pick you up?"

"If she has time, Lizbet. When she gets in, just ask her to phone me at Henry Thurston's place."

"Sure," Lizbet said, and hung up. Drum sighed, hefted his bags, and crossed the street to Highland Photography. He hoped Thurston had a bottle ready.

Polly rescued Drum from Thurston before they'd had time to get properly drunk, just shook her head at him on the drive home. "I hope you aren't starting down the road with James."

Drum was quiet. The whiskey hadn't helped his headache.

Back at Annie's house, Polly insisted on making a light supper from the groceries she'd brought. Whether from the food, or Polly's company, or the herbal tea she made him drink, Drum surprised himself by feeling better. After they ate, he sat on the floor spread a stack of black-and-white prints around him. "Look at these, before you go."

Polly sat beside him and they slowly sorted through the pictures of wounded soldiers in Army hospitals, unsparing and truthful images of broken souls and damaged bodies, portraits of pain. "So many," she said finally. "And you don't get paid for these?"

"Oh, I get paid. Eric says they are brilliant. But the Army didn't like them at all. They think it will hurt recruiting and encourage the enemy. So the magazine is scrapping the story."

Polly saw tears scrolling down Drum's face. She put an arm around his shoulder, "They're just pictures, Drum."

Drum gave her a look of utter despair. "You weren't there, Polly. You didn't hear their voices. These were only boys, most of them. I'm not crying for the pictures. I'm crying for Ben and Caleb and Ronan and all who are getting wasted over there."

Polly stood. It was time to go. "Are you sure it's all a waste, Drum?"

Drum shook his head. He did not look up, kept staring at his photographs. "Like Horace told us, this won't be the last time. It will all be done over again one day too soon."

#

A morning in March, before daylight, Drum's phone rang. Eric's voice sounded far away, "We need somebody to spend the summer in China, assuming we can get you in and out around the war. The State Department wants some friendly text with lots of touristy pictures. You interested?"

Drum didn't hesitate, "I'm already committed to a

book project down here this summer, Eric. Besides, isn't that Richard Holford's territory?"

A half minute of silence followed. Then, Eric's voice again, in the quiet paternal tone he used when he wanted to be serious and personal, "I'm sorry Drum, I assumed you knew by now. Richard died in China back during the winter. I had to call his fiancée. I think you know her."

"Emmalou Truelight. We went to school together as children. I haven't heard from her in years, but Richard talked about her when we were in London. He was obviously in love. What happened to Richard, Eric? I hear there is fighting in China."

Eric ventured an ironic laugh, which came out a hoarse bark, "There is fighting in China. Hell, the whole world is fighting now, but some local contagion got him, like some peasant farmer. It isn't fair."

Drum decided he wouldn't have taken this assignment if he hadn't promised Polly to help with her book, "It isn't fair to the peasant farmers, either, Eric. They have wives and babies who mourn them just as much as Emmalou mourns your precious photographer. I'm sorry Asian microbes have inconvenienced your magazine."

"Drum, I didn't mean..."

"I know, Eric, and I'm sorry. You're right. It isn't fair. Nothing in this poor benighted world is fair. Some of us have our life stolen from us, and the rest of us just throw it away."

Drum hung up. He waited a few minutes for the phone to ring, but Eric didn't call back. Drum wandered off to the kitchen to make his breakfast. He wished Polly were here to bear witness to his hurt. He wouldn't expect her to say anything. He just wanted somebody in his space who would give a damn.

After breakfast, Drum showered cold and drove off to Asheton to buy one of those electric water heaters he'd seen advertised in the Citizen. On the way back home in the afternoon, he stopped by to check on James Coggins. He found James slumped in the rocking chair on his front porch, asleep or drunk, an empty bottle on the floor beside him. Drum didn't wake him, got back in his pickup and drove away home. He was glad to have the best part of his day still ahead. Polly Coggins had invited him to supper again.

#

By the time he should leave for supper, fog and fine rain spilled from the gap down the cove toward the river. Drum debated with himself, finally decided to walk. He pulled his poncho over his head and stepped out into the wet. He needed a little air before he saw Polly and Lizbet, a little space to distance himself from his depressing day, make himself fit company. They were the closest to family he had in the world. He wanted every time he spent with them to be worth remembering if the day came when he, like Richard Holford, lay dead among strangers in some far place.

The rain in his face brought his mind back to the moment. Walking pushed his blood around, warmed his aching heart. As he came by Polly's mailbox he was almost ready to enjoy their company. Somewhere in the trees up beyond the house, Owl called his name. Drum laughed out loud at the absurdity of his life, at himself for taking it so seriously, "I'm coming," he told Owl, "But not before I've had my supper." As he crossed the yard, window light reached out to him like welcoming arms. Drum walked toward the light, expecting Lizbet would be watching for him and open the door when he reached the steps.

The door opened on cue and Polly leaned out and kissed him lightly, as he stood on the porch, shaking out his poncho,

"You're wet," she observed.

"Only on the outside."

Drum hung his poncho on a peg beside the door, and followed her inside. As he trailed her toward the kitchen, he noticed the table set for two. A young fire burned brightly on the hearth.

"Where's Lizbet?"

Polly answered over her shoulder, "Pajama party. She's staying over with the Bradley girls. Nobody here tonight but us old folks."

She handed Drum a bottle of merlot, "Open this. Anyway, I thought you came just to see me."

Drum astounded himself by blushing, tried to think of some clever retort, then gave her the simple truth, "I wouldn't have walked this far in the rain to see anybody else."

Supper consisted of another of Polly's salads, which she invented in endless variety as the output from her kitchen garden varied from day to day, and a frittata she had made in a covered iron skillet atop her stove. Polly's meals were always simple, always filling and tasty and colorful, pleasing the eyes as well as the stomach. *She cooks just like me,* Drum thought as he poured wine into their glasses, *except her kitchen's neater.*

They ate slowly, as the quiet house gathered love around them, drawing sustenance as much from the other's presence as from the food they shared. Polly explained her process for making a frittata. Drum told her about his encounter with James. Polly didn't comment, just shook her head and stared at her wine.

Trying to lighten their mood, Polly asked, "Are we still on for the High Balsam this summer?"

Drum nodded, "I've kept my card clear, Polly." Then he told her about his call from Eric, "Have you heard from Emmalou lately?"

"Only what Maude tells me, which isn't a lot. Maude doesn't get out much anymore. I used to see her at the grocery now and then. I ought to go by and check on her."

Drum's dark spell was beginning to settle on him again. When Polly offered spirits after supper, Drum refused. He was depressed enough already and whiskey would only push him further down the slope. He offered to help with the dishes.

Polly shook her head, "There aren't that many, I'll do them later."

Drum started toward the door. They could hear rain falling hard on the roof. Polly said, "You don't need to go out in this. You can stay here, don't you know?"

Drum shrugged, "If I hang around, I'll only depress you, Polly. I'm weighed down tonight with years and losses."

Polly stood with her hands on his shoulders until he met her gaze, "Then let me unburden you, Benjamin Drum."

Her fingers moved to the button of his shirt. As she loosed it, Drum gave her a look that might have indicated either amazement or panic. He spoke barely above a whisper, "I've never done this before, Polly."

"Neither have I," she admitted, "but we can learn."

TADAHITO

Drum woke tangled in a maze of golden arms and legs and scented hair. The face inches from his own looked familiar. It took a second to drag his mind to wakefulness and recognize Paulette. He had never seen a woman's face so close and unguarded. Her immediacy frightened him. Then he saw the strands of silver gray among the raven, the lines of a life lived deep inscribed around eyes and mouth, now softened by sleep. The face no longer young, not yet old, ageless and, Drum realized at this instant, beloved.

They had fallen asleep together atop the sheets. When Drum gained his feet, he paused a moment to look upon this body that had embraced him like a revelation. A loveliness that broke his heart and healed his life to behold. His photographer's mind snapped a picture and he drew the cover up over Polly's sleeping form, bent and kissed her brow. She murmured in her sleep but did not stir. Drum collected his clothes and went off barefoot to the kitchen to make their breakfast if he could find it.

When Polly woke and followed, she found Drum stirring a bowl of eggs with a fork. She took his face between her hands and kissed him. He set the bowl on the counter and kissed her back. They stepped arm's length apart and held hands and circled, laughing like children. Love was not what they had imagined it might be. Love had not driven them together with hunger or desire. They had not found love; they had been found. Love had waited for them here. They had seen the heart's door open and stepped inside and now it held them, stirring their souls together like the eggs in the bowl.

The new risen sun flooded the kitchen with golden light. There was no loneliness in the house at all. They made their breakfast, sat outside on the steps and ate it in the bright morning. Polly said, "If you don't have to rush away, walk up the creek with me and we'll check on James."

Drum could not think of anything requiring him to rush away. As the sun topped the trees, lifting the fog above the water, they slowly traversed the boulder field through which the creek descended. The water, high from the night's rain, created a tumult that didn't allow conversation, so they made their way in silence, as two familiar souls on a familiar path, now apart, now touching hands to stay one another on slippery stones.

When Drum saw the crested iris, on childish impulse, he bent to pick it for her, then, before he reached, he thought better of it; he'd never seen a vase in Polly's house. She would not approve of murdering a flower for momentary pleasure. Drum straightened, glanced sheepishly in her direction. Polly laughed. She knew.

The path along Sorrow Creek, kept clear by occasional hunters and more frequent trout fishers, ascended the cove toward the Shining Rocks more directly than the winding county road, lessening the distance between the Coggins households considerably. Along the way, Polly and Drum had to scramble up a couple of steeps to circumvent small waterfalls, but in the main, passage was relatively easy.

At one point, they came to a rickety bridge where the older road had once crossed the creek.

"This is where Horace and your uncle fished me out of the flood," Drum said. "It still makes me cold just to think about it."

Polly laughed, "Last night was all their fault, then."

Drum kept a serious face, though there was mischief in his eyes, "I give them more credit than blame for that."

At the place where Drum had rescued Emmalou, there was no log bridging the stream, but an overgrown path still led off from the far bank in the direction of Maude Truelight's place. When they turned to their right through the woods toward where Judy had kept her garden, they heard the sound of an engine ahead. When they came clear of the trees, James bounced along atop his little gray Ferguson tractor, plowing. When he looked up, Polly waved. James cut his engine, climbed down, and shambled toward them.

He was sober, though he looked to have had a long night. For the first time in months, he rewarded his sister with a smile, "I'm getting a late start here, but there's still time to make enough to keep us out of the grocery store this winter. I'll have to learn how to can things, unless you want to come help me."

"Oh, I'll help, James," Polly promised, "and Lizbet's a good hand in the kitchen. You grow it, and between us, we'll put it by."

James shook Drum's hand, "You keeping company with my little sister now? I'll have to keep an eye on you."

Drum grinned, a little self-consciously, "I'm harmless, James. I just do as she tells me."

James actually laughed, "Then I'd better keep close watch on both of you. Come up to the house. I need to tell youns about something."

James turned and they followed. Polly looked at Drum,

formed the question with her lips,

What? Drum shrugged, and took her hand as they walked.

In the kitchen, James gestured toward the table, and without asking, poured them all coffee, still almost hot on the stove. Polly and Drum sat obediently, looked at James expectantly as he sipped from his cup. Then he set it down and stared at them in wonderment, as if what he was about to tell was beyond even his own believing.

James took a deep breath, and spoke as matter-of-factly as if discussing the weather, "Judy was here last night."

Polly looked incredulous, "You mean you dreamed about her?"

"No, Polly, she was here, well and whole. I could have reached out and touched her, but I was afraid to." James looked at Drum, "You're thinking I was drunk, and I was drunk enough, but I sobered up quick after that. I know what I saw."

"James..." Polly began.

"She was here, Sister," James did not raise his voice, but there was iron in it, "She said she had always stayed close, even though I couldn't see her, but that if I kill myself, I'll do it alone. She said if I ever know any nearness of her, it will be by living out her love for all of us."

James gazed intently at the silent couple across the table from him, "That's what she said. I know it sounds crazy, but I believe it happened."

Drum nodded, glanced at Polly, then looked back at James, "Life seems craziest when it gets most real, James. I believe you."

After his confessional, James walked with his sister and Drum as far as his tractor. When they reached the creek, they heard it start again and drone away on another tack.

Polly seemed troubled, "Something's happened to James. He isn't a man to believe in spirits and ghosts."

Drum tried to ease her concern, "Well, Polly, he's certainly had some sort of psychological experience, maybe a psychic one. I've had stranger encounters. You shouldn't worry. When you've had his sort of trauma, sometimes things just shift suddenly."

"You don't think he's delusional or anything, then?"

"Polly, if his delusion keeps him away from his bottle, I don't think we'd do him a favor to try and cure him of it. He has to make his own sense of what has happened to him. He has to find his own reason to go on. He seems to be coming round. I think we need to give him some time and a little space."

Polly threw Drum a strange forlorn little smile, "I hope you're right. For his sake, and for Lizbet's. She needs her dad right now, and James hasn't been up to the job."

"How is Lizbet handling all this, Polly?"

"It's hard to know. She doesn't talk about Judy's dying, or James. She doesn't ever mention her brother. She is polite and friendly and helpful around the house. She reads a lot, spends a lot of time wandering the woods, but that isn't new. Somehow, though, she just seems detached. She reminds me of you when you were a boy."

"It's her way of coping with her losses, Polly. She'll reach out again when it is time."

"You sound so sure of that."

Drum smiled, "The voice of experience."

"Well, what made you reach out to the living, Drum?"

"You don't need to ask that, Polly. You did."

Polly stopped, and turned to face him, "I didn't make

257

you quit your job."

Drum felt vaguely like he'd been accused of something, "No, but you made me glad I did."

They walked on in silence until they reached the bridge at Polly's drive.

"You coming back up?" Polly asked.

It seemed to Drum like a rhetorical question. "I need to go home and check my mail."

"What do we do now, Drum? Is this what they call a relationship?"

"Well, Polly, I certainly feel related. What do we do now? I reckon we'll work on your book. If we are still speaking by the time we finish, we might just have a future."

Polly thought it didn't sound like a joke. She waved up toward her car, "You want me to give you a lift home.?"

"I need to walk in the sun, Polly. Come down tonight and I'll fix your supper."

Polly hesitated just an instant, "How about tomorrow?"

Drum leaned to her and kissed her on the cheek, "Tomorrow, then. Bring Lizbet if she's back, and invite James." He turned then and walked away toward the road. Polly watched with arms folded until he was out of sight beyond the trees.

#

The next night, Drum served the best beef stew he'd ever made, with potatoes and squash and green beans from his garden. Polly brought wine, but drank it alone as Drum declined due to his touchy stomach. James shook his head and held his hand over his glass when Polly reached the bottle toward him.

Lizbet looked surprised, "You quit drinking of a

sudden, Dad?"

Unperturbed, James just laughed, "I'm taking a vacation from spiritual drink until I can enjoy it again."

He and Lizbet drank tea with mint and lots of lemon. When he tasted, James nodded his approval, "I see my sister must have taught you how to make proper sweet tea, Drum. It ain't fit to consume unless it makes your teeth hurt."

They ate. Everyone had seconds. They talked about things vital and trivial, and although none there were oblivious to Judy's absence, her memory did not haunt them, but brought her love back to their company. She seemed a tiny bit less gone from them with every mention of her name.

Hours later, when James stood to go, they all stood with him. Drum shook his hand and Polly and Lizbet walked with him to the door. Lizbet and Polly bent heads together in whispered conference, and when Polly closed the door behind her brother, Lizbet went with him.

Polly came back to where Drum stood at the table, and was about to say something when the phone rang, one long and two short, Drum's ring. He picked it up, aware that Maude Truelight was probably listening on the line.

Polly could only hear Drum's side of the conversation, "Benjamin Drum...Yes... I'm definitely interested; this is just my sort of thing, but I have another project coming up right now. I'm not sure how we might schedule this... Let me see what I can work out at my end, and I'll call you back...Yes, Ron, I would like to do this, if I can. Can I get back to you? Goodbye, and thanks."

"Sounds like big doings." Polly said it like a question.

"Some guy named Ron Seward from the Sierra Club. They want to do a picture book on the Los Padres national forest and the Big Sur coast, and Eric, of all people, told them I'd be the man to make their photographs. Spectacular country, from the pictures I've seen. They'll pay travel and per diem plus my fee, but I don't want to put off our book any longer."

Polly launched a broad smile, "I think you should go."

"You do?" Drum looked like a child who had just been told he could keep the puppy who followed him home from school.

"And I think you should take me with you," Polly added.

"Sit," Drum pointed to her chair.

He picked up the phone, dialed, recited some numbers to an operator several times, finally, "Ron? Good, I'm glad you're still there. I'd be elated to do your project, and I have someone here who should do the text. We've worked together before. We see with the same eye. Her writing would be my images put to words... Paulette Coggins, *The Warwoman* and *Sorrow Creek*... Yes, I'm sure. I've just been speaking with her. She's my neighbor down here... Same as me, I'd think... Alright then, I'll have her call you in the morning and you can work out terms... Me too, Ron. Goodbye now." Drum hung up the phone, drank down his last swallow of tea, poured a little wine in the glass and lifted it toward Polly, "That was too easy. We're in, it seems."

Polly shook a finger at him, "You made up the part about us having worked together."

Drum grinned, "It's a lie right now, but it won't be soon."

#

It wasn't exactly easy, as things turned out. There were numerous phone calls and negotiations. Seward's people seemed on the verge of picking another writer, male, but Drum held firm, insisted he couldn't do the project without Polly, and three weeks later, Drum and Polly were walking barefoot along a sloping stony beach among boulders sculpted by the ocean into bizarre monuments, riddled with holes and small caves. They reminded Drum of the figures in Moore's sketch pad that appeared to have been shaped by time and weather more than any human hand.

Riotous surf thundered down on the beach. Through the sand underneath their feet, they could feel the interminable pounding, like the earth's beating heart. Past the beach the mountains reared straight up from the ocean. Three miles away, a cone shaped peak stood as tall as any of the ridges in the High Balsam. The sun came up over the mountain and ruby light flooded across the wet sand through a cavity in one of the great boulders. Polly ran and stood in the opening, her arms stretched out to reach the stone on either side as she gazed up at the mountain beyond. Her shadow spilled like dark water down the sand behind her toward the sea.

Instinctively, Drum raised his camera and removed the lens cap. He clicked off frame after frame as the sun climbed out of the mountain and the light shifted and flared while Polly stood transfixed, as if bound to the rock. Drum was reaching into his bag for a lens filter when he heard a voice behind him, "She looks like a crucifixion."

Startled, Drum whirled about. A small dark man, also burdened with camera and gear, also barefoot, with his shoes interlaced and hanging around his neck, bowed solemnly, then smiled apologetically, "Sumi masen. So sorry. I intrude." He started to turn away.

"Not at all," Drum waved his arm to take in the scene,

"Help yourself."

The man bowed again, but held out his hand rather than reaching for his camera, "Doomo. Tadahito is grateful to meet you. You are also a photographer?"

Drum shook the offered hand, "Drum. I'm here on an assignment from the Sierra Club, but this morning, I'm making pictures just for myself."

"So," Tadahito's eyes twinkled, "The best one's are always made for ourselves, so desu?"

Polly had been watching them from her perch, and came back across the beach to join them, "Are you two comparing notes, or just admiring the scenery?"

Tadahito, whom Drum had thought quaintly reserved, even shy, turned to Polly with a frankly admiring stare, "The most admirable aspect of the scenery has drawn near to us now."

Without waiting for an introduction, Polly thrust out her hand toward the new arrival, "Paulette Coggins, I'm writing words to explain Drum's pictures."

Another bow from the dark man, and another smile, "Tadahito."

Polly returned both, "I'm surrounded by photographers, it seems. Are you here on assignment, Tadahito, or is this a vacation?"

Tadahito shrugged, "Hai; work is the same as play for a photographer perhaps. Photographs for a magazine in Tokyo." Tadahito raised both hands over his head and turned in a circle, "All this. Mountain and sea. Very Japanese, but Japan is more green, perhaps." His *r*'s came out more like *d*'s.

Polly laughed, "So is Carolina, where we're from, but our mountains are not so robust as these, I think. Are you staying nearby, Mister Tadahito?"

Tadahito pointed to a cluster of low buildings visible among a crowd of huge boulders down the beach, "Just there, at Bixbe Landing, my home far from home."

Polly clapped her hands in delight, which seemed to startle Tadahito. He recovered quickly as Polly proclaimed, "So are we. You should join us for dinner tonight."

Tadahito bowed again. Drum wondered if he ever got tired of doing it. He looked at Drum. When Drum nodded and smiled, Tadahito turned back to Polly, "Your kindness honors this stranger on your shore. Dinner will be much anticipated."

Tadahito turned then and walked back the way he had come. As they stood watching him go, Drum punched Polly's shoulder playfully, "Why, Polly Coggins, I think you are taken with the little guy."

Polly leaned into an enthusiastic kiss, "Don't be silly, Drum. I'm taken with you. Tadahito is just interesting."

They continued up the beach where Drum had spied a relic in the distance, the half-buried skeleton of a craft run aground in some past season's storm, waiting for another storm to carry it back home to the sea. The sun rose higher. Gulls wheeled and cried. Away out on the water, Drum could see the spouting of whales, their huge dark bodies rising and falling away northward through the chop. Waves reared with menacing swiftness and crashed like accusations on the rocks. Drum felt the impacts through the soles of his feet, and a formless unnamable fear lay in his heart as cold as the ocean.

He trembled suddenly in the chill wind, saw Polly looking at him strangely. "Let's go back now," he said. "It's going to be a long day. I need a nap."

#

They had lunch on a terrace brinking a high bluff overlooking the beach and the azure ocean. As they ate, they talked little, preferring to listen to the liquid surge and sigh of the sea below. The fish was tasty enough, the wine better than the food, the grapes grown just eighty miles away, the waiter told them. After lunch, they met with Jake Reagan, their guide from the Sierra Club. They had three weeks to do this, he said. In the morning, they would be off to Cone Peak, just three miles from the shore but nearly a mile high. On the ascent they would pass through the whole range of habitat and terrain they would encounter in the Santa Lucia. It would be a good place to start, accessible, and give them a proper feel for the country.

Jake took them to an outfitters and helped them select their gear, although most of the things on his list, they'd brought with them.

"We'll give this one a day to start," He said, spreading out his map before them, "We can camp near the summit if you need more time up there, but with summer bearing down, once you get above the fog, the black flies will carry you away. I'd advise to come back down for the night, and go up again next day, if you want. It's only about a three hour walk."

The rest of the afternoon they spent exploring caves and rock formations along the beach north of the Landing. The sunset came on like the end of the world and consumed three rolls of Drum's precious Kodachrome. When they went in to supper, Tadahito was at the bar in animated conversation with two pretty young women dressed to maximize display of their tans. The women seemed anxious to make an impression on him, and Tadahito appeared confident that he was making his own.

When he saw Polly and Drum, he disengaged from his admirers with much bowing and clasping of hands, walked over to their table and sat down.

"Those lovelies seemed to have fancied you considerably, Tadahito," observed Polly.

Tadahito shrugged and smiled, "Gaijin with a camera, always a curiosity." He winked at Drum as he said it.

Polly thought Tadahito would excite curiosity whenever he came among youthful females. Dark and small, but fit and solid, he had what Polly thought of as presence. Quick and sure in his movements, he exuded purpose and mystery. He attracted.

He plied both Polly and Drum with a multitude of questions concerning what they were about and where they were from. When Polly described Asheton, Tadahito nodded enthusiastically, "Tadahito lives in a city among mountains, but there is also the sea. In Japan, like in this place, the sea is never far away, even on a mountain. There is a fine harbor there, also a famous church. In our Urakami District, most of the people have been Christians for hundreds of years. For a long time they were persecuted, but there is more liberty in these things now."

Drum asked Tadahito if he were a Christian.

Tadahito shrugged, "Mother and sisters are Catholics. I observe their practice."

"My parents were Baptists," Drum said, but I observe a photographer's practice." He spoke with a straight face, but Tadahito appeared to think his response hilarious.

When Drum told him about their plans to climb up Cone Peak next day, Tadahito beamed. Looking at Polly, he said, "That is where I go. Perhaps we may encounter along the way."

#

At the first hint of dawn, Jake met Drum and Polly outside the hotel. While the sky brightened above the mountains, they piled all their gear into his battered truck and drove away up the coast until the fog banked out over the ocean rolled in and devoured the sea and the beach below and all of the road more than fifty feet ahead of them. Jake set his headlights on dim, slowed and drove steadily onward into the murk. He seemed used to it.

When they reached the trailhead, Jake parked the truck in a small pull-off blasted out of the rocks. They could hear surf pounding and thumping at the foot of the cliff just beyond the road. The fog lifted only a little as they took up their packs and moved off up a steep, canyon-like valley, among firs and redwoods and ferns and flowers. A creek rioted alongside their path as they ascended. The mountain rose steeply to either side away up into the pervasive fog, her stony bones thrusting through her dripping green mantle, forcing them to scramble and detour continuously as they climbed. Unseen birds called to them, the songs familiar only to Jake. Once they crossed the tracks of a bear, and once heard the cry of a large cat from somewhere above them on the mountain.

They toiled upward through this rain forest a long time, it seemed, although it wasn't more than a couple of miles. Suddenly they emerged from the fog which spread away behind and beneath like a steamy sea. Ahead rose a different world. The sun crested the mountains eastward and burned like the eye of judgment over stone strewn slopes dotted with scrubby pine, chaparral, and tenacious grasses already browning with the relentless June sun and a drought that would likely go unbroken until fall.

As Jake had predicted, an omnipresent swarm of black flies settled around the three humans. The humans slathered on repellent, which made tiny fly corpses stick to their bodies when swatted. Polly endured the onslaught with a minimum of complaint. Jake was stoic, pretending they didn't exist. Drum seemed oblivious when he was manipulating his camera, which engaged more of his time than walking. They finally reached the summit past noon to find Tadahito there before them, sitting against a rock, eating a boiled egg, his gear piled at his feet.

He waved and smiled, as if waiting for them, "At last, we are all here."

At the summit, steady up-slope breeze from the ocean discouraged the flies. Jake began to lay out their lunch. Polly walked over to talk to Tadahito. Drum set up his tripod, put a long lens on his camera and began compassing the horizon. Blue ocean appeared to west as the morning's fog began to lift and fade. Thin shining tracery of surf writhed along the crests of waves just off the beaches. More rugged peaks and steep shadowed valleys ranged eastward, and far beyond those, higher mountains still, with white-tipped summits, sharp and precipitous.

Jake laid his hand on Drum's shoulder and pointed north, "Yonder's Pimkolam. Tomorrow we'll start heading up that way."

"Tell me about Pimkolam," Drum said, shading his eyes with his hand and staring off in the direction Jake had pointed.

Jake handed him a pair of binoculars, "It's the highest peak in the Santa Lucia. The First People, the Esselen , said it is where the world began."

Drum peered through the binoculars, "I see it." He said, and handed the binoculars to Tadahito, who had come up behind him and was looking over his shoulder.

Jake continued, "The First People were doing ritual up there two thousand years before the Brits put up Stonehenge."

The three foreigners stared and pointed and marveled while Jake brought out sustenance. When he had their provisions arranged, he called, "Let's eat."

Tadahito said he'd already had his lunch, but joined them, "for the fine company." He shared his tea from a thermos and some pickled plums he'd packed up the mountain. "The salt is good for the sun," he told them with his ever-ready smile. He fired a constant barrage of questions at Jake concerning the Santa Lucia, the weather, the animals, the best way to walk from here to there and what was to be found here and what was waiting there. Although Tadahito wasn't his paying client, Jake answered as readily as any Park Ranger.

After they packed away the remains of their lunch, Drum and Tadahito began making photographs of the surrounding ridges. A pair of hawks circled in courting dance high above and Drum removed his Leica from the tripod, changed the lens and began shooting at the pair one frame after another. When they plummeted down below the ridgeline and continued their play above a lake far below, Drum stepped out alongside a large boulder to catch the amorous raptors along with their shadows on the water.

"Careful, there," Jake admonished. "Those stones are loose, not as stable as they look."

Drum was careful, worked his way down the slope a bit for a clearer shot of the birds before they broke off their aerial ritual. Tadahito and Polly walked to the brink to get a better view. As Jake had advised, the stone was loose underfoot. Tadahito slipped, and would have fallen if

Polly had not grabbed his arm to steady him. He managed to keep his feet, thanks to her, but unleashed a shower of shards down the slope toward Drum. Drum, his eye to his camera, heard the rattle above him, and looked up just in time to try to dance out of the way. His footing gave way and he toppled. Drum had a split second to toss his camera up to Tadahito, saw him catch it, and then was down, sliding along the steep slope amid a swarm of small stones and dust, first on his belly, then on his back, the sharp rock tearing and bruising as he went. He flailed about trying to grab something stationary to anchor himself, only succeeding in wounding his hands on jagged edges. Suddenly, he was airborne.

Drum landed on his back, heard an audible snap, and his right hip and leg exploded into consuming agony. Utterly winded, he gasped for breath and every breath wracked him. Maybe a dozen feet above, he could see the ledge he had fallen from, shimmering as if he were looking through water. Shards and pebbles peppered down upon him. A large rock came bounding over the edge and thunked about a foot from his head, and all was still. Polly and Jake and Tadahito were nowhere in sight. Somebody called his name.

Drum tried to shout, "I'm here!" It came out like a scream. The effort brought unbearable pain to his hip. It hurt to breathe. It hurt to move so much as a finger. Drum did not try to speak again. He lay very still and took shallow breaths. His right side was in flames. The whole world slid off into darkness.

#

A month later, Drum was getting around fairly well with a cane. He did not remember Jake and Tadahito carrying him down the mountain on an improvised litter. He had only the vaguest recollection of his time in the hospital. He did remember telling Polly a week after the accident that somebody needed to call The Sierra Club people and tell them he couldn't finish the assignment.

"I've taken care of it," she said, "I told them you'd been hurt, but we'd hired you an assistant, and that we would have the project done on time. We have the photographs you made, and Tadahito is shooting the rest."

"But he's doing practically the whole thing, then," Drum protested, "How much is our assistant going to cost us?"

"He doesn't want pay. He's working on his own assignment at the same time. Says he's doing this for friendship."

Drum did not feel reassured, "It must be for your friendship, then; I hardly know the man."

When he began to see the photographs they brought in from their forays, Drum grudgingly admitted they were as good or better than anything he could have done himself. Polly's text was poetry. When he read the words, he was there in the mountains with them. But it rankled him that he was getting credit for being a bystander. He was surly and testy with them, and Tadahito's unfailing good humor and generous spirit whenever they met only made him feel worse about himself.

Eventually, Drum's work had been done for him and it was time to go home. He packed, knocked on Polly's door on the way to breakfast. There was no answer, so he went down to the dining room, found Polly sitting at a table waiting for him. Tadahito wasn't there.

"I can't believe this is done," Drum said, "I'm ready to see the Cove again."

Polly looked him in the eye as she said, "I'm staying here."

Drum couldn't say exactly why, but he wasn't surprised, "Tadahito?"

"I can't close the door on this Drum. He's shown me a world I never thought I'd see." Drum tried to swallow the sickness he felt, but his face betrayed him.

Polly reacted almost angrily, "Don't look so hurt, Drum. You've had your chance to engage the larger world. This is mine."

Drum gazed at her in silence for a moment, until he believed what she was telling him. He gave her his tourist smile, "Enjoy it while you can, Polly."

He went back to his room, leaving his breakfast untouched, called a cab. Although it made his leg hurt fiercely, carried his bags out himself to wait in the fog for deliverance.

#

When Drum stepped out onto the rail platform at Asheton, his leg ached from the ceaseless jostle of the train. He took a cab to High Country Photography, where he had left his pickup under Henry Thurston's watchful eye.

"How was the trip?" the old man asked over his glasses when Drum dragged his bags through the front door.

"About as interesting as I could stand," Drum answered with a wry grin, "You still want to sell this place?"

Thurston didn't sound surprised, "I want to sell it to you. What happened to your leg?"

"Fell off a mountain. Busted my hip. I'm mending, but hurt like hell right now. You got a chair?"

Thurston rolled a desk chair from behind the counter, and Drum eased himself down into it with an utterance more than a sigh but not quite a moan.

"Where's your lady friend?" Thurston asked.

"She found herself a man who wasn't broken. If I buy this place, will you stick around until I get the hang of the business?"

Thurston laughed, "Long as you need me. Maybe longer than you want me. After all these years, it will be hard to keep away."

"You won't wear out your welcome," Drum assured him, "I'm going to stay in town tonight. My stiff leg needs some rest before I wrestle that pickup home. Come over to Millie's this evening, and we'll talk out our deal over supper."

"I'll get out of here around six, Drum. I'll come straight on over. I have a bottle of something in back that might make your leg feel better. I'll bring it along."

"Don't tell Miss Millie," Drum laughed, "We'll slip it into our coffee."

"Hell, Drum, We'll just tell her it is coffee."

#

The locals claimed Millicent Robbins' inn had been in Asheton forever. Her mother, who had named her after a character in an English novel, started the business after Millie's father disappeared with the Methodist minister's wife. Millie remembered Horace Kellett as one of the boarders when she was a girl, and Mura had been a regular at the table. Whenever he was in town, Drum liked to eat there, as much for Millie's tales as for her edifying and comforting cuisine, which James Coggins affirmed was "pure mountain." She was about Drum's age, had married young, to a logger who died underneath a spilled load of timber a few months after their wedding. Millicent was an amateur historian of the area and had stories aplenty for anyone with inclination to listen.

Intensely religious, Millie, was not prone to judge any who weren't. Actually, her personal theology was decidedly unorthodox by local standards. She took a spiritual view of almost everything, and when Drum let slip that his grandfather had been a Baptist preacher, Millie pegged him as a kindred spirit. Whenever he ate alone in her establishment, Millie would, if she had time, pull up a chair to his table and engage him in conversations which required he mainly be an attentive listener. Still, Drum liked Mad Millie, as even her friends called her behind her back. She was funny, smart, possessed of a quirky sort of beauty. Drum thought if she had ever learned to stop talking occasionally, she would have found another husband by now.

#

Lizbet didn't go up to the Shining Rocks after her mother died. Judy had been the anchor and compass for her days. Without her, Lizbet felt her already tenuous hold on the world slipping a bit every day. Her father seemed to her suddenly fragile in some way she couldn't define to herself. He needed her here. Lizbet was certain of that.

Her aunt had gone off with Drum to California, then phoned to say he had been hurt, perhaps crippled. Later she wrote that she wasn't coming back with him. Nothing held solid. Nobody in Lizbet's life remained as she had always known them. The world was no longer real. If she had to stay in it, for James' sake, she would stay away from the Shining Rocks. If she went through the Stones again, Lizbet doubted she could summon will to return. She had reached the place where most people arrive in old age, when the heart holds more love for the dead than for the living.

James, miraculously, Lizbet thought, stayed sober. The bottles disappeared. That was James' way with things. Whatever became a problem in his life, he avoided or put away. He looked normal. He acted normal. He tended to his business, took care of himself and his daughter, tried to be good company to her. But Lizbet could see that something was missing. There was a joylessness about him, even though he smiled when he spoke to her and laughed at her jokes. The feeling part of him, the alive part, had gone somewhere. Lizbet thought it had gone wherever Judy was now.

Lizbet figured she had a pretty good idea about where the dead go. She had seen Horace there. She had never seen Annie there, though, or her sisters. That was another reason she didn't go to the Shining Rocks anymore. If she went through to the Other Side, and didn't find Judy, what would that mean? Of course the Other Side was probably just as big at this side. She had not seen many people over there at all. If she ever did go back there, she intended to ask Horace about her kinswomen and Annie Starling. She wished Drum would come back. She would ask him. Lizbet had a nagging suspicion he might know something. She hoped he would still be able to walk on the mountain with her.

Sometimes, Lizbet rode her bike down to Annie's house, Drum's house now, and filled her basket with vegetables from the garden. It was getting overgrown with weeds now that Caleb was gone to the army and Drum wasn't here to take care of it. It was in the garden that Lizbet saw the Dark Man for the first time. She was picking grapes and looked up and he was standing by the river, watching her. She thought at first, he was Drum.

"Hello," Lizbet said. "I'm surprised to see you. Nobody told me you were back."

"I'm surprised you can see me," The Dark Man answered. His voice was almost like singing, flowing up and down, and the words were not English, his lips moving hardly at all as he spoke, but, strangely, she knew what he said. She could see then that he wasn't Drum. He looked like Drum, darker maybe, and a little younger, but definitely not Drum.

Lizbet tried a smile, "I can't help but see you. You're standing right in front of me. How come I can understand you?"

The Dark Man smiled back, "We are speaking the One Tongue. We can do that because this is a sacred Telling Place. Even the animals and birds can talk to us here if they want to."

The Dark Man walked up to her and lifted his hand toward her. He was small, like Drum, not much taller than Lizbet, and his clothes looked like some kind of soft leather. Lizbet raised her hand and touched his, palm to palm.

The Dark Man looked surprised, "I thought you were a ghost," he said. He reached up again and brushed the tips of her fingers with his, just to be sure.

The breeze gusted and the Dark Man seemed to flicker slightly before her, the way Annie had done.

Lizbet wondered and pondered a moment. "If one of us is a ghost," she asked the Dark Man, "How would we know?"

The Dark Man hesitated, as if he had just thought of something that had never occurred to him before. He reached down to pick up a pebble, but couldn't seem to get a grip on it. Then he stepped back and pointed at it. "Throw that stone at me," he told Lizbet.

She bent and picked up the stone.

"Throw hard," he said.

Lizbet threw the pebble as hard as she could at his chest. The stone passed right through him and bounced off the trunk of a sycamore by the river.

#

The sign in front of Millie Robbins' inn said *Hillhaven*. To Asheton locals during the forties, it was just Millie's place. Tourists occupied most of the rooms in season, and the food, plain and good, drew enough diners from the townfolk to fill the tables for several seatings every morning and evening. At noon, the "roomers and streeters," as Millie called them, were on their own. Millicent only ate twice a day herself. "I can't cook when I'm not hungry," she said whenever someone complained that she didn't serve lunch.

She presided over the rambling Victorian structure like a capricious but benevolent monarch. Her eccentricities were more endearing than irritating often enough that her roomers came back year after year. The diners forgave her for occasionally ushering them from their chairs as soon as their plates were empty because people stood waiting in the hall for a table. They knew that should they be late in line themselves, Millie would make straight their path to nourishment.

According to local legend, a noted writer had shot himself on the upper level of the double veranda that wrapped around two sides of the house. The natives told the tourists that the inn was haunted. When curious visitors asked her about the resident spirit, Millie told them she didn't believe in ghosts as a rule, but she had seen him a few times. None of the guests ever reported a sighting, although a few said they had heard things in the night.

#

Drum had difficulty starting his old pickup after it had been sitting so long, but just when he was about to give up, the engine caught, and he drove over to Hillhaven where he found the parking lot nearly full. He locked his bags in the pickup, braved the porch steps, and went in through double stained glassed doors to a high ceilinged hall, dark as a cave after the bright sunlight outside. The door clicked behind and quiet enveloped him. A large fan whispered and purred faintly overhead, slowly slicing shadows. When Drum's eyes adjusted to the dim, he spied Millie at her little desk, sorting through her mail.

She looked up when she heard the door, pulled her glasses down to the end of her nose, and inspected Drum closely, noting his cane, "Well, then, you seem worse for wear. Must have been a tough trip."

"It was interesting, Millie, and my hurt leg doesn't feel up to driving home tonight. I was hoping you might have a place at your table for supper and a bed to sleep in before morning."

"Just for tonight?"

"Just for tonight, though your cooking is a lot better than what I get at home."

"Well, Drum, the rooms are all booked, but if you don't mind sleeping on a daybed out on my little porch upstairs, I can keep you. It's trellised with trumpet vines and up off the street. You'll have your privacy, but you'll have to share a bath."

Drum reached for his wallet, "I'll take it. How much, Millie?"

"It isn't proper lodging, I'll not charge you for camping, but you can pay for your supper."

"Thanks, Millie; you're a saint."

"We're all saints, Drum. Some of us just don't know it yet."

Leaving his cane beside the door, Drum went back out to his pickup, slung his gear bag over his shoulder, hoisted a suitcase in each hand, gritted his teeth, and limped toward the house. At the top of the steps, he put down the luggage to rest. Millie came out the door, handed him his cane, took the suitcases and went back in. By the time Drum got through the door, she was halfway up the stairs just inside.

Without looking around, Millie called back to him, "When you are able, Drum, follow me."

Drum sighed, and meekly pursued, while Millie traipsed up the stairs as if carrying pillows. She waited for him when she reached the second floor. When Drum grimaced his way to the upper landing, Millie, still holding his luggage, wheeled and led him off down another hall to a door opening onto a small porch at the back of the house. Through thickly laced trumpet vine bedecked with a constellation of scarlet blossoms, Drum glimpsed rising above the intervening ridges, the distinctive profile of Myrtle Mountain, purple with distance.

Millie set down the suitcases and herded Drum past a curtained window, a small table with two chairs, a door, and a daybed already made for sleeping. She opened a door at the far end of the porch, which had been enclosed to improvise a bath.

Inside the bath, she pointed to another door, "That's to my room. There's no lock on the outer door, so be sure to knock before you barge in."

Back out on the porch, Drum collapsed onto the day bed, groaning softly in spite of himself.

Millie, hand on hips, appraised his condition, "You're hurting some, boy. There's a ceiling fan up here to keep the mosquitoes off. It'll be cool enough for comfort. We'll bring your supper up here so you won't have to ply the stairs again tonight."

"I've asked Henry Thurston to join me for supper, Millie. We have some business to talk over."

"When he gets here, Drum, we'll send him right up. Youns can eat up here and scheme in private. That way, Thurston won't have to hide his bottle."

Before Drum could speak, Millie was gone, closing the door behind her. He heard her bounding off down the stair like a girl at play. He wondered where she found such energy. Traffic murmured in the street, sounding far away. Drum listened to a cook scolding his helper on the porch below, but couldn't make out the words. A mocking bird called from an old pine across the yard. Drum looked at his watch. Two more hours before Thurston showed up. Drum took off his shoes, a task that brought pangs to his insulted hip. He lay back on the day bed, sank his head into a feather pillow, and before the mocking bird sang again, was oblivious.

Drum sat in the circle on the ridge above Horace's hideout. The night, moonless and dark, kept whispering something to him he couldn't understand. Annie, Horace and Mura were in the circle with him. In the dark, he couldn't see their faces but he knew who they were. No one spoke. Drum wondered if they were waiting on him to say something, but he could not bear to break the holy silence.

After a year or two, Mura said, "I'm sorry, Drum."

Drum's response came out like a scold, "Don't be sorry for anything, Mura. You taught me all the skill I have. I've lived my whole life by your example. You, Annie, Horace have made me who I am. Don't any of you be sorry on my account."

"I'm sorry," Mura said again, and Drum was alone.

When he realized he wasn't alone anymore, Drum opened his eyes. The ghost leaned against the porch railing, smoking a cigarette, watching him with a strange expression that could have expressed either pity or envy.

Drum closed his eyes, opened them again. The ghost was still there.

Drum said, "You must be the writer."

The ghost drew deeply on his cigarette, expelled a cloud of smoke, itself a wee ghost in search of form, "And you must be the photographer."

"Guilty," said the photographer.

"Everybody's guilty," said the ghost

Drum sat up. The sudden movement pained, made him wince. The ghost faded into the vines. A single firefly drifted across the porch, flashing longing and loneliness against the dusky air.

Drum gathered some clean clothes from his bag, went to the bath, knocked dutifully, and when there was no answer, went in to wash for supper. The shower finally began to warm by the time he finished. Drum looked in the mirror, wondered if the dark mark on his forehead would ever fade, rubbed his scratchy chin. He really should shave before dinner. He decided to grow a beard, instead.

When he came out of the bathroom, someone had set the table, and lit several large Japanese style lanterns hanging from the ceiling. An open bottle of wine stood waiting beside his plate. Drum poured some into his glass, looked out at the last of day fading over Myrtle Mountain. The wine was good.

"Save that for your dinner, Drum." Henry Thurston stood in the doorway, holding up a paper shopping bag, his fist clenched tight around the contents, "I have something more therapeutic here."

When Thurston finished his second shot of therapy and was about to polish off a third, Millie, trailed by one of her helpers, pushed open the door and supper descended upon the two men, green beans, stuffed squash, country ham steaks, fresh tomatoes and cantaloupe, and a huge salad with radishes and pickled beets.

"Too much green stuff," growled Thurston good naturedly, "What's for dessert?"

Millie rapped his balding pate with her knuckles. "If that plate isn't cleared when I get back, you don't get any."

"Ouch!" Thurston strove to appear injured. "You abuse all your guests like this? No wonder nobody wants to eat here."

Millie pointed to Thurston's coffee cup, "Drink the rest of your poison, so Alice can pour something to keep you from falling into a drunken stupor before you finish your dinner."

Thurston obeyed enthusiastically. Drum turned his cup upright and Alice filled them both. Millie replenished their water glasses, and admonished Drum, while directing a mock glare at Thurston, "Don't let this pirate cheat you Drum; I know he's trying to sell you that floundering business of his."

Thurston affected an indignant scowl, "If you minded your own business like you mind everybody else's, Millie, you'd be the richest woman in Asheton. Anybody ever tell you you talk way too much?"

"None who love me," said Millie over her shoulder as she pushed Alice through the door ahead of her.

When they were gone, Thurston walked over to the railing and emptied his water over the side. Then he retrieved his bottle and poured another shot of whiskey into his glass. "Let's eat, he said, "I'm starving."

They ate and talked, and Thurston drank a little more of his whiskey, although he seemed to realize when he had reached his maximum capacity. They discussed the sale of High Country Photography as if they both weren't already decided. The price was less than fair and Drum didn't quibble. Payment would be in a percentage of the profits and Thurston would stay on as a "consultant," until he received all his money.

"If I die in the meantime," he told Drum, looking deadly serious, "I'll will you the rest."

They did clear their plates and wished for seconds. While they were waiting for Millie or Alice to appear with dessert, Thurston reached back into his shopping bag and pulled out a bundle of folded paper, tied with a string. "I found these stuffed in a box with some old plates and negatives, thought you might be interested."

He handed them to Drum. There were letters sent to Mura from various unknown correspondents. Mura had written notations on the back of some of the pages. A few still had their envelopes and Drum was intrigued with the old stamps and postmarks. Some of them had been mailed from Japan. The address on one caught his eye. *Tadahito Kitamura, C/O Mr. Oren Shorts, 36 Mountain View Avenue,*

Asheton, North Carolina, USA. He shuffled back through the stack to find a sheet Mura had written on. He recognized the handwriting.

Drum forgot to breathe as he studied the envelope, Tad ... Ted ... Kitamura ... Mura. It seemed so obvious now. How had he never noticed the resemblance? But Tadahito seemed younger than Mura, more lively, more...lusty. Drum had never guessed, would not have guessed in a thousand years. Even with his own impossible history, he could hardly accept what his eyes were telling him to believe. He understood now the severe courtesy Mura always exhibited toward him, as if his mentor had something he wanted to apologize for.

He didn't see Millie coming through the door behind him with a huge chess pie in one hand and saucers and forks in the other. "Holy Shit." he said aloud, staring at the papers he held.

Millie kicked his chair as she set down the pie, "Don't be profane under my roof. It's ungracious."

Thurston lifted his glasses, peered sharply at Drum, "What's that about?"

"I've seen a ghost," said the photographer.

#

Drum woke next morning with a buzzing in his head. When he opened his eyes, a hummingbird with throat the color of the blossoms was inventorying the trumpet vines. Sunlight filtered down through the vines. The brilliant colors of the shadowed bird flared whenever a ray touched her. Drum tried to recall something about a firefly, remembered the ghost, who, Millie had explained over dessert, was Gerald Fox, a self-destructive writer and all the rage during the twenties. He had a lover in Asheton. Millie seemed to know who, but she wasn't saying. He had a wife in New York who wouldn't grant him a divorce. He lost all his money during the Crash. His last novel was a huge flop, and he shot himself on the porch where they were eating, not on the veranda, as they told the tourists.

Drum had mentioned seeing the ghost because there was no way he could explain his reaction to Mura's letters. By the time he told his tale of haunting and Millie told all hers, nobody seemed to remember what had sparked the conversation.

This was the first morning since his accident Drum had come awake without his leg hurting, and although by the time he had showered and dressed, it had begun to twinge again, he was glad and grateful for this sign of his healing. Today was Sunday. Millie's dining room was closed on Sunday. Maybe he would stop off and breakfast with James and Lizbet if they hadn't eaten already. He'd phone them before he left town. He supposed Millie would be at church somewhere, but when Drum gathered his bags and started down the stair he met Millie coming up with their breakfast on a tray.

"I thought you'd be off to church," he said, putting down his bags as she handed him the tray,

"I don't go to church," she answered, "I close the restaurant so the help can worship if they like, and have a family day." Millie came past him and opened the door as he turned to follow.

"But you're religious, I know. Don't you belong to a congregation?" Drum asked her as he set the tray on the table.

"I believe in God," Millie sat down and began laying out their plates, "I don't much believe in church. That has more to do with human pride and prejudice than with divine love and mercy."

Drum couldn't argue. He eased into the chair opposite. Millie poured their tea. Drum reached to butter his toast, but she lay her hand on his to stay him and bowed her head, "Lord, we receive unworthily, and we are thankful as much as we know how."

"Amen," said Drum.

"Amen," said Millie

They ate slowly and with many pauses as Millie talked and talked and talked and Drum listened and remembered every word.

It was nearly two hours later when Drum drove across McMinn Gap and the sheriff's car came up behind him and passed, crowding him slightly on the curve. The cruiser disappeared round the next bend, but as he came up on James' drive, he caught sight of it again, turning up the hill toward the house. When Drum pulled up in front of the house, the car sat with door open, lights still flashing, and the brand new sheriff, Marcus Dill was talking to James. The sheriff looked serious. James looked traumatized.

As he walked toward them, Drum heard James say to the sheriff, "She got off the school bus with the Bradley girls and walked up the drive. That's the last they saw. I don't know where she could be. We looked all over for her yesterday, and then I called you."

"What's going on here, James?" Drum asked.

James' voice trembled, "Lizbet's gone, Drum. We don't know where."

MILLICENT

Unless she was exhausted, Lizbet couldn't sleep after her mother died. She'd lie awake at night, prey to dreams and waking visions. Sometimes she dreamed she was awake. Sometimes awake, she felt in a dream. When she thought James was asleep, she walked through the darkened house, listening, watching for some echo, glimmer of Judy. But however late, when Lizbet passed the door to her father's room, she might hear him talking, as if in conversation. Once or twice she heard another voice that sounded like her mother. Lizbet never asked James about it. She tried her best to forget what she had heard.

Lizbet longed for her aunt's return until Polly phoned to say she was not coming home. Every day after that, Lizbet rode her bike down to Drum's house by the river and tended the neglected garden as best she could. Gardening, though, was just her excuse. She went in hopes of seeing the Dark Man again. She still thought of him as that, although he'd told her his People had named him Talks To Trees. More often than not, she was disappointed, but once in a while, when the fog rolled in off the Long Broad, she would find him standing under the trees at the water's edge, staring up the hill toward the house, as if waiting for her. Other times he waited with his hands behind his back, looking out over the river as if he could see through the fog to the other side. Lizbet would toss a pebble at him then. It would sail through his body and crack against a tree trunk or splash in the water

286

beyond, and they would laugh and lift their hands to touch the other's palms. Then they would talk for as long as the fog held him there.

This day Lizbet found Talks To Trees gazing out over the river and very quietly, she walked up behind him. He didn't look around, didn't appear to know she was there. She threw the pebble she had carried down from the road and watched it bounce off his back. He turned around very slowly then, as if he had been expecting it, walked up to her and closed his fingers tight around hers when she lifted her hand. His skin felt warm with life, almost hot, and his touch made Lizbet shudder with something not quite fear and close to delight. He dropped his hand and looked deep into her with his gray eyes and his smile flashed like the sun on the river.

Then Talks To Trees sang the words to her, "I am whole again now, Elizabeth, and it is time for me to go beyond, to the Other Side where my People are. You can come with me, if you want to."

She wanted to. She did.

#

James Coggins received one more letter from his little sister. She wrote in September, telling him she was going to Japan with the photographer she had met in California, that she planned to live there indefinitely. In December the country was at war with Japan. After that, no one heard anything more from Polly Coggins.

No one heard anything from Elizabeth, either. She had simply vanished from the earth, it seemed, with not a trace left behind. They searched. No one had seen her. No one knew why she might leave. There was no place that James knew of for her to go. There was a scary time when the new sheriff, who didn't know James from Adam, thought he might have had something to do with his daughter's disappearance. James endured the brutal questions, the persistent prying into his private life, such as he had left of it, hoping that Marcus Dill's zeal for the truth would lead him to find Lizbet. In the end, Marcus apologized sincerely and profusely for his misdirected suspicions and his failure to find the lost girl. James realized the man had been doing his job as best he knew, but he never learned to like the sheriff.

Early on, James tried to get drunk. Maybe he intended to drink himself to death that night, but the alcohol made him suddenly and violently ill, something that had never happened to him before. After that, he never touched spirits.

Judy saved his life. He never told anyone about her visits, but he would sometimes wake in the dark and feel her presence in the room. He would call her name and hear her voice then, telling him that she loved him, that she was never far away, that Elizabeth was safe and would not be gone forever, and that Ben would come home whole from the war.

Three times, in broad daylight, James had come out his front door to find his dead wife sitting in her rocker. She would turn and smile up at him and reach out her hand, and James would sit down beside her, afraid to touch her, and she would talk to him until his eyes closed and he drifted off into sleep.

When all the searchers had gone home and sheriff Dill had turned his attention to other crimes and misfortunes, James still took long treks through the ridges and hollows, searching, calling, listening, watching for his lost child. When the last faint hope of finding Lizbet faded, James still took his walks, spending days on the mountain sometimes, gathering the peace and comfort that only wild places could give him. He felt closer to Judy there than even in his own house. He felt her smile in the sun, her breath on the wind, heard her laughter in the creeks, and her movement in the trees. He knew she had walked these hills with her friend Drum when she was young, and now James was walking them with her.

When he wasn't walking, James pretended to run his business, did all the ordinary things a man must do to get through his day. Sometimes he would go down the creek and have supper with Drum, or Drum would come up to his place. They would sit out on the porch after they ate, drinking strong coffee. They agreed that, strangely, the coffee helped them sleep. James would smoke his pipe. Drum didn't smoke.

The photographer was dealing with his own loss. James tried to ease his hurt.

"She took after her mother, Drum," James said once, after a long silence when they both seemed to be waiting for some other beside themselves to speak, "Our mother left us, you know, when we were small. Dad raised us pretty much on his own. He didn't talk about her much, but once he said, "If you gave her the moon, she'd want the sun and all the stars.""

As soon as the words were out, James wanted to call them back, but Drum looked up, smiled and nodded, and seemed to rest lighter in his chair as if he had finally decided to let go a weight and a burden. That was the night James decided to move out of the house, though he didn't tell Drum until later. The next morning, James drove into town, talked to a realtor about selling the property, and came home and packed away all Judy's clothes. The following week, he moved down to the smaller house he'd built for Polly on Walt's old place.

With the war on, people weren't much interested in mountain real estate, and it would be several years and three realtors later before James finally sold the rambling old house his father had built for Annie Starling. Janice Smiley, the realtor phoned him gleefully one day to say a retired college professor from Virginia had put down earnest money.

Eventually Ben did come home whole from the war, as did Caleb Two Trees. Ronan Darner came home, too, not quite whole, but mending, and immediately moved over the mountain to South Carolina to marry a nurse he'd met in an army hospital. Ben went off to university to complete his forestry degree, and when Drum moved to Asheton to occupy Mura's old apartment over the photography studio, Caleb rented Annie's house by the river, and James took him in as a partner in his contracting business, which gave James more time to walk in the woods. It was his plan they would find him one day on a mountain somewhere. He hoped when they did, they might just bury him where he lay.

#

Millicent Robbins was eating her Sunday supper alone in her kitchen when she smelled a cigarette. Since she forbade smoking in her kitchen she knew the transgressor without looking up. When she turned around, the ghost leaned against the counter behind her. His cigarette flared in the dim light as he inhaled, then he expelled a great cloud of smoke that made it appear his foggy form was turning itself inside out. After the cloud expanded and dispersed, he stood three or four feet closer to Millie than he had before, and looked to have gained a degree of solidity from the process.

"Hello, Gerald," Millie said to the ghost, "I'd offer you some supper if you had any use for it."

"Sweet thoughts count," said Gerald, "I do miss the taste of a good venison stew, though."

Millie laughed, "And the taste of bad whiskey, no doubt."

Gerald drew again on his cigarette, "Actually, I drank whiskey purely for the effect. I never learned to like the stuff."

"What do spirits nourish themselves on?" It was a question Millie had often wanted to ask before. "What does your kind thirst for?"

Gerald's cigarette dissolved into a little puff of smoke. As it drifted up and away Gerald reached out and closed his hand around it, and it was gone, "For love, Millie. That's why I keep hanging around. Your house is full of it."

Millie pondered that for a second before she spoke, "The whole world is full of love, Gerald. Most souls are oblivious. But what does a ghost know about love? Love is incarnate, requires bodies and breath for exchange."

Gerald took his turn to laugh, "I was embodied enough for your mother in my day, Millie. Surely she must have told you something of that. I loved her more than even she knew. She was not much younger then than you are now. Her loveliness is in you. Unfleshed and breathless though I am, love remains. I stay, dear child, because I love you."

Gerald was telling her something she had known since childhood, but had never spoken aloud. She tried to put the truth at a comfortable distance, "Gerald, any sane person would say you're just my imagination."

The ghost began to fade before her eyes, "You really

don't think I'm real?"

"You were real enough to my mother, Gerald. That I know, and Mother is real to me. Maybe that makes you real enough to get by."

Millie could barely see the ghost now, but she heard Gerald's voice before he vanished completely, "I'm as real as love, Millie. As long as you can love, I'll be around if you need me."

#

After the Los Pedros fiasco, Drum took few assignments that carried him away from Asheton and the surrounding mountains. He immersed himself in the routines of a small-town photographer, making pictures of weddings, graduation ceremonies, portraits of beautiful young daughters and athletic sons, manicured moms and old dads and grandfathers. He did occasional shoots for tourism magazines and brochures. He had lived a wider life. Now he sought a deeper, quieter one. Drum wanted peace.

Most mornings he cooked breakfast for Henry Thurston, who showed up unfailingly for work each day, and behind the scenes, continued to run the business while Drum scurried around town manipulating his camera. When Thurston's arthritis made it a chore and a pain to climb the stair to Drum's apartment, they met for breakfast at Hillhaven or the Riverside Cafe. On Sundays, Drum had breakfast with Millicent Robbins. When the weather was warm, they ate on her porch. In the winter, when it was cold, they ate in her kitchen. Then later in the day, Drum would usually drive over to Sorrow Cove and visit James Coggins. They pondered the absurdities of their lives and shared a meal in the evening. Usually Drum cooked.

#

Horace was exasperated, "Li, why can't I get a straight answer about where this place is? Doesn't anybody know where we are?"

Li smiled patiently, as if he were a slow child, "Horace, I keep trying to tell you that you are in the same place you've always been; You're just on the Other Side of what you're used to."

"So why can't I go back?"

"You can go back anytime you want to be dead."

"But you go back all the time."

"I'm a different case. I started from here. Besides, I don't really go back; I just follow the lines."

"But I don't follow you."

Li set aside the note she was writing, took a blank sheet of paper, wrote Horace's name on it, flipped it over, and slid it across the table to Horace, "Read that to me, friend Horace,"

"I can't see it; the writing's on the other side."

Li laughed, "But it's still there, isn't it? Hold the paper up to the window."

Horace lifted the paper, saw the sunlight shining through, and the reverse of his name, "It says *Horace.*"

Li, took a sip of her tea, "How can you tell when it's on the other side?"

"Because the light shines through, and I can read backwards."

Li, set down her cup, clapped her hands, looked delighted as a child, "When you learn to follow the Light and read time backwards, Horace, you can touch the place you left, but…"

Horace waited for her to finish, but Li gave him only her inscrutable smile. "But what?" he asked finally.

"But it won't be home anymore. When you learn to travel lightly, you can go anywhere you want, but you can't go home again."

"I give up, Li; would you like some breakfast?

"Horace, that would be ever so appropriate."

Horace got up, went across the kitchen and broke some eggs into a bowl. He noticed as he laid the shells aside that his weathered hands looked younger. The longer he was in the Laurel, the stronger and healthier he felt, in fact. His memories of his former life also dimmed day by day. He was afraid if he did not return soon, he wouldn't even know he'd been there. Maybe this would be home by then. Maybe that wouldn't be so bad. He beat the eggs with a fork, added a little ground cayenne, and began to chop an onion.

Li broke into his musing, "Have you let Ernest show you that place by the river I was telling you about?"

"Yes, it's good ground, has a nice spring. I'm not sure I'm ready to settle down here yet, though."

"Horace, you still don't get it, do you?"

#

A year after his accident, Drum retired his cane, although for the rest of his life, whenever he got cold or wet, his hip ached and his leg throbbed. Few ever noticed his slight limp. The photographer led a decidedly ordinary life, had no urge for it to be any other way. He had found love and lost it. He had found friends and kept a few. He had a place among people who would miss him if he were not there. Drum thought that was home enough.

The day after his birthday, Millie Robbins threw him a surprise party at Hillhaven. James was there. Caleb came with an impressive young woman he introduced as Wilma. Wilma, Caleb said, was Lucas Dill's new deputy.

Willard Hoots and Stephen Nodine showed up bearing flowers and gifts. James reported that he had finally sold his old house on the hill. Henry Thurston wasn't among them. He died from a stroke three months before.

That night Drum chased sleep and fled from dreams and visions. Dawn brought him awake to headache and depression. He was fifty years old. Two thirds of his life lived and gone, he reckoned, and what had he to show for it but failed relationships, missed and broken connections? When he looked around at his friends, none his age seemed to be doing much better. They were a little pack of refugees, huddled together against the final unraveling.

All morning long, as he worked in his darkroom, he had a creepy sensation that the air was stirred by wings. He worked on billing in the afternoon, a task he hated, but forced himself to do every Monday, now that Thurston wasn't here to do it for him. As he added a column of figures for the third time, his first two efforts not in agreement, a brash young woman with red hair steamed through his door with a portfolio under her arm.

She was a student at the university, majoring in math and physics to please her father, but really wanted to be a photographer, and there were no photography courses offered at the school. Her calculus instructor had told her about Drum, said he used to be a famous photographer with National Geographic. She wanted to sign on as an apprentice.

Sharon Suttles was very earnest, Drum thought, too pretty for her own good, and very sure of her ability to persuade him to her way of thinking. He motioned toward her portfolio, cleared a space on his desk, "Let me see your work."

She opened the portfolio and turned it to face him. Then, without trying to explain or justify her images to him, she stood silent, watching his face, waiting for his reaction. Drum pushed back his chair, stood, and slowly went through her pictures, one by one. Occasionally, he would go back to one he had seen previously and look at it again, compare it to the other he held in hand. They were mostly landscapes, images of the mountains around Asheton, a few portraits, all older people. Teachers, perhaps, or relatives. Long minutes passed, neither spoke.

"Did you do these?" He asked finally, his code for admitting he was impressed.

Sharon killed a smile almost as soon as it flickered, "All by myself."

"Who's been teaching you photography?"

"I don't have a teacher. I look at photographs. I read. I try to do what I've read. I only make pictures of what I care about."

"Who's your favorite photographer, Sharon?"

"Nobody you've heard of, a local man. I found some of his pictures in the school library. He's been dead for years and years."

"Try me."

"Do you know of Ted Mura?"

Drum managed not to cry in front of the girl. He carefully stacked the prints, closed the portfolio and secured the ties. "Mura was my first teacher, Sharon. I've spent thirty years trying to be as good as he was."

Drum sat down, motioned Sharon to a chair, "My partner died not long ago. If you can keep regular hours, take some of this damned book work off me, and keep on making photographs as good as these, we can work something out. I can't pay you much, but I can teach you

296

something about darkroom technique, which is your biggest weakness, judging by your prints."

Sharon didn't hesitate. "My classes are all in the morning. I can work every afternoon."

Drum reached across his desk and shook her hand. Her grip on his arthritic fingers made him wince. "Let's make it three afternoons for the first week or so, Sharon, let us both get used to working together and see how you'll best fit in here."

"Thank you, Mr. Drum. I'll make you glad you did this."

"Just Drum will do."

"Yes, sir, Just Drum," Sharon said brightly.

"Just call me Drum."

"Okay, Drum."

#

When Drum met Millie for breakfast on Sunday morning, she looked tired. He asked how she was feeling. Millie gave him a self-deprecating chuckle, "I guess it shows. I haven't been sleeping well at all."

"What's wrong, Millie?"

"I've been having wild dreams. I wake up exhausted from them."

"Nightmares?"

"No, not really, but visions full of tumultuous and fantastic things. When I wake, I'm worn out."

"What kind of things?"

"Most slip away once I'm awake, but in one that recurs, I'm flying high up over a wide river. Sometimes I feel like I'm being carried by a huge bird; sometimes I feel like I am the bird, have great wings. When I wake, my shoulders are sore. Always at the end of the flying dreams, I start falling toward the river, but I always wake up before I reach the water."

Drum stared at his hands. "You won't believe this, Millie."

"Let me decide that, Drum."

"I've been having that same set of dreams since I was a boy."

"Well, I've not had them until recently. What do you suppose they mean?"

"I don't know, Millie. I can't even figure out what my waking life means. My dreams are a deep mystery."

"Well, Drum, I do believe life has meaning, whether we are asleep or awake. Don't you?"

"I suppose it does, Millie. It's just that I've never had a clue as to what it is. We go round and round, but to what end?"

Millie sipped her tea, gave him a speculative glance over her cup, "This doesn't sound like the Drum I know. What brought this on?"

Drum showed her a bleak face, "Nothing and everything, Millie." He told her then all the details of his life he had never breathed aloud to another living soul. He went on and on, while breakfast sat cold and forgotten between them.

Of all the people Drum could have told about his life between times, none would have been as prepared to receive his witness without bias or skepticism as Millicent Robbins, who had lived her life in the company of her father's ghost. Millie didn't interrupt or question, just sat still and listening, her eyes fixed on Drum. She nodded occasionally to encourage him to continue. When he finished, church bells were ringing as congregations fled for home and dinner. Drum saw tears trailing down Millie's cheeks, reached up to wipe his own wet face. His voice came hoarse and raspy. He had poured out his soul and felt spent and empty and strangely at peace.

Millie reached across the table and covered Drum's trembling hand with hers, "You're coming home to yourself, Drum. Now you can live your future."

Drum gathered himself as they began picking over the cold remains of their breakfast, "Speaking of the future, Millie, I've hired a part-time assistant, a student at the university. Willard Hoots sent her to me. If she works out, I'll be able to leave the business for a couple of weeks now and then and start looking for Horace, as Polly Coggins and I planned before she ran off with Tadahito or Mura or whoever he was."

Millie poured fresh coffee, "Horace has been lost for so long most people have forgotten him. Do you really think there's any trace of him left to find?" She was always intrigued by any historical puzzle and by this one in particular.

Drum sat back and spread his hands, "I doubt it, Millie, but I've always fancied spending a good chunk of time with a camera in that high lean place. Something has always happened to make me put it off. I saw it the first time from afar with Horace at his hideout. Ever since I've been homesick for the High Balsam, if you can be homesick for some place you've scarcely set foot on."

Millie pushed her plate aside, folded her hands under her chin and leaned across the table, her blue eyes intense, "Drum, we both have experience to know that time folds in strange patterns. Maybe you have been there in some moment you've forgotten, from some other age, some other life."

"Who knows? I don't know enough to deny it. But if I'm going to go up there in this life, I dasn't put it off much longer. I'm passing fifty and have a gimpy leg. I really should do it while I can still walk."

"Walking on a mountain is what that leg needs, Drum. More to the point, it is what your spirit needs. That place has been calling you since time before time. I think you should get off your duff and go. Tell me about this student of yours. Is she a photographer?"

"Sharon Suttles. She's a better photographer than I let on to her. She's also brash and pretty and has an ego that requires no propping up on my part. She has a lot to learn about craft, but she has an eye for subject and composition and knows what she wants her camera to do even though she isn't yet adept at making it do all she wants. I'm hoping she's as good at the business end of photography, and shows up at work regularly enough that I can leave it with her on occasion. I want to ramble a bit, choose my own subjects and make some images to please myself in my old age. I've drug off all over yonder and never gotten to know my own yard."

"Bring her by for lunch sometime, Drum; I'd like to meet her."

"I will. You know, Millie, you could use some time off, too."

Millie laughed, "I don't know what time off is, Drum. What do you have in mind?"

"I'm thinking Alice could handle things for you for a few days. You could come with me up to the High Balsam and we'll look for Horace together. Don't tell me you're not interested."

"Oh, I'm interested, but I'm a respectable single woman, Mister Drum. I'm not going to loiter on the mountain for days on end with some man I'm not married to."

"You're teasing me now, Millie."

"Yes, I'm teasing you, but I'm also telling you the truth."

"Will you go with me if we get married first? I've been meaning for a good while now to ask you about that."

Millie looked at his face, saw that he was quite serious. "Drum, dear man, I thought you'd never ask. Yes, I'd love to."

Drum and his future spent the rest of the afternoon and evening getting better acquainted. The next morning, Drum's pickup wouldn't start. When he found out what it would cost to get it fixed, he bought a new one, a green International. Caleb made a weather proof box for it large enough to hold all Drum's photography gear.

Drum and Millie plotted their expedition as they planned their wedding. Drum felt in his gut that in some form or another, Horace Kellett was waiting for him on the High Balsam. After all this time, they still called. Remembering a boy who had stood outside Horace's hideout watching the sun go down over the far mountains, Drum thought Millie was right. It was past time he answered.

#

Coming home from Caleb's place with his new gear box, Drum passed the drive where James and Judy had lived, saw stenciled on the mailbox, *J Bear.* Thoughtless, Drum stopped his pickup in the middle of the road, suddenly enough that Caleb's box slid across the bed and bumped the cab. Drum looked in the mirror and was relieved to see nobody was behind. He backed down the road, then pulled up the drive.

There was no way he could tell Bear who he really was. He'd just introduce himself as a former neighbor, maybe ask permission to take some photographs. They might laugh about the coincidence of the name. Drum wondered if the artist who had welcomed the boy would be as quick to befriend the man. Drum stopped in front of the house, got out of his truck. It was as it had been forty years before, except he didn't see Bear's jeep. When he saw the boy standing on the porch, Drum felt like a ghost.

He wanted to flee the scene. Instead, he said to the boy, "Hi, is Mr. Bear at home?"

The boy looked at him, seeing too much for a child, Drum thought, as he felt or imagined a flicker of recognition pass between them. The boy answered, "Bear had to go to town; he'll be back soon if you want to wait."

Drum gazed all around the yard, taking in the precious scene, "No thanks," he heard himself saying, "I've come too soon. I'll catch him another day."

He wanted to tell the boy to stay where he was loved and spare himself hurt and loss he couldn't begin to fathom, or at least, assure him that while he was trying to find himself, his life would find him, that love lost would claim him back in the end, that the peace that ever eluded his grasp, would pursue him, finally holding him fast and unshakable. But Drum cherished this place and these souls his life had brought him to. He was glad and grateful to be the man he had become. He feared he might let slip some slight word that would alter it all, so Benjamin Drum got back into his pick-up, waved to himself and drove away down the hill into the rest of their life.

ABOUT THE AUTHOR

(photo by David Longley)

Henry Mitchell's family has lived in the mountains and foothills of the Southern Appalachians for eight generations. Currently, he resides in Greenville, South Carolina with his wife, Jane Ella Matthews, a Feldenkrais teacher, and their German Shepherd and spiritual guide, Simon. Between Times is Henry's second novel. He is working on a third novel to complete the trilogy, and a fourth, a fairytale turned murder mystery.

ALSO BY THE AUTHOR

The Summer Boy
the first novel in the Benjamin Drum series

Alfie Dog Fiction

Taking your imagination for a walk

For hundreds of short stories, collections
and novels visit our website at
www.alfiedog.com

Join us on Facebook
http://www.facebook.com/AlfieDogLimited

Made in the USA
Lexington, KY
12 November 2014